BEACH DREAMS

Praise for Tammy L. Grace

"I had planned on an early night but couldn't put this book down until I finished it around 3am. Like her other books, this one features fascinating characters with a plot that mimics real life in the best way. My recommendation: it's time to read every book Tammy L Grace has written."

— Carolyn, review of Beach Haven

"This book is a clean, simple romance with a background story very similar to the works of Debbie Macomber. If you like Macomber's books you will like this one. A holiday tale filled with dogs, holiday fun, and the joy of giving will warm your heart."

— Avid Mystery Reader, review of A Season for Hope: A Christmas Novella

"This book was just as enchanting as the others. Hardships with the love of a special group of friends. I recommend the series as a must read. I loved every exciting moment. A new author for me. She's fabulous."

—Maggie!, review of Pieces of Home: A Hometown Harbor Novel (Book 4)

"Tammy is an amazing author, she reminds me of Debbie Macomber… Delightful, heartwarming...just down to earth."

— Plee, review of A Promise of Home: A Hometown Harbor Novel (Book 3)

"This was an entertaining and relaxing novel. Tammy Grace has a simple yet compelling way of drawing the reader into the lives of her characters. It was a pleasure to read a story that didn't rely on theatrical tricks, unrealistic events or steamy sex scenes to fill up the pages. Her characters and plot were strong enough to hold the reader's interest."

—MrsQ125, review of Finding Home: A Hometown Harbor Novel (Book 1)

"This is a beautifully written story of loss, grief, forgiveness and healing. I believe anyone could relate to the situations and feelings represented here. This is a read that will stay with you long after you've completed the book."

—Cassidy Hop, review of Finally Home: A Hometown Harbor Novel (Book 5)

"Killer Music is a clever and well-crafted whodunit. The vivid and colorful characters shine as the author gradually reveals their hidden secrets—an absorbing page-turning read."

— Jason Deas, bestselling author of Pushed and Birdsongs

"I could not put this book down! It was so well written & a suspenseful read! This is definitely a 5-star story! I'm hoping there will be a sequel!"
—*Colleen, review of Killer Music*

"This is the best book yet by this author. The plot was well crafted with an unanticipated ending. I like to try to leap ahead and see if I can accurately guess the outcome. I was able to predict some of the plot but not the actual details which made reading the last several chapters quite engrossing."

—*0001PW, review of Deadly Connection*

Beach Dreams
A Novel By
Tammy L. Grace

BEACH DREAMS is a work of fiction. Names, characters, places, and incidents either are products of the author's imagination or are used fictitiously. Any resemblance to actual events, locales, entities, or persons, living or dead, is entirely coincidental.

www.tammylgrace.com
Facebook: https://www.facebook.com/tammylgrace.books
Twitter: @TammyLGrace
Instagram: @authortammylgrace
Published in the United States by Lone Mountain Press, Nevada

ISBN 978-1-945591-33-4 (eBook)
ISBN 978-1-945591-34-1 (Print)
FIRST EDITION
Printed in the United States of America

ALSO BY TAMMY L. GRACE

COOPER HARRINGTON DETECTIVE NOVELS

Killer Music

Deadly Connection

Dead Wrong

Cold Killer

HOMETOWN HARBOR SERIES

Hometown Harbor: The Beginning (Prequel Novella)

Finding Home

Home Blooms

A Promise of Home

Pieces of Home

Finally Home

Forever Home

CHRISTMAS STORIES

A Season for Hope: Christmas in Silver Falls Book 1

The Magic of the Season: Christmas in Silver Falls Book 2

Christmas in Snow Valley: A Hometown Christmas Book 1

One Unforgettable Christmas: A Hometown Christmas Book 2

Christmas Wishes: Souls Sisters at Cedar Mountain Lodge

Christmas Surprises: Soul Sisters at Cedar Mountain Lodge

GLASS BEACH COTTAGE SERIES

Beach Haven

Moonlight Beach

Beach Dreams

WRITING AS CASEY WILSON

A Dog's Hope

A Dog's Chance

WISHING TREE SERIES

The Wishing Tree

Wish Again

Overdue Wishes

Remember to subscribe to Tammy's exclusive group of readers for your gift, only available to readers on her mailing list. **Sign up at www.tammylgrace.com. Follow this link to subscribe at https://wp.me/P9umIy-e** and you'll receive the exclusive interview she did with all the canine characters in her Hometown Harbor Series.

Follow Tammy on Facebook by liking her page. You may also follow Tammy on her pages on book retailers or at BookBub by clicking on the follow button.

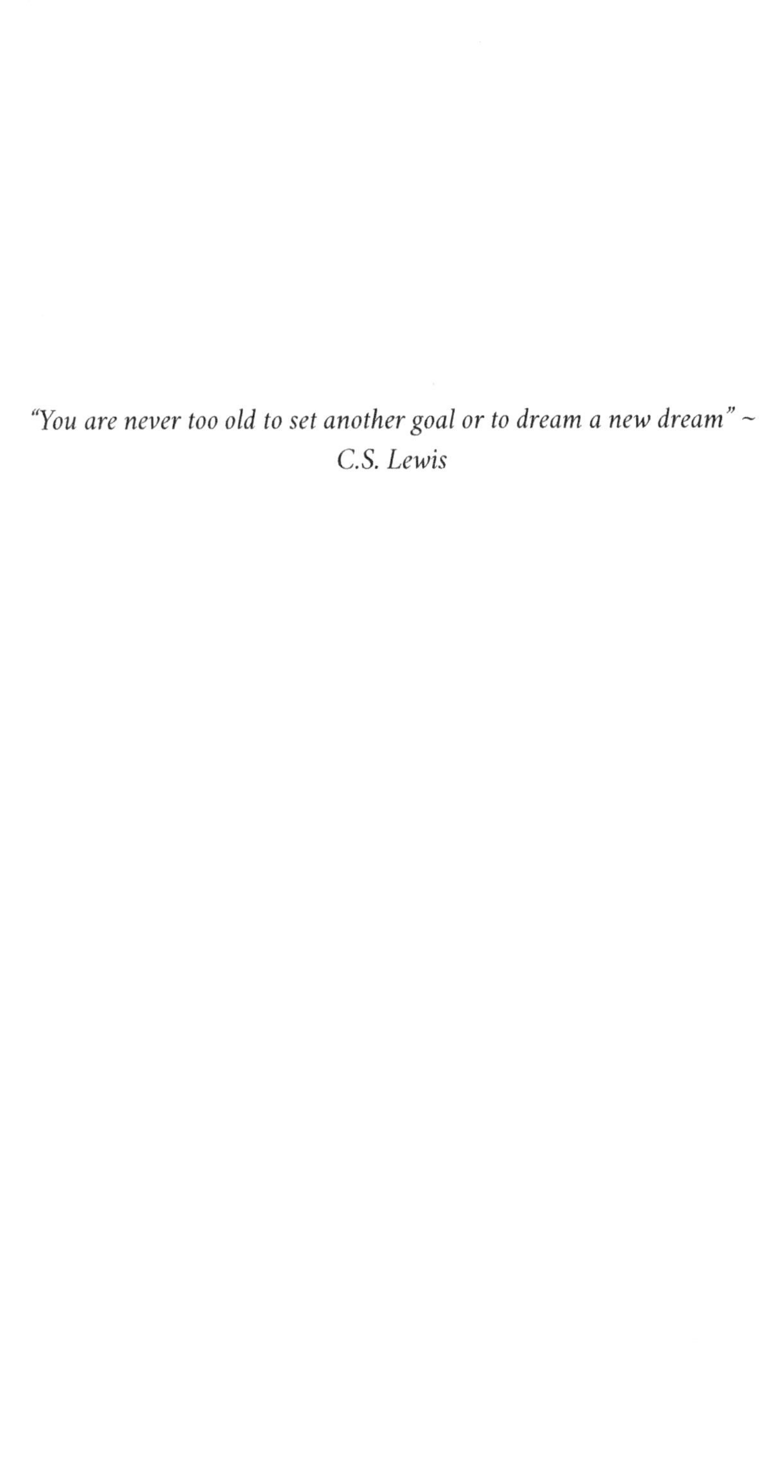

"You are never too old to set another goal or to dream a new dream" ~ C.S. Lewis

BEACH DREAMS

GLASS BEACH COTTAGE SERIES BOOK 3

TAMMY L. GRACE

LONE MOUNTAIN PRESS

1

Lily glanced over at Mel in the passenger seat and smiled. Mel's long hair shined in the sunlight coming through the window, her shoulders relaxed, her eyes heavy—such contentment.

Lily loved seeing her relaxed and happy, but her heart still ached for the young woman who had found her way into Lily's life. The last few days had been filled with a mixture of emotions. Lily had promised Mel a trip to Seaside to pay homage to her aunt who had passed away over two years ago, without Mel knowing of her plight.

They had taken advantage of Mel's spring break from school and squeezed in a trip before Lily's busy season would kick off in May. The first stop on their list was the cemetery. Mel had taken great care in selecting colorful blooms at the flower shop to place at the grave. All of them were pink—Aunt Tricia's favorite color.

Lily's heart broke when she saw the tears streaming down Mel's face as she bent to place the flowers on the grass. Mel spent several hours there staring at the plain, flat headstone wedged into the thick lawn, touching the cool stone, and gazing across the grassy expanse. She was quiet except for the few times she would mention a memory of her aunt. Nothing earth shattering, just tidbits and flashes of Tricia buying her those pink and white frosted animal cookies or telling her about the flowers she liked to plant in pots on her front steps.

After Lily was sure she was strong enough to be left on her own, she gave Mel some privacy and took a walk. The cemetery was only a couple of miles from town, but it was quiet and nestled in the trees. It was maintained by the city, meaning it wasn't extravagant, but it was clean and peaceful. Once she left the gates, she made her way along the pathway bordering the nearby creek.

The dogs would have loved the trail, with all the vegetation offering what Lily could only imagine would be irresistible scents they would have to explore. The slow flow of the water sloshing among the rocks made for a pleasant sound. After she wandered down the trail, she circled back to the road and made her way to Mel.

She found Mel with her eyes red and puffy, but she was ready to go. Her mission was complete. She had said her goodbyes. That day had been a rough one, with Mel more subdued than usual and emotionally spent with no interest in going anywhere or exploring more of the town.

After takeout dinner in their room, on the balcony overlooking the ocean, Lily let Mel talk about how she felt. Her grief was so heavy, leading Mel to complain about the pain in her shoulders and in the gnawing pit of her stomach. It was the finality of it all.

The last hope Mel had clung to for a semblance of a family had evaporated without Mel even knowing. She talked about feeling guilty and abandoned. Lily, more than anyone, understood.

Lily, too, had felt the weight of guilt and the fear of the

unknown, facing a new life without Gary. Their future had been snuffed out, and the days of anger and disbelief that followed his death wouldn't soon be forgotten. At least she had enjoyed the years they had together and had nothing but good memories to comfort her. Mel's life, on the other hand, had been filled with tragedy after so many losses that someone her age should never have to experience.

Mel was far more resilient than Lily and the next morning, she was up early and excited to begin their tour. The days that followed their visit to the gravesite had been filled with outings to the aquarium, walks at the beach, and window shopping along the promenade. The views were gorgeous, and they even took a ride further south to Canon Beach, where they had a picnic.

As Lily watched Mel delight in perusing some of the whimsical shops, she was struck once again by the young woman's innocence and almost childlike reactions to fun. Each time Lily realized all that Mel had missed out on and all that she had endured, she felt a pang deep in her chest.

True to her inquisitive nature, Mel had studied and researched the town and all it offered before they left Driftwood Bay. The simple things, like an outing to the aquarium or the beach, where they worked to build sandcastles, brought overwhelming joy, almost disbelief, to the young woman's face. Lily missed her sweet dogs and Mac but seeing the smile still on Mel's face as they made their way back home had been worth it.

Lily pulled off the highway and into a convenience store to grab a drink and use the restroom. The change in speed and turns the car took startled Mel from her nap. She blinked her eyes several times and took in the store.

Mel insisted on treating Lily to her drink and a snack. "You've paid for the entire trip, it's the least I can do. I appreciate you taking me to see where my aunt lived... and died. I'm not sure why it was so important to me, but I feel better having gone there."

As they walked back to the car, Lily put an arm around Mel's shoulder. "I understand, believe me. I hope you had some fun. It's such a beautiful area."

Lily slid behind the wheel and steered the car back to the highway. Mel took a drink of her hot chocolate. "It made me happy and sad. Happy that Aunt Tricia had found such a lovely spot to live and sad that I didn't get to visit her there. I wish I would have known."

"Just remember what Dr. Clay said about getting stuck in the past. Trust me, I've lived there too long myself. You've come so far from where you were. Celebrate that and be happy about your progress. Your aunt would be so proud of you." She reached across and patted Mel's knee, which earned her a smile and an eyeroll.

After she finished her drink, Mel dozed and didn't even budge when Lily slowed down as they entered Driftwood Bay. She checked the time and let out a breath. She had a couple of hours to get settled and order the pizza she had promised Mac before he would arrive with the dogs.

Despite talking to him each night, she had missed him over the past five days and looked forward to one of his legendary hugs. She'd only been in Driftwood Bay a year now, but it felt like home. She never imagined feeling comfortable in the arms of anyone but Gary, but Mac changed all that. It was like she had known him forever, and he made her feel safe again.

As she made her way to the house, and they unloaded the car, Lily's thoughts drifted to Mac. With the cottages closed for the first three months of the year, they had spent much more time together. Mac had even taken extra days off, and they had enjoyed several long weekends exploring nearby areas. The weather wasn't ideal, but they made the most of their time together. The bonus of snuggling by the fireplace came with the cooler days, many of them rainy and gloomy, which made the warmth of indoors even more inviting.

They had spent most of their days off together going to breakfast and wandering downtown, taking the dogs on a walk along Mac's property and visiting the llamas and alpacas, then starting a fire and watching movies or binging a series while they waited for whatever Mac decided to make for dinner. It was Lily's idea of perfection. Their love wasn't all fireworks and excitement, but it was deep and real and something she never expected, but now couldn't imagine being without.

At Cyndy's urging, they had even joined a pub quiz team that met at a local tavern along the waterfront. It would soon disband for the summer in May, since Driftwood Bay would fill with tourists for the high season, and the tavern would be much too busy to allow their tables to be taken up for hours by locals whose bar tabs were nowhere near those of the summer visitors.

Mel's offer to take the laundry downstairs drew her from reminiscing and back to the task at hand. Lily unpacked her suitcase and put it in the closet. She sniffed and wrinkled her nose at the musty smell throughout the house. She opened a few windows and the door off the deck to let in some fresh air.

She filled the dogs' water bowls and called in an order for pizzas, while she rifled through the stack of mail Mac had collected. Once that was done, she made a quick shopping list and hollered down to Mel to let her know she was leaving to run errands.

After buying more than she intended at the market, she hurried to pick up the pizzas and made the turn to her street, smiling when she spotted Mac's SUV in her driveway.

Before she could get out of the car, the dogs bolted through the door, and her heart fluttered when she saw Mac standing there, grinning at her. He unloaded her groceries and the pizzas, while the dogs, including Sherlock, mauled her with kisses and thwacks from their tails.

Lily grinned, knowing in her heart she would always own golden retrievers, just to make sure she'd never feel unwanted or unloved. She finally gave up trying to stand and sat on the garage floor to let them hug her more. Fritz put his front legs around her and rested his head against her shoulder, while Bodie zoomed around her in circles. Sherlock stood in front of Lily taking in the antics, no doubt thinking the puppy should calm down. Pure love radiated from all of them.

"Have you two been good boys for Mac while I was gone?" Lily tried to calm the exuberant and jumping Bodie and gave him the signal for sitting. It took a couple of tries, but he finally calmed down and sat in front of her, next to Sherlock.

She couldn't help but forgive his excitement and less than stellar behavior. He was just too cute and cuddly.

After a few more minutes of petting and belly scratches, she rose and led the three furry friends into the house. Mac had already put away the groceries, and he and Mel had the table on the deck set and ready.

The dogs were at Mel's heels, noses in the air sniffing at the savory aroma coming from the pizza boxes Mel carried outside. Mac reached for Lily's hand and engulfed her in a tight squeeze, holding her close for longer than usual before placing a gentle kiss on her lips. "I've sure missed you and am so glad you're home."

She smiled. "I was thinking the same thing. It was a good trip, especially for Mel. I'm glad we did it, but I couldn't wait to get home to you and my sweet boys."

They made their way outside, and Mac engaged Mel in talking about everything she saw in Seaside, while they ate slice after slice of the warm pizzas. Lily eased back into her chair and watched as Mel became more animated, telling him about the colorful fish in the aquarium.

It warmed her heart to see the young woman smiling and Mac's gentle way with her. Seeing him with her, Lily couldn't imagine his own daughter missing out on being part of his life. Their estrangement was hard on him and although he didn't talk about Missy much, Lily knew it hurt.

As dusk settled over them and the sky darkened, Lily had a hard time keeping her eyes open. The drive had exhausted her, and she looked forward to sleeping in her own bed and getting caught up over the weekend. Mel would be working both days and once Lily had her housework done, she'd dig into the reservations and begin the process of getting the cottages ready for their first guests of the season.

Mac was cooking dinner tomorrow night. She didn't have any burning obligations outside of lunch with Cyndy on Sunday, and she longed to spend a few hours in her window seat, reading a book she had taken on the trip. She began clearing the table and putting the leftover pizza on paper plates.

She hated to make Mac rush off, but she was tired and wanted nothing more than to slip into her cozy pajamas and sink into her bed. After she had the kitchen tidied, she went back outside and found Mac and Mel still talking. She stood behind him and kissed the top of his head. "I hate to be a party pooper, but I'm beat. I'm going to hit the hay. I'll see you both tomorrow."

He leaned back and looked up at her. "Go on and get some rest and just relax tomorrow. Come out whenever it works for you, and we'll plan to eat around six."

Mel nodded. "I'll make sure to lock up when I go to bed. I work early tomorrow and then go back for another evening shift." She stood and moved next to Lily, wrapping her arms around her shoulders. "Thanks again for the trip. I had a great time."

Lily squeezed Mel tighter. "It was my pleasure."

She said good night and wandered through the kitchen on

her way to her bedroom, grabbing the cup of tea she had left to brew. As she passed by the living room, the doorbell rang.

She shook her head and glanced at the clock. It was late for a visitor. She flipped on the entryway light and looked through the glass window in the door. "You have got to be kidding me." She took a deep breath, wishing she could pretend she wasn't home.

2

As soon as Lily opened the door, her sister's sad eyes met hers. Lily glanced down the steps at the designer suitcases she recognized from her sister's last visit. "I'm back," Wendy murmured.

In her tired state, Lily didn't have the patience for her sister. "Your timing isn't ideal. I'm just heading to bed. I thought we talked about this last time, and you agreed to let me know if you were coming for a visit."

Tears glinted in Wendy's eyes. "I don't think it's just a visit. I'm stuck and need to stay here."

Lily's heart sank. Her head began to throb. "I'm too tired to talk about it. You can set up downstairs in the guest room and fill me in tomorrow."

Mac and Mel came from the kitchen. Even in the low lighting, Lily saw the shock on their faces. Mac composed himself first. "Hey, Wendy."

She nodded at him. "Would you grab my bags for me? They're at the edge of the driveway where the shuttle driver left them. I don't think I can carry them another inch."

He stepped between the two sisters. "Sure thing. I'll just put them downstairs in the guest room." It wasn't an actual question, but his eyes met Lily's with a quizzical look.

"That would be great." Lily turned to Mel. "You can help Wendy find some towels downstairs and get her anything she needs. I've got to get to bed."

Mel smiled. "Sure, come on in, and I'll help you get settled."

As Mac came through the door, lugging Wendy's bags, he swiped a quick kiss across Lily's cheek. "Just go to sleep and call me tomorrow. We'll figure it out together."

Lily shut the front door, listening to Mel chatter on and offer Wendy pizza. She stifled a laugh as she padded down the hallway to her bedroom. Wendy would have to starve tonight since Lily was fresh out of kale and soy milk.

Lily's eyes shot open. She couldn't sleep. The soft snores coming from Fritz's bed surprised her. She must have dozed, at least for a bit, since she hadn't noticed Mel letting the dogs into her room. Knowing Wendy's aversion to them, Mel probably put them in there to save them from her.

After staring at the ceiling longer than she wanted to, Lily punched her pillow to make a better spot for her head. Then, she jabbed it several more times.

It wasn't the pillow's fault. Her irritation with Wendy overrode her body's desire for sleep. She couldn't shut off her brain. Now, her weekend was ruined. Ideas of relaxing and reading, interspersed with a bit of work on the cottages, disappeared with the arrival of her high-maintenance sister.

She remembered Wendy's incessant whining and complaining when she had arrived several months ago and wasn't sure she could forgive her for the way she treated Mel. The last thing Lily needed was someone else to take care of right now.

She tossed and turned, finally turning on the lamp and reaching for her book, hoping to escape reality. The sudden light earned her a bloodshot eyeball from Fritz, who scrunched further into his bed. She stared at the same page for ten minutes and then slammed the book closed and put it on her night table.

She had to get some sleep or risk being even crankier than she anticipated at having to listen to Wendy's latest excuses and hear whatever sad story she would share that brought her to Lily's doorstep.

Lily had tried to be patient last time, hoping to forge some semblance of a relationship with Wendy, and it hadn't worked. Just when she thought she might be making headway, Wendy had up and left, without so much as a goodbye. She had been living with Chad's wealthy sister back in Dallas, which was a much better fit for the lifestyle Wendy enjoyed.

Lily was accustomed to being used by Wendy, but Mel was hurt, especially when Wendy left behind the Christmas gift Mel had put so much thought into for her.

Lily wasn't up to suffering more of Wendy's arrogance and condescending attitude. She couldn't turn her sister out into the street, but there had to be some ground rules this time.

After a fitful night, Lily woke later than she wanted. There was no sun to shine through her window to roust her from bed this morning. Gray gloom filled the sky, and it looked like rain would arrive soon.

She sighed.

The day matched her mood.

She padded out to the kitchen and got the boys their breakfast, letting them out into the yard to romp together. On her way back to the kitchen to brew a cup of tea, she noticed the sticky note on the counter and recognized Mel's precise handwriting. *I hope you have a good day. I'm going to grab dinner with Elsie from work, so I won't be home until late tonight—Mel.*

They had come a long way from the first day Mel arrived. To say the young woman had been withdrawn would be like saying a sloth was sluggish. With what Mel had endured, it was understandable that she would recede into her own little world. Lily understood the allure to stay within the safety of her own cocoon. Mel had blossomed since she started attending classes at the local community college in the fall and working at the coffee shop.

She was bright and talented, and Lily hoped having a safe place to call home played a role in Mel's transformation. She still wasn't like other young women her age, but she was beginning to spread her wings and become more confident. Lily considered it an honor to be part of Mel's newfound family.

Now, she'd have to tackle her own flesh and blood and see if she could make any inroads with Wendy. She didn't hold out much hope and was dreading the conversation that would have to take place. First, she had to have a shower and a cup of tea. She wasn't much of a drinker but saw a glass of wine, maybe two, in her future tonight.

It didn't take Lily long to get ready and make her bed before emerging to wrangle the dogs and see if Wendy was up and coherent. The house was quiet, and there was no sign of her sister. As the dogs made a mad dash for the deck, Lily's stomach growled. She watched them romp through the yard, wishing she could be as carefree as they always were.

After she dried their paws, wet from the grass, and herded them into the house, she popped in a slice of bread to toast. Tired from racing around the yard and chasing each other, Fritz and Bodie stretched out in the living room, in search of their favorite patch of sunlight to sleep in, but with the cloud cover, they were out of luck.

While Lily nibbled on her toast and sipped on another cup of tea, Wendy wandered up the stairs. Dressed in her silk robe, her hair stuck out all over with her face streaked with makeup and mascara. She wasn't the picture of perfection she always sought.

Lily offered her a cup of tea, and she nodded her head, while tapping her freshly manicured nails on the granite counter. Wendy let out a long sigh and cupped her hands around the warm mug.

"So," Lily said, her brows raised. "What brings you here?"

"It's horrible, really. Chad's trial was a disaster. He was found guilty and will be in prison for ten years. That was the best his useless lawyer could do." She shook her head.

"What about his sister Constance? I thought you were staying there so you could be closer to your friends."

Wendy rolled her eyes. "Yeah, it didn't work out so well. Once Chad got sentenced, she got cranky with me. She's always been bossy, but she took it to a whole new level." She took a long sip from her cup. "She told me I had to get a job and contribute to household expenses. She went so far as to call me a mooch."

Imagine that. Lily reached for her tea before she said something she would regret.

Wendy's shoulders slumped, and she shifted her hand to support the side of her head. "The worst part was my so-called friends just ghosted me as soon as Chad was convicted. They blocked me on their phones and social media. It was like I was shut out from everything. My entire life."

"I'm sorry, Wendy. That can't have been easy."

"Constance was going on a Mediterranean cruise with two of her friends and told me I had to move out. She didn't want to leave me alone in the house. What does that even mean? Does she think I'm going to steal from her? I offered to watch the house and take care of things, but she wouldn't budge. I finally had enough and told her I would just come back out here. She paid for my ticket and is shipping all my things here. Not that they amount to much more than my clothes and accessories."

Constance was no dummy. "I feel for you, I really do. I'm sorry Chad's trial didn't go well."

Wendy interrupted, "That lawyer had the gall to tell me I was lucky I wasn't brought up on charges. Can you believe that?"

Why, yes, I can. "Like I was saying, I'm sure it's difficult for you. The reality is you'll have to figure out how you're going to live and adjust while Chad is in prison. You could make your own life. A new one. But you'll need a job to support yourself."

Wendy slammed her hand on the counter and pushed her chair back, flouncing out of the room with a huff. "You're just as bad as Constance."

She hurried to the stairs and slammed the door shut.

The dogs rushed to Lily's side, alerted by the commotion. Lily's head throbbed again, and she reached to pet Fritz's head. "What are we going to do with her?"

As much as Lily longed to lounge around the house, she sat in front of the computer in her office off the kitchen and brought up the reservation system. Technically, she opened in May but had a few reservations sprinkled in the last weeks of April. One lodger had booked the entire last two weeks of the month, starting on Monday. She was an author working on a book deadline and wanted peace and quiet.

With Wendy here, Lily hoped she could deliver on her promise of a quiet stay. She needed to find something to keep her sister busy and out of her hair.

Jobs weren't in abundance in Driftwood Bay, especially in

the off-season. Maybe Cyndy or Mac would have a good idea about where Wendy could look. Even better, maybe they could help think of a place she could move to, far away from Driftwood Bay. Maybe they knew someone in Rhode Island.

She rinsed both cups and put the dishes in the dishwasher, telling the dogs they'd soon be taking an excursion out to Mac's. Fritz's eyebrows lifted when he heard Mac's name, and Bodie's tail thumped against the floor. She felt the same way.

She went downstairs to the laundry room and saw that Mel had set out freshly laundered linens for the cottages. She took her role as a helper seriously, and Lily's heart lifted, thankful for her work around the property. She grabbed the linens and her keyring and headed down to the cottages.

She made quick work of getting the beds made with fresh sheets and taking the comforters from their storage bins. She'd dust and vacuum everything tomorrow, so it was ready for her one guest arriving on Monday. She sprayed a bit of the rose water she liked to use on the bedding and nodded her head with approval. She'd have time to add finishing touches tomorrow before her lunch date with Cyndy.

She wasn't in the mood to deal with Wendy's attitude or complaining. Rather than hang around the house like she'd planned, she packed up a few things to take to Mac's. She loaded the car, including Bodie and Fritz, then hurried downstairs to let Wendy know she was leaving.

Guilt niggled at her as she raised her hand to knock on the guest room door. It wasn't very hospitable to leave her sister on her own, but it served Wendy right for not even calling and showing up out of the blue. Lily rapped on the door.

"What?" snapped Wendy.

Lily opened the door a crack and saw Wendy sprawled across the bed. "I have plans today, so I'm heading out to Mac's. You've got my cell number if you need anything. Mel's working, and neither of us will be back until late tonight. I went to the market yesterday, so there's plenty of food in the fridge." She failed to mention there wasn't much Wendy would eat, but that was beside the point.

"So, you're just going to leave me stranded here with no car or anything?" Her whining was already grating on Lily.

"Afraid so. I have plans tomorrow so I'll be gone again, and Mel is working. I left a spare house key on the counter in the kitchen. If you leave, just make sure all the doors are locked."

"What am I supposed to do?"

"I don't know, Wendy. You could get online and check out the job listings or take a walk downtown. It's not that far."

"I hope you're taking your dogs with you. I can't deal with them."

Lily bristled at her snide comment. "Don't worry, they'll be with me, but you need to keep in mind, this is their home. I won't tolerate you being mean to them. They're sweet souls." She didn't wait for a reply and closed the door.

Lily rushed up the stairs, not wanting to wait around for any more questions or arguments.

She climbed behind the wheel, comforted by the cheerful faces that stared back at her in the rearview mirror. The boys were secured, and she was ready to get away from her sister. She resented being forced out of her own house, but the idea of listening to Wendy a minute longer was too much to bear.

As she made the drive to Mac's place, she took deep breaths, hoping to slow her heart rate and not spend the whole day yapping about what a pain Wendy was. Mac always went to the trouble of making something delicious, and she didn't want to spoil his welcome-home dinner.

A long walk and visiting the sweet alpacas and llamas would be just what she needed to clear her mind of Wendy.

3

It didn't take long for Lily's mood to improve. Just being at Mac's property offered a gorgeous retreat and was enough to lift her sprits. No rain had fallen, and the morning's ominous clouds threatening a dark day had been replaced by friendlier looking, puffy ones.

She noticed Sherlock in the grassy pasture and led Bodie and Fritz to join him. Once she had them secured behind the gate, she headed back to the house. The aroma of rich tomato sauce, fragrant with garlic and Italian herbs, greeted her as soon as she opened the door.

She found Mac in the kitchen and looking over his shoulder, she saw the huge lasagna he was putting together. He greeted her with a smile, and it was enough to make her forget her troubles. "What can I do to help?"

"Not a thing. Just relax. Pour yourself some iced tea or whatever you want to drink. I've got wine, too." He gestured toward the counter next to the fridge. "I didn't expect you so early."

She poured a glass of tea and topped off his glass. "One guess."

"Wendy," he said with a grin.

"Yep. I just couldn't hang around any longer. She's already getting under my skin." While he layered noodles, meat sauce, and cheese, she filled him in on Wendy's latest drama.

"So, she hasn't changed her tune since she left. That's too bad."

"It's like she doesn't live in reality." Lily took a long swallow from her glass. "I figured Chad would serve time and hoped she'd snap out of it and figure out she had to grow up. I don't want to fight with her or argue. With the season gearing up, I don't have time for her antics."

He slathered butter and garlic onto a fresh loaf of bread. "Like you said, she needs a job and needs to be responsible. Hopefully, she'll get on her feet and out from under your roof. I'm trying to think of anything she might be able to do."

Lily rolled her eyes. "That's part of the problem. Along with her unwillingness, she has almost no experience and very few marketable skills. She's going to be stuck with retail or food service. With her people skills almost non-existent, those aren't ideal options."

"Her time at Poppy's wasn't exactly great, was it?"

Lily shook her head, still embarrassed to go into the tea room. "Wendy hated it, and I think Poppy only tolerated her. It wasn't a good match." She sighed. "Wendy honestly believes she's above working, especially in any position that's service related. I'm not sure what she thinks she can do, but I'm afraid a strong dose of reality is about to smack her right in the face."

Mac chuckled and untied his No Prob Llama apron with a goofy, smiling llama on it that Mel had given him for Christmas. "Shall we take a walk? It's a bit cool, but that will make us walk faster and burn more calories, right?"

He had a way of making everything better. His thoughtful gestures made Lily happier and lighter. She loved that about him.

Soon, they and the three dogs set out for a jaunt around the property. The dogs were free of their leashes, since they were used to roaming Mac's acreage, and he had a whistle that never failed to bring all three of them running, should he need to get their attention. Their three tails wagged from side to side, in perfect unison, as they plodded along just a few steps in front of Mac and Lily.

He reached for her hand and smiled. "Do you need any help getting the cottages ready tomorrow?"

She wrinkled her nose. "I don't think so. Mel surprised me and had all the bedding laundered and ready for me this morning, so that's the worst of it. Just some light housekeeping tomorrow. Not that I'd refuse your company if you have nothing better to do in the morning."

He winked at her. "Cyndy said you two have big lunch plans, but I'll stop by in the morning. Maybe with some snacks from the bakery. I could take the boys back home with me, so you don't have to leave them with Wendy. I know that makes you uneasy."

She leaned her head against his upper arm. "Thank you. I'm not sure how I got so lucky, but you always know exactly what to do or say to make me feel better."

"I wish the same could be said for my daughter. I seem to have the opposite effect on her." He sighed. "I called Missy last week, just to say hello. While you were away, Cyndy and I talked more about it, and she encouraged me to reach out again."

Lily winced. "I take it things didn't go well."

He nodded. "You could say that. She's so snippy and acts like I'm disturbing her. I can imagine her rolling her eyes the whole time I'm talking. It wasn't much of a conversation. I tried to keep it upbeat and just asked her how she was doing and if she had any plans to visit."

She squeezed his hand. "I'm sorry."

"It's the same old story with her. If I call, I'm bothering her or butting into her life. If I don't call, I don't care about her. I can't win."

"For what it's worth, I don't think it's you."

He blew out a breath. "I know, but my heart still longs for the little girl I remember. Jill would be devastated to see us now."

The pain in his voice made Lily's heart break. "I'm sorry I was away when you were dealing with that."

He shook his head. "I purposely did it while you were away. I hate how it makes me feel after we talk and wouldn't want you to have to deal with it. Cyndy was there when I called her, so she helped me lick my wounds." He chuckled, but she knew it was only to cover the pain.

They walked a few hundred feet in silence. When they reached the fenced pasture where the llamas and alpacas stood, Mac leaned against the railing. "I want Missy to be part of my life and for so long, I've wanted to be included in hers. With how I feel about you and all the time we're spending together, I wanted Missy to know about you. About us."

She felt the angst radiating from him.

"She was less than supportive and was as hateful as she's ever been. I swear she delights in making things tough for me."

Her stomach lurched. Was he trying to tell her it was too hard, and he couldn't be with her if it meant losing his daughter? She couldn't imagine having to choose between Mac and Kevin but knew she could never give up her son.

The dogs sniffed along the fence line, and the animals moved closer, looking for the treats Mac always seemed to have in his pocket.

She hung her head and took a deep breath. "I understand if you need to step back and take a break from us. I don't want to come between you and Missy." Her throat burned, and her voice wobbled. At that moment, she understood the depth of her love for him. She was willing to let him go so he wouldn't have to suffer choosing.

His blue eyes, full of anguish, stared at her, and he wrapped his arms around her. "Aww, Lily, I'm not trying to tell you any such thing. You're the reason I'm so happy now, and I'm not giving that up. Ever."

He squeezed her even tighter, and Lily swallowed hard, hoping to squelch the tears that burned in her throat and eyes. She couldn't speak, just sighed, and let herself melt into him.

Hearing his words brought such comfort. She had no idea how she would be able to let him go. She'd been trying to be brave. Trying to be strong. For him. She didn't want him to be torn. She wanted to make it easy for him.

He continued to hold her as he spoke, "Before you, my life was hollow. Meaningless, really, except for my work. I'm not sure I knew how unhappy I was. I worked as much as possible, had Sundays with Cyndy, volunteered with the hearing dog project, and that was it. It was my normal. Now, with you, it's a thousand times better."

His words gave her chills. She lifted her head from his shoulder and looked into his eyes. "I wasn't looking for this. For you. I was just looking for somewhere new. To survive and maybe build a new life. I never dreamed I could find happiness again. I honestly thought it was over for me."

The clouds were rolling in again, and a chilly breeze ruffled Lily's hair and made her shiver. Mac rubbed her arms. "Let's get inside and start a fire. I need to put the lasagna in the oven, anyway."

Arm in arm, they made their way back to the house, the dogs following. Once inside, Mac got their dinner in the oven to bake and lit the kindling he already had prepared in the wood stove.

As the fire took hold, he added a large log, and the orange flames curled around it. The dogs settled in next to it, and Lily carried in two steaming mugs of tea. She sat on the couch next to Mac and snuggled under the thick blanket he had warmed in front of the stove before placing it over them.

She took a sip and reached for his hand. "So, back to Missy. What are we going to do?"

He smiled and brought her hand to his lips, kissing the top of it. "I like that you said we."

4

Lily made sure she and the dogs got home late from Mac's, hoping to avoid another conversation with her sister. After she got ready for bed, she tiptoed downstairs and saw the light coming from under the guest room door, where she pictured Wendy pouting behind it. She let out a quiet breath, happy she hadn't found Wendy in the living area where she would have been forced to talk to her.

As she was contemplating turning in for the evening, the front door opened, and Mel walked through it. She extended the cup she held to Lily. "I brought you a chai tea latte. I thought you might need one." Her voice almost a whisper, she darted her eyes toward the kitchen. "Is she here?"

Lily took a sip from the cup. "No, she's downstairs in the guest room." She pointed at the cup. "This is delicious, thank you." She gestured toward her bedroom, and Mel followed her and the dogs.

She and Mel sat in the window seat, overlooking the backyard and beyond to the beach. The hint of light still lingering on the horizon held the promise of summer days stretching longer, giving her more time to enjoy the beauty of the backyard and the firepit that would soon be used.

"How long is Wendy staying?" asked Mel, as she folded her legs in front of her and leaned against a pillow.

Lily shrugged. "She no longer has a place in Texas, so I would say indefinitely. We've only talked briefly, but she'll need to find a job so she can support herself. I don't have much patience for her, so I'm just hoping she figures things out quickly."

Mel smiled. "She probably just needs time. I'll keep my eye out for any job postings."

Lily admired Mel's innocence and willingness to help Wendy. Her kindness made Lily want to try harder to be there to help her sister. Years ago, she'd had the same optimism, but Wendy's unending rejections had turned Lily into a cynic.

She leaned against her side of the window seat and listened as Mel chattered on about her day at work, happy to sip her latte and soak in Mel's happiness.

Their conversation was about absolutely nothing, yet everything. Last year, Mel would have never sat with Lily, smiling and babbling on about customers and coworkers. She had come so far in a short time.

Mel's tone became more serious, and she let out a long breath. "So, there's a guy I work with, Tony Burns."

Lily nodded. "I don't think I know him."

"He's tall with sandy-colored hair and deep blue eyes."

Lily's heart skipped a beat. She saw the flicker of interest in Mel's eyes. "He sounds cute."

Mel's cheeks blossomed as she nodded. "Well, he asked me about going to pizza and the matinee at the theatre next week. They're doing an Alfred Hitchcock tribute."

"That sounds wonderful. Did you say yes?"

Mel's nose wrinkled, and she chewed on her bottom lip. "I

told him I'd check. I've never been on a date with a boy. I'm not sure what to do."

Lily pondered what to say. She tried to remember what it was like when she was young. "I guess my first question would be is Tony a nice person? Is he someone you enjoy spending time with?"

Mel nodded. "He's great. A hard worker and always polite, plus he likes to read."

"Well, he sounds like a nice guy. If you like being with him, I think you should say yes and see how it goes. Movies are a great date because you don't have to fill all that time with conversation. You can comment on the film a few times. I know you love pizza."

She smiled. "I think I just feel sort of awkward. I've never even thought about going on a date, and I'm not sure what to do or say."

"Just be yourself. You are a lovely young woman. So smart and have the kindest heart I've ever seen. If you have a shared love of books, I know you can talk about all the many books you've read. You love Alfred Hitchcock, so you'll already have lots to talk about. Ask Tony questions about himself, that always helps me relax when I'm with new people. Does he go to college with you?"

"Yeah, I forgot to say that."

With Mel's tragic history, Lily suspected nobody had ever told her she was beautiful or smart. It was easy to see the results of young people without anyone in their lives to encourage them, and she wanted to make sure Mel knew, no matter what happened with Tony, that she was intelligent, kind, and capable.

"I think you'll have loads to talk about with work and school, plus the movie. It's a good way to get to know him better. I'm sure in all your reading, you know how hormones can get carried away, especially with young men and women. He may want to hold your hand or kiss you, or you may want to kiss him. Just be true to yourself, only do what you know is right, and if you feel uncomfortable with him, call me or text me, and I'll come and get you."

Mel leaned against the pillow and smiled. "I think I'm a bit worried about that hormone stuff."

"That little spark of attraction is part of our biology, but you don't ever have to let a boy kiss you or touch you in a way you don't want. If it doesn't feel right to you, just say no. And Tony may not do any of those things. I'm just preparing you, like I would my own daughter. You may find out you're good friends, which is sometimes the best relationship to have with a boy."

Mel cocked her head as she listened. "What you said makes sense. I think you're right, and it would be fun. Tony isn't a jerk like some of the other guys who make fun of people and talk about girls all the time. I wouldn't go with him if he was like that." She talked more about what she should wear, since it would be right after she got out of class.

Relieved that Mel recognized the good guys from the slimy ones, Lily relaxed. She didn't relish having anything close to a sex talk with Mel but also wanted to keep her safe.

Lily helped her with ideas for outfits and encouraged her not to worry too much and choose something she liked and felt comfortable wearing. Thank goodness, Mel had weakened her stance on not accepting any gifts, and Lily had given her several new articles of clothing to add to her meager closet. Mel had also used some of her earnings to buy a few things on sale.

After twenty more minutes, Mel wound down, unfolded her legs, and stood next to Lily. "I work early again tomorrow, so I'll see you tomorrow night." She bent and petted each of the dogs. "Good night, boys."

Lily waved at Mel before the door clicked behind her. Thinking of the lovely day she had spent with Mac, she smiled as she turned off the lamp and snuggled under her blankets. The boys were tuckered out from their long day and nestled together in Fritz's bed.

After her sleeplessness the night before, she willed her mind to empty and relaxed against her cool pillow. The dogs were already sleeping and instead of thinking about her sister and Mac's daughter, she let her shoulders sink into the mattress. As her eyes closed, her mind raced with thoughts of where Wendy could get a job.

She couldn't stop thinking.

The idea of Wendy living under her roof with no plan was enough to make her pulse race. Lily's patience for her sister had run out after years of dealing with her self-importance and lack of interest in Lily's life. Wendy had a knack for only appearing when she needed Lily's help, and it didn't make it easy to welcome her.

Along with the frustration came waves of guilt. Lily's mother would be hurt and disappointed to see the relationship between her two girls had deteriorated to such levels. If her parents had still been alive, Lily was sure things would be different. Her mom, especially, was the glue that held them together and without her, it wasn't easy.

Wendy's disinterest in Lily's life and her sister choosing not to be even a tiny part of Kevin's life, hurt more than she liked to admit. Lily had written Wendy off long ago and had no expectations, but now, with her back and seemingly not just for a visit, old wounds were opened.

Her lack of genuine care when Gary was killed was the last straw. Wendy didn't do family. She was always too busy wrapped up in her extravagant life with Chad and their elite circle of friends. Now, with all that gone, she was back, looking to Lily to fix things.

As much as Lily tried to channel her mom and what she would do, her heart wasn't in it. She wanted nothing more than to find a solution that would send Wendy far away and keep her out of her life.

The realization brought more guilt. She didn't like feeling that way, but she'd been burned too many times.

~

The next morning, Lily woke later than usual, beckoned from sleep by a wet tongue on her hand and sunlight already streaming through her bedroom window.

She opened her eyes and saw the sweet faces of the two dogs who never failed to cheer her. Bodie was doing so well in his training, and it would soon be time for him to leave his puppy home with her and Fritz. The only thing that made it easier to bear the thought of giving him up was knowing he'd be going to Andy.

Bodie would make Andy's life so much bigger, so much fuller. And she and Fritz would still get to see Bodie all the time. Giving him up to a stranger or to someone out of town would be so much harder. The people involved with the hearing dog program had been hinting they would like her to take another puppy later this year, but she wasn't sure her heart could handle it.

She smiled as Fritz let Bodie smother him and sighed. She wouldn't be the only one who would suffer when Bodie had to leave.

After getting ready for the day, she padded out to the kitchen and let the dogs out while she prepared their breakfast and set the coffee to brew.

As soon as they finished eating, and she scooted them outside, the doorbell rang. She smiled when she opened it to find Mac and Sherlock. As promised, Mac was holding a box from the bakery.

He greeted her with a sweet kiss, and Sherlock thwacked her

legs with his tail. She led the way to the kitchen and opened the door to the deck so Sherlock could play with her boys in the backyard.

The faraway look in Mac's eyes made her reach for his hand. "Are you okay?"

He shrugged. "I just got some bad news this morning. A friend of mine passed away. A buddy I went to school with, Joe. He lived outside of Boston. Had a massive heart attack and died yesterday."

She squeezed his hand and led him into the kitchen. "I'm so sorry. Are you going to his service?"

He shook his head. "His family is going to do a celebration of life later this summer and just have a private service now." His voice cracked.

"I wish there was something I could do for you." She embraced him in a long hug. "I can reschedule lunch with Cyndy and spend the day with you."

He kissed her cheek. "No, I think some time with the dogs will be just what I need. We hadn't seen each other in a long time. I'm not sure why it hit me so hard, but it did. I guess it's a harsh reminder that our time is short."

She kept hold of his hand. "Sometimes way too short."

He smiled at her. "I'll be fine. It's just the initial shock of learning about it. I think when we lose people our same age, it makes us feel vulnerable, you know?"

She nodded. "Yes, I agree. It's like that now that we're in the age group where we lose friends more often. It has a way of making you face your own mortality."

He nodded and let go of her hand while he poured two cups of coffee.

As soon as they sat with their pastries and coffee, the door to the downstairs opened, and Wendy came through it. "Morning, Wendy," said Mac.

Still in her robe, she mumbled something and made her way

to the counter. She picked up the tea kettle and sighed. "You haven't made tea yet?" She turned her attention to Lily.

"No, but there's fresh coffee."

"And I brought plenty of stuff from the bakery." Mac turned the box so she could see into it.

She shook her head. "Too many carbs for me." Wendy looked at the carafe and wrinkled her nose. "I prefer special beans from Jamaica. That doesn't smell like what I drink."

Lily pointed at the cupboard. "The bag's in there. It's the last thing Costco had on sale."

With a huff, Wendy filled the kettle with water and rummaged through the boxes of tea in the cupboard.

Lily cut off a chunk of her croissant and looked at her sister, leaning against the counter, waiting on the kettle. "Did you have any luck on the job front?"

With a roll of her eyes, she shook her head. "I was too tired to even look. All this stress and travel has done a number of me. I could use a spa day and a massage."

Shoving another bite into her mouth to keep herself from weighing in on that idea, Lily reached for her cup of coffee.

Mac finished the last bite of his cinnamon roll. "With the tourist season starting next month, businesses will be looking for extra help. Hopefully, that works in your favor."

Wendy poured the hot water into her cup. "All I know is I'm not going back to Poppy's, and I'm not taking a job waiting on people. I hated it there."

Lily kept her hands wrapped around her cup. "The shops along the waterfront are usually the busiest, so it might be a good place to start. You could see if any of them look like a good fit."

As she lifted her cup, the three dogs stampeded up the stairs and onto the deck, where they stood at the glass door.

"I cannot deal with those dogs today. I'll be downstairs. I

really need to do some shopping. There's nothing in your fridge I'll eat."

"I'm visiting Cyndy later and can drop you by the market then."

Wendy shrugged and then nodded before she took her tea and disappeared downstairs.

When the door clicked closed to the downstairs, Lily got up and let the three dogs inside, taking care to wipe their paws before she let them through the door.

Mac raised his brows over his cup of coffee. "Glad I'm taking the boys home with me. She's in a prickly mood."

Lily laughed. "Welcome to my world. I hate that I have to disrupt my schedule and theirs to accommodate Wendy. She is a horrible houseguest."

Mac glanced at the clock. "Looks like she'll need a job that starts in the afternoon if this is her normal routine."

Lily took their plates to the sink and chuckled. "She'd never make an eight o'clock start time. That was the good thing about Poppy's."

The dogs stood at the end of the island counter. Despite their expert begging eyes, neither of their humans gave them a nibble of their breakfast treats. Mac offered to stay to help her with the finishing touches in the cottages, but she insisted he take the dogs and try to relax.

"I'll come by later this afternoon and pick them up. If you need anything, just call me."

He hugged her close. "I need you. Come for leftovers. I have a ton of lasagna left, and I'll send some home for Mel. I'm sure it's not up to Wendy's standards." He chuckled and herded the dogs to the front door.

"You don't have to twist my arm. I'll be there." She kissed him goodbye and watched from the front step as all the men she loved in Driftwood Bay piled into Mac's SUV.

It didn't take Lily long to dust and vacuum the cottages. She plumped the pillows and took the covers off the small table and chairs that graced each of the back decks of the cottages to wipe them clean. Once she was satisfied everything was ready for the first guests of the season, she walked back to the house.

After washing her hands in the laundry room and tossing the soiled cleaning cloths in the washer, she knocked on Wendy's door. "I'm heading to town in a few minutes, if you still want a ride."

Her sister shouted through the closed door. "I'll be up in a minute. Keep your dogs away from me."

Lily counted to ten. "Mac has the dogs." She didn't wait for a reply and hurried up the stairs.

She changed her clothes, made sure there was no dust in her hair, and added a swipe of lip gloss before she grabbed her purse and headed to the garage. As she started the engine, Wendy came through the door, taking her time getting to the car.

Lily backed out of the garage and turned toward downtown. "I'll be a couple of hours, so if you want to check out some businesses and do some job research before you do your shopping, I could pick you up on my way home."

Wendy fiddled with her designer purse. "I don't have much choice without a car."

Her tone reminded Lily of a two-year-old child gearing up for a tantrum.

Lily pulled to the curb and let Wendy out in front of the waterfront area. "Just call my cell if you need anything. Otherwise, I'll pick you up in about two hours, probably a little more."

Wendy left with a huff and slammed the passenger door. The sound rattled her head. Lily gritted her teeth and pulled into the street.

Thankful Cyndy suggested lunch at her house instead of a restaurant, where Wendy might find them, Lily drove the short distance to her house.

Cyndy's porch boasted containers of colorful tulips in bloom, and a gorgeous wreath of purple hydrangeas hung on her front door. Cyndy greeted her with a hug and a smile.

Lily handed her a bottle of wine from the cases she had purchased from Izzy's family winery in Friday Harbor. "I know this is one of your favorites."

Cyndy motioned her inside. "I haven't met too many wines I wouldn't drink, but you're right about this one." She led the way to her kitchen.

As usual, Cyndy had worked her magic in the kitchen. She had chicken salad sandwiches on flaky croissants, along with a fresh fruit salad and a beautiful lemon cake. With it being a gorgeous spring day, they ate on Cyndy's back porch.

As they nibbled at lunch, Cyndy asked how it was going with Wendy visiting.

Lily's shoulders sagged. "I hope it's only a visit, but realistically, I don't see her moving on anytime soon. I left her downtown today so she could check out the waterfront and hopefully get some leads on a job."

"Well, the good news is most of the retail stores will be looking for their seasonal help next month." She speared a grape with her fork. "Oh, you know, there's a new boutique opening, Marla's. She's new to town and stopped in to say hello this week. I'm not sure of the details, but she mentioned she would be looking for someone."

Lily chuckled. "New to town might be a bonus. Less chance she's heard of Wendy."

Cyndy chuckled as she refilled their iced tea glasses. "I suspect she's having a hard time adjusting to the fact that she's on her own. It sounds like her husband took care of everything, and she lived a life of luxury without having to worry about how to pay the bills."

Lily rolled her eyes. "Yep. Chad took care of everything, all right. I just don't see how she's going to find a job that pays enough to support herself. Without specialized skills, she'll be in retail work. I did a quick scan of available jobs in the area, and there wasn't much for someone without some type of training or education. Lots of manual labor jobs, but nothing that suited her. The pet grooming assistant made me laugh. The only possibility was a bank teller."

"Well, tell her about Marla's. Wendy might be able to talk to her before she advertises for help. I know she loves nice things and her designer clothes, so it might be a better fit than the bank or Poppy's."

Lily nodded, as she slipped her fork into the luscious cake. "She is frustrating because of her attitude. I've been through too many dramas with her and while I don't want to be the mean sister, I want to make sure she understands that if she's going to stay with me, she's going to have to pitch in and help." She sighed and took another bite. "Honestly, I'm not happy she's disrupted my world. She's not nice to the dogs and doesn't lift a finger to help."

Cyndy's forehead creased. "Maybe she could earn enough to afford a room. Like look for roommates."

"That's probably the best she can hope for at this point. I'm just not looking forward to the constant turmoil and stress she brings to my life." She chuckled and added, "Maybe I can find her a roommate in Texas and send her back."

5

Monday morning, Lily was up early to get ready for her guest who would arrive in the afternoon. The woman had paid in advance, and Lily added the breakfast vouchers to her folio while she sipped her first cup of tea.

The house was quiet, except for Bodie and Fritz lounging at her feet. Satisfied she was ready for Rebecca, the author who would be working to finish her book over the next two weeks, Lily slipped into her jacket and led the two dogs outside for a walk to the beach.

Last night over leftovers, Mac invited her to join him on Friday night at Noni's. He had already arranged with Mel to stay with the dogs, since she had a rare evening off from the coffee shop. Lily couldn't resist the delicious Italian food or the man who asked her and was already looking forward to the end of the week.

She gazed at the water and sighed. After trying to reason with Wendy last night when she got home, she needed the tranquility and peace the soft lap of the tide delivered. The sun was just peeking above the sea as they set out on the trail.

The dogs, loving the freedom to explore, wagged their tails as they trotted a few steps in front of Lily. She walked to her favorite driftwood log and sat to watch the sun rise above the water.

The wonders of nature, especially at the edge of the water, never failed to calm her mind. She focused on the ribbons of light that danced atop the water. She let go of the heaviness in her neck and shoulders, picturing her worries about Wendy flowing out with the ripple of the tide.

Sometimes, like today, she wished she felt Gary with her. His presence had been so strong when she first moved to Driftwood Bay and sat on the old log each morning. Not only was it beautiful and peaceful, but all those mornings last year, she swore Gary was with her. Sometimes, she even smelled him in the space next to her.

She was stronger now and liked to think he knew that. She brought her hand to her heart. He would always be with her because a part of her heart belonged to him forever.

Escaping all the memories that were too hard to bear had brought her here. A change of scenery, a new career in her retirement years, and a chance to reconnect to the cherished memories of her youth beckoned her to the small town she remembered. She never imagined finding a second chance and a future with someone she loved.

She was happy.

Sometimes that happiness made her feel guilty.

Sometimes she even believed she was happier now than she had been for years. Not because of losing Gary, but because of living a different life. Gary and Kevin had been her whole life, along with a career she could now admit she didn't love but stuck with for the retirement benefits.

She had more friends in Driftwood Bay than she ever had back in Virginia. She missed Kevin, sometimes so much it ached, but she would have missed him no matter where she lived. Her life now, although perhaps smaller, was fuller, deeper.

The dogs stuck their snouts in her lap, jarring her from her morning therapy session.

She rubbed the top of their heads. "Are you two ready to go home? Our first guest arrives today, and you must be on your best behavior."

They were good boys for the most part, especially Finn. Bodie, still a youngster, could get into trouble. Looking at their expressive eyes and sweet faces, she knew there was nothing they couldn't get out of with a tilt of their head.

She stood and led them back to the house. As they climbed the trail up to her yard, she glanced back and sighed. She would never tire of the pristine view.

Once back at the house, she fed the dogs breakfast and brewed some tea. While she waited for Mel to come upstairs, she took her cleaning supplies to the deck and wiped everything down, looking forward to warmer weather and spending part of her days enjoying it.

She brought her tea outside and watched the dogs play in the yard below, while she contemplated a trip to the nursery. She needed some plants to fill the containers on the deck. Maybe that was something she and Wendy could do together.

She wanted to avoid a conflict with Wendy, but at the same time, wanted her to understand the house rules.

Lily's line in the sand was about to be announced.

While she was cleaning the outdoor furniture, she made up her mind to approach her sister today. Wendy was struggling, and Lily didn't want to add to her angst, but from experience, she knew her sister could take advantage of her.

As she was contemplating, Mel came through the door, dressed and ready for her first day back at school after their break.

"Morning," she said, sliding into the chair next to Lily. "I'm heading out and won't be home until later. I've got to work at the coffee shop, and then we're meeting there tonight to work on our group project."

"That sounds fun. I don't have any plans today. Just the one guest arriving, so I'll get her settled this afternoon."

Mel's eyes widened. "It's exciting that she's a real author and going to be staying here. I hope I can talk to her while she's here, but I don't want to bug her."

Mel's enthusiasm for all things reading hadn't waned. Lily smiled and nodded. "I'll be sure to ask her if she has time for a chat. Maybe we can talk her into joining us for tea and snacks, since I won't have the firepit weekends yet."

"That would be great. I'm working a ton but left my schedule on the fridge." Mel checked her watch. "I better get moving. Hope you have a good day." Mel gave her a quick hug and left.

Mel didn't mention Wendy, but Lily appreciated the little hug of encouragement. She would need it to get through the conversation she was dreading.

By the time Wendy emerged from downstairs, Lily was ready for the day, had caught up with emails, and checked her reservations, which were filling up for the summer season. From her desk, Lily hollered out, "Good morning, Wendy. The kettle is full if you'd like tea."

She didn't answer, but Lily heard the clink of the cup on the counter. She took a deep breath, steeling herself for the talk.

Lily poured herself a cup of tea and joined Wendy at the island counter. "Did you give any more thought to getting in touch with Marla about her new boutique?"

Wendy shrugged. "I saw the coming soon sign in the window but couldn't tell much about it. I guess I could stop by and look. I just don't want to work at some dowdy store."

"Cyndy thought it would be stylish things that you might like. I think it's worth checking out, especially before she advertises for help. Plus, it's close enough you could walk to and from work. I'm happy to give you a ride if it's convenient, and I know Mel would help, too, but there are times we won't be available."

Wendy sighed and sipped from her cup.

Lily set her cup on the granite counter. "I know it's going to take some time for you to figure out what you're going to do, Wendy, but you need a job. There's no getting around that. Driftwood Bay doesn't have much to offer, but if you start working, you could save up enough to move somewhere that might have more job opportunities."

"I know. I hate this little town. There is nothing here."

"Where would you have looked for a job back in Texas?"

She rolled her eyes. "I didn't need a job in Texas."

"Yes, I understand. I'm just trying to figure out what interests you. Since you liked the big city atmosphere, I thought brainstorming ideas might help you figure it out."

She sighed and gazed across the kitchen. "Oh, well, I know quite a bit about fashion and jewelry, along with cosmetics. I probably would have looked at something in that arena, maybe a designer shop. I'd really excel at being a personal shopper." She shook her head. "Not much chance of that in this place."

"You'd have to go to a larger city, Seattle or one of the suburbs to find a clientele for that." Lily reached for the notepad at the end of the counter and flipped it open. "I did some looking online for costs for rentals." She slid the information across to her sister.

Wendy's eyes widened.

"On the next page, you'll see a sample budget of what you will need to support yourself in a small apartment." She reached and flipped a page. "I did a comparison between something close to the city and something more rural, like Driftwood Bay."

Wendy eyes flicked from page to page.

"You'll see the housing costs are about double in the cities. You may want to think about looking for a roommate situation, which could cut your costs. Bottom line, you'll need to work at least full time to be able to afford the basics."

Wendy's bottom lip quivered. "I don't even have a car."

"Right." Lily tapped her finger on the notebook. "This is your new reality. You can stay here while you figure out what you're going to do. I do have some house rules and conditions you'll need to agree to and follow."

Wendy continued to stare at the budget sheets as Lily continued, "First, you'll need to pitch in and help around here, which means cleaning, yardwork, fixing meals, and being helpful to my guests. If you need special food, you'll need to buy it and prepare it. Also, and this one is a deal breaker, you must treat the dogs and Mel with kindness. I won't tolerate anything less, and you'll find yourself without a place to stay if you're anything but kind and gentle with them. Think of them as my children and treat them as such."

Lily took a sip of tea. "With the busy season coming up, it will mean cleaning the cottages and doing laundry, making sure things are set for new guests and generally helping guests with anything they need. They have access to the downstairs living room with the television and all the games and books, along with the makeshift kitchen and refrigerator."

Wendy wrinkled her nose. "Eww, you let those strange people in your house. I'm not sure I can deal with that."

"Well, that's how it works. I lock the house by around nine or ten o'clock, but until then, they can come and go. If you aren't comfortable, I suggest you start looking online and in the paper for a place to stay."

Wendy shoved the notebook across the counter, knocking it into Lily's cup and splashing tea all over it and the counter. She stood and glared at her sister. "You're making this impossible for me. You're not helping at all."

At her shouting, the dogs, who had been resting on the deck, came to the door, their faces pressed against the glass.

Lily kept her voice calm. "I'm not going to argue, Wendy. If you want to stay here for free, which according to you isn't helping, those are my conditions. This is my home and my business. If it's too much for you, you'll need to find another solution and a different place to stay."

"And where would that be?"

"I don't know, but that's for you to decide. I've got a guest coming this afternoon, and she'll be here for two weeks. There are a few other guests who will be staying a night or two and then starting in May, I'm booked almost every single night. So, I don't have much time for histrionics. I'm fine if you want to stay here, work, and save up so you can find something more suitable, but while you're here, my rules stand."

Wendy took her cup of tea and stomped downstairs, slamming the door behind her.

Lily's stomach clenched. Her home was her haven, and Wendy brought only chaos to it. The resentment she held for her sister brought such sadness.

She let the dogs into the kitchen, wiped the mess from the counter, and took her tea to the living room. She curled into the corner of the sofa, and both dogs climbed onto it, snuggling close to her. She ran her hand over Fritz's head and gazed at Bodie's sweet brown eyes.

Staying sad wasn't an option with the combined weight of one hundred and forty pounds of golden love leaning against her and doing everything in their power to dispel her sour mood. The cute wooden sign she had picked up at Cyndy's store was right. All dogs were indeed therapy dogs.

Sitting around and wallowing wouldn't solve her problem. She thought of Mac and the loss of his old friend. Nothing would help him, but she put in a call to the florist to send him something for his office, hoping it would brighten his day.

Lily finished her tea and got the dogs ready for a walk to the park. Her guest wouldn't check in until mid-afternoon at the earliest, which gave her hours to enjoy the spring day and sunshine.

The dogs were beyond excited for an adventure, tails wagging as they made their way to the park. Bodie walked next to her and wasn't tugging at his leash any longer. He stopped when she stopped and was making excellent progress with his training.

The park was quiet and almost empty, so finding a spot was easy. Lily took off her backpack and retrieved the dog toys she had packed. The moment she took hold of the colorful balls, Fritz and Bodie danced in circles. Their favorite game was about to commence.

After dozens of retrievals, Lily's arm was ready for a break. She led the dogs to the nearby watering station and filled their travel bowl, while they slurped at the water as it came out of the spout.

With some of their energy burnt off, the two dogs were content to rest on the grass at Lily's feet, while she sat on a bench in the sunshine. The cool breeze coming off the water wicked at the sweat on the back of her neck.

Her phone buzzed with a message, and she smiled when she saw Mac's name. He thanked her for the thoughtful arrangement and included a photo. The florist had chosen succulents potted in the back of a small ceramic vintage truck planter, and it was perfect.

After drinking the bottle of water she brought with her, Lily attached the dogs' leashes and set out for home. Each step that brought her closer to the house filled her with dread. She didn't want to fight with Wendy or subject her first guest of the season to any unpleasantness. Being relatively new to the business, she couldn't risk negative reviews.

When they arrived, she used the keypad to open the back gate and left the dogs outside, while she climbed the stairs to the deck. She blew out a breath and opened the door to the kitchen.

The house was quiet. Too quiet.

Lily went downstairs and put her ear to Wendy's bedroom door. Silence.

She knocked on it and got no response. She cracked it open and saw the unmade bed and clothes and makeup strewn about on every surface. Wendy wasn't there.

She climbed the stairs and walked through the house and even checked the garage, but there was no sign of Wendy. Lily's stomach growled, reminding her she hadn't had any breakfast, and it was well past the lunch hour.

Lily opened the fridge and smiled when she saw the containers of leftovers Cyndy had sent home with her yesterday. She reached for a plate and enjoyed the delicious sandwich and salad from her table on the deck.

Bodie and Fritz were stretched out on a sunny patch next to her. They were tuckered out from their morning adventure.

As soon as she finished her lunch, her phone dinged with a motion alert. She looked and saw a car parked in the guest parking area. Rebecca had arrived early.

She ushered the dogs into the house and went downstairs to help her guest with her bags.

Rebecca greeted her with a smile and an apology for being early. Lily grabbed her bag and said, "No worries at all. We're ready for you, and you're our only guest until next week."

She led Rebecca along the walkway to the downstairs and showed her the common area. Lily discovered Rebecca enjoyed tea and wine. With her being the only guest, Lily promised to leave her a bottle that she could enjoy in her cottage. She explained the intercom system and the security code before giving Rebecca the guest folio. "You'll find your breakfast vouchers and some local information, should you want to explore a bit."

Rebecca chuckled as she followed Lily to the first cottage. "I am not allowing myself to do anything but write. I'm on a deadline and crunched for time, so I'm hoping the seclusion and beach air will do the trick. I'm on a strict word count schedule each day. If I'm on track at the end of the week, I'll be sure to reward myself with a look around town."

"There are lots of places to eat along the waterfront, and some of them will even deliver, if you don't want to leave the property." Lily pointed back at the house. "I know we discussed dogs when you booked, but I've got two golden retrievers, and they think everyone is their best friend, so you probably won't escape meeting them if you're outside."

Lily opened the door and waved Rebecca in first. "Oh, I love dogs, so that won't be a problem."

"I've also got my sister Wendy staying with me. She and Mel, a young woman who helps me around the property will be in the downstairs bedroom areas. And only if you have time and are up to it, I'd love to have you up to the house for tea. Mel loves all things books and is dying to talk to you."

"That sounds wonderful. I'll chat with you on Friday and see what I can make work with my schedule." She took in the space and sighed. "This is perfection. I can already feel the words flowing."

Lily made sure she knew how things worked before waving goodbye and leaving the author to write.

Her shoulders relaxed as she made her way upstairs. Rebecca would be an easy guest. As long as Wendy behaved, it promised to be a quiet week.

6

s Lily contemplated what to have for dinner, growing concerned about Wendy's whereabouts, her phone rang.

Wendy needed a ride home from town.

Lily hopped in the car and picked her up in front of the market. Lily's mouth fell open when she saw her sister, dressed in a black animal print dress with magenta high heels and a matching bag. Lily loaded the grocery bags at Wendy's feet in the back and then slid behind the wheel.

A hint of a smile formed on Wendy's face as she told Lily about her day. "I stopped by to see Marla, and she hired me on the spot. She needs help getting all her inventory received and priced and wants me to help stage and display things to get ready for her opening in ten days."

"That's good news," said Lily, as she turned onto her street.

Wendy straightened the skirt of her dress. "She liked my sense of style, I think."

Lily glanced over at her sister. "I don't know how you can walk in those heels. Did you walk to town?"

Wendy chuckled. "They're comfortable, but no, I didn't walk

to town in them. I called a ride share car." She rolled her eyes. "Apparently, there are only two such cars in Driftwood Bay."

Lily pulled into the garage. "The dogs are upstairs, just so you know. They'll be excited to see you, so keep that in mind and be nice to them."

Wendy rolled her eyes. "You and your dogs. Just you being here is sooo unbelievable. I still can't see how you're happy in this tiny place that has almost no real shopping. It's so inconvenient and... ordinary." She wrinkled her nose as she added that last word.

"I love it here, but it's not for everyone." Lily got out of the car and grabbed the grocery bags, since Wendy was already opening the door to the house. Those high heels must exempt her from carrying anything.

Lily lugged the bags into the kitchen and noticed the dogs standing at the door to downstairs. She reached out to pet them both. "I'm sure Wendy ran away and didn't want to risk any dog slobber on her beautiful clothes."

In response, they both licked her hand.

Lily led the dogs to the deck, grabbed a bottle of white wine for Rebecca, and went downstairs. With a guest on the property, hollering at Wendy from the kitchen wasn't an option.

She slipped the wine into the refrigerator and went down the hallway. Lily called out to her sister as she tapped on the bedroom door, before opening it a crack. "I left your groceries on the kitchen counter. You'll need to come up and put them away. I'm just getting ready to make something for dinner."

"I'll be there in a sec," Wendy said, from behind the door.

Lily went back upstairs and rummaged in the fridge. She still had another chicken salad sandwich left from Cyndy's, so she put that on a plate and added the rest of the fruit salad.

As she was finishing her meal, Wendy appeared. Lily made the dogs stay seated by her while her sister went about putting away her groceries. Wendy waited for her tea to brew, took it and a plastic container of salad, and headed downstairs.

Lily opened the door for her since her hands were full. "Why don't you stay up here and eat, and we can watch a movie or something?"

Wendy shook her head. "I'm beat, and Marla wants me there at nine o'clock. I've got to get some sleep. Can you give me a ride down there in the morning?"

"Sure, Bodie and I have training, so that works out well. Mel could probably drop you in town on the days she has classes, since they usually start at nine."

Wendy shrugged.

"I'll mention it to her tonight when she gets home. On Fridays, she doesn't have class, so that would be your only problematic day."

"I'll be working on the weekends too, just because Marla has so much to get done, and I could use the money."

"That's great. I'm sure we can work it out most days and if not, you can walk or call a ride share." Wendy started down the steps. "I'm very happy you found a job that suits you."

When Wendy reached the bottom level, she turned. "It's a job I can probably tolerate. We'll see. I just need to save up enough money to see about moving somewhere else."

"Have a good night," said Lily, as she shut the door. Prickly had been the word Mac had used, and it was a good description of Wendy. She wasn't as cranky as she had been yesterday, but her comment about moving gave Lily hope that she wouldn't be stuck with her forever.

Lily didn't smother the flicker of hope she had but was a realist. The sad reality was it would take Wendy months to save enough money to move.

~

The next morning, Lily was up early, put together soup in the slow cooker, took the boys for a walk on the beach, and got ready for the day. She put Bodie's harness on to get him ready for their trip to the training facility. Fritz was staying home, lounging in his favorite patch of sunshine, and Lily had seen Rebecca outside the cottage and waved at her from the deck, but she was proving to be the least demanding guest to have ever stayed at the cottages.

Bodie and Lily waited in the SUV, and Wendy finally emerged, dressed in pants and more sensible shoes today.

While she drove, Lily let her sister know that Mel was willing to drop her off on Mondays, Wednesdays, and Thursdays. "Mel starts class at nine, so you'll need to be ready to go by eight thirty."

Wendy shook her head and blew out a long breath. "That's terrific. I can barely make it by nine." Her sarcasm hung in the air. The shine of her happiness at finding a job had already worn off, and Wendy was back to her thorny self.

Lily didn't respond and pulled to the curb in front of Marla's, where Wendy got out without so much as a goodbye.

Lily glanced in the rearview mirror and saw Bodie's happy face, his tongue hanging out of his mouth, and eyes full of excitement. Wendy's petulance didn't bother him. She needed to be more like her dog.

During their training, she learned Bodie was on schedule and would be continuing his professional portion of the program starting in August. That would take about five months, and then he'd be matched with his new owner.

It was all good news, but she found herself crying on the drive home. They had asked her about signing up to raise another puppy, and she couldn't do it. The only thing keeping her from breaking now was knowing Andy would get Bodie, and she'd be able to see him as often as she liked.

She knew this day would come, and Andy was so excited

about it. She blamed her tears on the upheaval Wendy had caused and seeing Mac so sad about losing his friend. Loss was difficult and surrendering Bodie was something she didn't want to face.

Days like this made her feel like a wimp.

She pulled into her garage and used a tissue to blot the tears from her cheeks. They found Fritz waiting at the door, wagging his tail to greet them. She led the pair outside, and they took off chasing each other around the yard.

Glad she didn't have Wendy underfoot, Lily made herself a cup of tea and curled into the corner of the couch with the book she had been reading. She longed to escape into the pages and leave behind real life for a few hours.

Along with reading, she and the dogs squeezed in a long nap and when Lily woke, it was close to time to pick up Wendy.

She fed the dogs before she made her way downtown, where Wendy was coming out the door of the new boutique. The look on her face made Lily brace for impact.

Wendy slammed the passenger door, causing Lily to wince. Exhaustion came over her as she steered the car back toward home. Wendy was huffing and doing all she could to elicit a response from Lily, but Lily focused on the road, choosing to ignore her.

When she pulled into the garage, Lily said, "I've got some soup ready if you'd like some."

Wendy followed her. "Is it organic?"

As she opened the door to the house, Lily took a long breath. "Not one hundred percent."

Like always, the dogs were waiting, their tails wagging in anticipation of Lily's return. She bent down and urged them to their beds, not wanting to have to deal with Wendy's reaction to them.

She needn't have worried since Wendy went downstairs without a word.

Lily ladled the chicken soup into a bowl and plopped onto a chair at the island counter. Despite doing almost nothing all day, she was overwhelmed with fatigue.

As she finished her meal, Wendy emerged from downstairs. She wandered to the fridge and looked inside for several minutes before shutting the door. Her eyes glanced at the slow cooker full of soup.

She lifted the lid and took a sniff at it. After stirring it, she scooped out a serving and brought the bowl to the counter.

She met Lily's eyes. "I'm too tired to make anything else." She ate a few bites and then said, "Marla told me today that once the store opens, she probably won't need me full time, unless it really takes off. She wants me to learn how to do everything but thinks she'll only need me on weekends."

Lily took her bowl to the sink. "Oh, that's not great news. I'm so sorry. I'm sure she's just trying to make sure the business is successful. It's hard to make ends meet when you're new."

"That's not my problem, is it?" Wendy snapped at her.

Lily poured the leftover soup into a container and went about washing the dishes. "You might be able to find another part-time job to pair with it if you enjoy working there. So many small businesses are run by owners who work in them each day, and they don't need full-time employees. Or you could check out the job listings again."

"Well, part-time there, I'll barely make enough to cover my food. Do you know how expensive things are?"

Lily wiped off the counter and counted to ten. "Yes, I'm fully aware of how much it costs to live. How much electricity, heat, insurance, maintenance, and groceries cost. I know you're disappointed, and I hope the new boutique is super busy so you can work full time, but you might want to consider checking around for alternatives or a second part-time position. Sadly, that's your reality right now."

The spoon clanged against Wendy's empty bowl, and she dashed downstairs.

Lily had never had to raise a petulant teenaged girl, but she imagined it was exactly like this.

7

Thursday was Mel's big date. Lily got up extra early in case Mel needed help picking an outfit or anything else. She needn't have worried. Mel came up for breakfast looking very stylish in a blouse Lily had given her and a matching sweater. The teal color reminded Lily of some of the darker-colored sea glass in her aunt's jars and looked magnificent with Mel's dark hair.

She noticed Mel was wearing the silver chain with a dainty sea glass charm Lily had given her. "I think you chose the perfect outfit. Not too fancy or fussy, but very classy."

Mel smiled as she sipped a cup of tea and nibbled on cinnamon toast. Before long, she was packing up her bag and heading for the door. Lily hugged her goodbye and whispered, "If you need me, call me."

Mel smiled as she headed out the front door.

A tear trickled down Lily's cheek as she watched her drive away. Mel was a grown woman, but to Lily, it felt like her own child taking her first steps into a new world. Mel had endured so much, and Lily didn't want to see her hurt. She closed her eyes and said a little prayer that Mel would be protected and enjoy her outing.

As Lily kept busy throughout the day, she reminded herself that Mel had proven to be resourceful and after her brush with danger last year, was even more aware of her surroundings and people. Lily trusted her judgment, and it didn't hurt that she had checked with Jeff and found out Tony was a good kid. His mom was a single mother who was a local real estate agent and well respected.

Once a cop, always a cop.

After dinner was over, and she took the dogs for another walk, Lily settled into her chair to wait for Mel to return home. She tried to concentrate on her book but was too nervous to get far.

She drank several cups of tea, scanned through the television channels, and finally found a new episode of a series she knew Mel liked. She queued it up to have ready in case Mel felt like watching it when she got home.

Knowing her, she'd probably want to tackle her homework. She was very disciplined, and, with going to the movie and pizza right after school, she wouldn't have had time to do any schoolwork.

The dogs heard Mel long before Lily and rushed to the front door to welcome her home. It was only a few minutes after eight o'clock.

Mel came through the door, bent down to pet her furry fan club, and set her bag in the entryway. Lily stared at the open book she had on hand and pretended to be nonchalant and engrossed in the story.

Mel came up to her chair, all smiles.

"Oh, you're home early. How did it go?"

She took a seat on the couch and grinned. "It was great. We

saw *Rear Window*, which is one of my very favorites and turns out to be Tony's, too. You were right about having lots to talk about."

She went on, chattering non-stop, while Lily fixed them both a cup of tea. "Tony's mom sells real estate, and he helps her put up signs and get houses ready and things like that. It sounds fun."

She told Lily he would be working more for his mom and the other agents at the real estate office during the summer, along with his barista job.

Not lazy, check.

Helps his mom, check.

Lily was liking this kid the more Mel talked.

Mel prattled on, giving Lily a detailed description of her entire evening. Turns out they both like the same pizza toppings. "Oh, and he was a perfect gentleman. We held hands during the movie, but he asked me first, and then he kissed me on the cheek when he walked me to my car. He even held the door for me."

Gentleman, check.

"Tony sounds like a great guy. Maybe you can invite him over for dinner one night." She remembered Wendy. "Well, let's see how things go, and we might invite him when we're going to Mac's house. With Wendy here, it's a bit unpredictable right now."

Mel smiled and yawned. "I'm beat and need to get my homework done, so I'm not behind." She retrieved her bag, stopped, and gave Lily a hug. "Thanks for encouraging me to go. I had a good time, and I think we'll do it again soon."

"Night, Mel. I'm glad you had fun."

Lily was exhausted from worrying about Mel and then listening to her rapid-fire chatter. She turned off the television and herded the dogs to her bedroom. She smiled as she crawled under the covers. She loved seeing Mel so happy and spreading her wings. She was tired, but it was the best kind of tired.

~

Friday, Lily dropped Wendy at work and returned home where she and Mel changed out the bedding in Rebecca's cottage while she was at breakfast.

Mel beamed with excitement since Rebecca had spoken with her and suggested they have tea on Sunday to discuss books and anything else Mel wanted to know.

As they worked together to clean things and replace the towels in the bathroom, Mel chatted about school and the coffee shop. "Oh, my shift tomorrow starts at nine, so I can run Wendy to the boutique and bring her home."

"That's nice of you. I appreciate you doing it. I know she's not the easiest person to be around right now."

Mel shrugged. "She's going through a tough time. She's been quiet each day I've driven her this week."

"Has she mentioned any new job leads?"

Mel shook her head. "No, I suggested a few places, but she's not interested in working in a restaurant setting. She's not super people oriented, so it's tough to find something."

Lily chuckled. That was a tactful way of putting it. They finished up the cottage, and Lily added another bottle of wine to the fridge in the common area, while Mel got the laundry in the washer.

With the major chores done, Mel helped Lily get the lights she liked to string in the yard out of storage. Lily checked the bins and smiled. "I'm going to get started on these tomorrow. They always make the yard look so festive."

"I'm off on Sunday and could help you."

"That would be great. I'll do what I can tomorrow, and then we'll finish it up on Sunday before our tea with Rebecca."

Mel grinned. "I can hardly wait. I've never met a real author in person before."

"Are you interested in writing a book someday?"

She shrugged. "I'm not sure, but books have been my best friends for most of my life. They're like magic to me." She checked the clock and gasped. "I better get going. I have a short shift today and will be home in time to watch the dogs while you and Mac go on your date."

"I appreciate that. I still don't trust Wendy around them. I wish she'd relax and realize how gentle they are and how much comfort they offer. I know she's stressed, and there's nothing better than those two to ease your troubles."

Mel nodded. "She's pretty uptight around them, that's for sure. I'll see you around five o'clock and will be here as soon as I pick up Wendy from the boutique."

"Thanks, you've been a real trooper when it comes to pitching in to help her. She may not always tell you thank you, but it's truly kind of you."

With a quick grin, she trotted up the stairs.

Lily carted the storage bins outside, so they wouldn't be strewn about the downstairs area and took one of the smaller ones upstairs so she could work on stringing them along the deck. It made the evenings so enjoyable to sit among the twinkling lights.

As she surveyed the deck, she remembered that she needed to make a trip to the nursery and get some flowers to plant in the large pots she liked to place around the edge of it. She had intended to ask Wendy to help her, but with her new job, working was a priority.

Bodie and Fritz loved to visit the nursery and take in the tantalizing scents that beckoned them to explore every bush. The nursery was dog friendly, except for a certain area that was fenced off and contained plants that were toxic for pets.

The boys enjoyed their time romping through the pathways,

while Lily juggled their leashes and the wagon she pulled behind her. After less than an hour, she had selected a pile of colorful blooms and couldn't wait to get home and get to planting them.

Minutes after pulling into the garage, she saw Andy's truck swing into her driveway. The young man waved at her and rushed to help her with the dogs and the plants.

She wasn't overly skilled in sign language, but because of Andy, she was committed to learning it, and his visits helped her exercise her skills. She had more laundry to do and while she was busy with it, he dug in and got the flowers planted in the pots. Once she was done downstairs, she joined him and between planting, they talked.

He was a master lip reader, so despite her lack of skills, he had no problem understanding her. He was excited to let her know that his parents had agreed to him finding a place of his own, once Bodie was placed with him. His smile made her heart full.

Their situation was a bit unusual and unorthodox, in that recipients usually didn't know their hearing dog before they were matched, but with the urgent need for a volunteer foster trainer and Mac's long-standing relationship with the non-profit organization, they had agreed to honor Lily's stipulation that Bodie be placed with Andy when he graduated from the program.

Last year, when she had taken Bodie on, she never imagined how much having him would open her heart and connect her with the young man who was currently rolling on the deck and playing with Bodie and Fritz. There was nobody more deserving of a hearing dog and partner than Andy, and it made the bittersweet thought of giving him up, much sweeter.

As much as she hated the thought of sweet Bodie not being with her, seeing the excitement and love in Andy's face helped ease her burden. Bodie would love Andy forever and would make such a difference in his life. Andy looked forward to having more freedom, and Bodie was his ticket to a fuller life. Lily could only imagine how much his parents worried about him and wanted to keep him safe. The small part she played in helping foster and train Bodie would rank in the top experiences of her life.

She and Andy made quick work of getting the pots filled with colorful flowers and when they finished, Andy offered to put up the twinkle lights along the railing of the deck. He had them installed in no time. Lily looked forward to seeing them lit up tonight.

She paid Andy in cookies and iced tea before he scooted out to get back to the job he was supposed to be at and helping his dad. He gave both dogs more belly rubs before he left and promised he'd stop by again soon.

With a bit of extra time and thankful she didn't have to worry about collecting Wendy tonight, Lily lingered under a hot shower and took her time getting ready for dinner at Noni's. She had limited her lunch to a snack of cheese and fruit, since the meals at their favorite restaurant were so filling.

As she perused her closet, the beautiful tank she had purchased on sale caught her eye. It was in shades of blue and teal with shimmering beadwork in sea glass colors down the front of it. She paired it with a blue cardigan with a stylish waterfall hem and her favorite jeans.

She had time to feed the dogs before Mac was due to arrive and with any luck, he'd get to the house before Wendy returned and spoiled what had been a lovely day.

As if reading her mind, the doorbell rang, and she found Mac waiting for her, more handsome than ever. The deep-blue shirt and matching jacket made his eyes stand out, and his smile melted her heart.

He greeted her with a brush of his lips against hers. "You look lovely, as always."

Not to be left out, the two dogs came running to say hello. Fritz dashed outside the open door, searching for Sherlock.

"Hey, get back in the house, you silly boy. Your friend isn't here this time." She led them back to their beds, rewarded them with a treat, and collected her purse.

She turned to Mac and said, "Let's get out of here before Wendy gets home. Mel's picking her up from work."

He grinned and opened the door. "I take it things haven't improved on that front?"

She shook her head as he held the passenger door for her. "Today was great because she was at work, and I did some planting. Plus, Andy came to visit."

As he drove to Noni's, she asked about his day. "It was busy, but I was able to sneak out early like I planned. I'm working tomorrow morning but thought maybe Sherlock and I would get some takeout and come by for lunch tomorrow. The weather is supposed to be fantastic."

"That sounds like a plan. I'm going to put up some more lights in the yard. I'm trying to get ready for the busy season. We can check out the deck tonight. Andy strung the twinkle lights on it today."

He pulled into Noni's parking lot and took her arm as she got out of the car. The hostess greeted them with a warm smile and led them to a corner table in the parlor room. A candle flickered atop the table.

The tiny restaurant, situated in an old house, was always in high demand and had only a few tables in each of the rooms, which afforded an almost private dining experience. The décor was all velvet, wood, and crystal. It was old-world elegance.

After they ordered, Mac smiled at her. "So, how's your lone guest?"

"She's quiet and low maintenance, so I'd say she's perfect. Mel is chomping at the bit to visit with her and so excited to meet an actual author. Rebecca kindly agreed to have tea with us on Sunday."

They chatted as they ate Noni's famous to-die-for garlic bread, along with their crisp salads. As Lily finished her last bite of salad, she said, "Oh, the arts center called, and they need a volunteer for tomorrow night, so I've got to work for a few hours. I figured I better say yes, since I'll be too busy during the high season to be much help to them."

"I can stay with the dogs, or you can bring them by the house, whatever works for you."

She wrinkled her nose. "I might take you up on that. Mel's working a split shift, so she'll be out, and I'd feel better if they weren't alone with Wendy. I'd like to acclimate them to her and her to them, but she tends to rush downstairs when she gets home."

"How's the job going?"

Lily rolled her eyes. "I'm not holding my breath. Marla told Wendy she wouldn't have enough work for full-time, once the store opens, since she'll be working most of the time by herself. That was a blow to her, which I understand. With Wendy's attitude, it's almost impossible to discuss it with her."

Their entrees arrived, and the enticing aroma of the herbs and tomato sauce wafting from her plate of chicken parmesan made Lily forget all about her sister.

They took their time, enjoying the always delicious food, talking about the dogs and the upcoming summer season. Lily was looking forward to June, when Kevin would be visiting for a couple of weeks between school and work.

Lily took a sip of water and raised her brows. "Oh, I forgot to tell you. I got an email from Izzy, and she invited us to spend the Fourth of July on the island. I'd love to do it and could probably arrange with Mel to watch over the cottages, since she won't be in school."

"I think that sounds like a great idea. We can take the dogs, so all Mel would have to worry about is the guests, and she's so responsible, that should be easy."

After such a heavy meal, they resisted the temptation of the decadent tiramisu. Mac slipped his credit card into the leather folio and caught Lily's eye. "How about a walk around the waterfront, then we can grab a coffee?"

"I'd love that." He collected his credit card and took her hand as they left the restaurant. After a week of angst with Wendy, the idea of spending time with Mac, just the two of them, like a proper date, appealed to her. Being with him brought out the best in her. He made her laugh and lifted her spirits. His strong hand in hers made her feel safe.

He drove downtown and found a parking spot along the waterfront shops. He offered her his arm, as she stepped from the car and led her down the street toward the fountain in the square. The evening was mild and perfect for walking along sidewalks where the trees twinkled with white lights. Spring flowers burst from containers on every corner, and the fresh aroma of pear trees in bloom filled through the air.

The locals were out in force enjoying the weather and the relative quiet in Driftwood Bay before the sidewalks would be bustling with tourists. Hand in hand, they made their way to the square, where they spotted a table near the fountain. Mac pulled out the wrought-iron chair for her. "You can take a seat, and I'll grab our drinks. Any special requests?"

"Surprise me."

Lily did a bit of people watching while the scent of the lilacs that surrounded the square drifted around her. Lilacs always reminded her of her mom. She closed her eyes and could almost feel her presence.

Moments later, Mac returned and handed her a chai tea latte with a heart poured into the froth. He took a seat and sipped his mocha.

He set his drink down and reached across the table to take

Lily's hand in his. He gave a soft whistle, and Sherlock appeared at their table. Lily gasped when she saw him. "Where did he come from?"

Mac chuckled. "He's here because we have a very important question to ask you."

As she glanced between the two of them, her forehead furrowed. Mac cleared his throat. "Remember on New Year's Eve, when I told you I wasn't popping the big question and that I just knew I wanted you in my life? We agreed to take things slowly, but Joe's death made me realize time is limited."

He paused and took a deep breath. "I admire your strength and love the feel of your hand in mine, your leg touching mine, your lips against mine. I think of you every single second that I'm not with you. I don't want to waste another month, another week, another minute without you."

He stood and reached for Sherlock's neck and untied a small velvet box that was attached to his collar. He bent on one knee, next to Lily's chair.

The people in the area who had been chatting and moving about quieted and stilled, and Lily felt all their eyes on her. Her mouth went dry as she focused on Mac.

"Lily, I'd be the happiest man alive if you'd do me the honor of marrying me." He plucked the shiny ring from where it nestled between the blue-velvet cushions.

Her heart fluttered as she let his words pour over her like warm honey. As she looked deep into his eyes, she saw the sincerity, the gentleness, the desire. She had those same feelings and thoughts.

She nodded her head and whispered, "Yes, Mac. I love you, and I'll marry you."

He slipped the ring on her finger and wrapped her in a tight hug. As he squeezed, he whispered, "I called Kevin to ask his permission, and he was thrilled and wants nothing more than for you to be happy."

Tears leaked from her eyes. "That's so sweet, Mac. I must admit, as much as I want this, I was a little worried about telling him."

The crowd that had gathered around them broke out into applause.

Mac got to his feet and ran his hand over Sherlock's back. "Good boy, we pulled it off."

Lily bent forward and touched her forehead against the top of Sherlock's. "You're such a sweet boy. I bet you can't wait to get home and tell Fritz and Bodie about what a good secret keeper you are."

His pink tongue poked out of his mouth, and his jaw moved into a smile. She laughed and reached for Mac's hand, holding her other hand out in front of her to admire the ring. It had a vintage vibe and was stunning, especially when the streetlights hit it.

She leaned her head on his shoulder and said, "You caught me by surprise. I had no idea you had all this up your sleeve."

Mac's grin filled his face, all the way up to the tiny crinkles on the sides of his eyes. "I was going for a big surprise, but low key." He moved his chair closer to hers and sat, wincing as he rubbed his knee.

She frowned. "Are you okay?"

"Yep, just not as nimble as I used to be, and there was a tiny rock under my knee."

She sighed. "I'm trying to figure out if I'm dreaming or if this is real." She smiled at him. "I can't believe I'm getting a second chance at love with a man like you. After losing Gary, I figured I'd grow old alone. I never thought I'd feel those warm and bubbly feelings for another man. Then I met you. I feel like I can tell you anything and while I pride myself on being independent, I know I'm better with you."

She leaned closer and kissed him. "And I could stare into your pretty blue eyes forever."

He grinned. "It's the same for me. From the first day I met you, I haven't been able to quit thinking about you. I haven't felt like this since losing Jill. You make me happy, and I know we'll have to figure things out, but I want the rest of my life to be the best of my life."

As they sipped their drinks, with Sherlock settled at their feet, Lily's heart quivered in her chest. "What about Missy?"

Mac's jaw tightened. "I'm hoping she comes around to the idea, but I'm not building my life around her approval. She's had the control over me since Jill died, and I'm done waiting. Over time, I've finally realized she delights in making sure I'm alone and does everything possible to thwart any chance of a relationship."

Lily's stomach lurched at the idea of their marriage being one that was the target of her malice. "I just don't want to cause more stress between the two of you."

He shook his head and brought her hand to his lips, kissing the top of her knuckles. "It's the reverse, really. With you by my side, there's nothing we can't weather. Even hurricane Wendy."

She finished the last of her latte. "You said you don't want to wait long. I'm not much for a big wedding. What do you think about trying to plan something for when Kevin is here in June? Is that too soon?"

His smile grew wider. "I'd roust a judge out of bed and marry you tonight if you want, so June sounds great. I'll leave it all up to you. You decide when and where."

"I want to keep it simple. Just a few close friends and family. Maybe we could get married on the beach?"

He leaned close and kissed her. "That sounds like a dream wedding to me."

8

After staying up late, talking more with Mac about the wedding, and showing off her ring to Mel, whose excited yelps threatened to wake Wendy, Lily slept later than normal.

Mel and Wendy were already gone by the time she emerged from her bedroom. Mel had left a note letting her know that she had fed the dogs and didn't tell Wendy the exciting news, leaving that for Lily to share.

As Lily made her tea and toast, the ring caught her eye. She held it up in the sunlight streaming through the window and admired the cushion-cut stone and platinum setting. It sparkled even more in the light of day, and her heart did a tiny flip when she gazed at it.

As she glanced out the window, she saw Rebecca leaving for breakfast and hurried down the stairs to take care of servicing her room while she was gone. As she wrestled the sheets on the bed, she missed Mel's help. It went much faster with the two of them, but Lily made quick work of the process and tossed the laundry in the wash before heading upstairs.

She checked the time, while not sure what Kevin would be

doing in the early afternoon, risked it, and connected a video call. He appeared on the screen and greeted her with a huge smile. "Hey, Mom, what's new?"

She flashed her hand in front of the camera. "I think you know, but I wanted to call to tell you the latest. Mac said he talked to you before he proposed."

He nodded. "He sure did. I'm so happy for you, Mom." He paused and added, "I know Dad would be too. Mac's a good guy, and you deserve to be happy together."

Tears stung her eyes as she listened to her son, who seemed much older than his years.

"We want to have a small ceremony and decided to do it when you're visiting in June. I want you to be there."

"Sounds great to me. Uh, I was going to ask you if you would mind if Brooke came with me?"

The nervousness in his voice betrayed his feelings for Brooke. Lily knew it was serious if he was asking her to join him on a visit. "That would be wonderful. I'd love to meet her and between Mac and Cyndy, we've got plenty of room. I'm not sure if Aunt Wendy will still be here or not."

"How's that going?"

"She's at work right now, so that's a step in the right direction, but it's not all that much better, attitude-wise. She's not a fan of Driftwood Bay and is hoping to save up some money and move somewhere larger."

Kevin's eyes widened. "That's going to take some time. Housing prices are crazy."

"Well, you know her, she doesn't always embrace reality. She hasn't had to worry about money her entire married life, so it's going to take some time for it to sink in. Enough about all that, I'm just so excited you'll be here in June. Mac and I will work on the details, and I'll let you know the date for sure. We're just going to have a ceremony down on the beach." She paused. "I'm going to email Nana and Pop and let them know."

"Sounds great, Mom. I need to run, but I'll talk to you soon. Tell Mac congratulations again from me. Love you."

She disconnected the call and blotted her eyes. There was something wonderful and heartbreaking about seeing Kevin grow into an adult. The shift in their relationship was good, and she was so proud of him. At the same time, her heart longed for the little boy he had been. She had a hunch she'd be attending his wedding before long.

She settled in at her office computer and composed an email to Gary's parents. They didn't keep in touch much, but they did check in on Kevin, and she appreciated that. She kept it short and to the point, just to let them know she had met a lovely man who was a widower, and they were planning a wedding in June when Kevin would be visiting. She wished them well and signed off, letting them know they were welcome to visit but knowing that would never happen.

After breakfast, she tossed the wash into the dryer, watered her new plants, and then wrestled the ladder from the garage. Mac had told her he'd help her hang the lights when he was done at the clinic, but she wanted to get started on them.

Andy and Wade had installed some hooks in strategic places to make the process easier. She plugged in the string to make sure it worked and attached it to the first hook on the edge of the deck. She climbed down and moved the ladder to the next spot.

The string slipped out of her hand, and she leaned to reach for it. Before she knew what happened, she yelped in pain as her wrist and the rest of her hit the ground. In the process of falling, the ladder toppled and was on top of her legs. The dogs rushed over from the other side of the yard.

Fritz put his snout in her face. "It's okay, Fritzie. I'll be okay. I just need to get up."

She used her good hand to try to reach for the ladder and

move it. As she tried to do that, Rebecca rushed from her cottage. "Lily, Lily, are you okay?"

"I think so, but I've hurt my right wrist. Could you help move the ladder?"

Rebecca bent and lifted the ladder off her. After inspecting her new ring and making sure it hadn't suffered any damage, Lily used her left hand to help lift herself up. When she stood, she winced in pain. Her right ankle had taken the brunt of the ladder, and she couldn't stand on it.

Rebecca reached for her to help steady her and support her weight.

"Oh, man. My ankle is hurt, too. This isn't what I needed right now."

"Shall I call someone or call the ambulance?"

"My cell phone is up on the deck. On the table. If you can get that for me, I'll call Mac."

Rebecca helped her walk over to the area under the deck and settled her into an outdoor chair before hurrying up the stairs to retrieve her phone.

Moments later, she returned and handed it to Lily. "You should get some ice on those injuries right away."

Lily nodded. "I'm so sorry to have disturbed you. If you don't mind, I've got some ice packs in the freezer in the kitchen."

Rebecca shook her head. "It's no problem at all. I'll run to get them for you."

While her guest went to find the ice packs, Lily put in a call to Mac's office. He didn't usually answer his cell phone when he was working, but his receptionist connected her within a few minutes.

"Hey, I was just getting things wrapped up. Sherlock and I will be there within the hour."

Lily grimaced. "Slight change of plans. I took a tumble off the ladder and probably need to get checked out. I hurt my wrist and ankle."

"Oh, no. We'll be right there. Don't worry."

His calm, reassuring voice eased her worries. Fritz and Bodie kept circling her chair, and Bodie even whined. She reached out with her good hand and petted them. "Don't worry, guys, I'll be okay."

Rebecca returned with the gel ice packs Lily always kept in the freezer and helped situate one on her ankle, while Lily held the other around her wrist. Lily shut her eyes and between berating herself for being so careless, prayed neither was broken.

A few minutes later, Mac and Sherlock came through the side gate, sprinting toward Lily.

Lily shrugged and smiled at him. "Mac, this is my guest Rebecca, who was kind enough to help pick me up off the ground." She tilted her head toward Mac. "This is Mac, my... well, as of last night, my fiancé."

It was the first time using that word and Mac in the same sentence. It sent a tingle through her as she saw him grin and extend a hand to Rebecca.

"Well, congratulations to both of you. That's such exciting news," said Rebecca, smiling at them.

"Thank you for helping me, Rebecca. I'm sorry to interrupt you but appreciate it."

The woman waved away Lily's concern. "Don't worry about it. I needed a break. I just hope you're okay."

Mac put a hand on Lily's shoulder. "We'll get you down to the hospital and get you checked out." He bent to look at her ankle. With gentle hands, he moved it a bit and asked her to let him know when it hurt.

Lily looked up at Rebecca. "He's a veterinarian."

The woman smiled. "I'll leave you to it, but if you need anything, please just ask. I'll wait to hear from you on our tea for tomorrow."

Lily gasped. “Oh, Mel has been looking forward to it. It will happen, one way or another.”

Rebecca smiled. “If you don’t need any more help, I’ll get back to work.” She waved as she took a few steps toward her cottage.

“We’ve got it, but thank you,” said Mac. “I’m going to get her down to the hospital right now.”

Lily sighed. “I feel so foolish. I know I should have waited for you to help. This isn’t going to be good.”

“I don’t think the ankle is broken,” he said, as he bent and put an arm around her to lift her from the chair. “Just lean your weight on me, and we’ll get you to my car. I called ahead and let them know we would be coming in.”

“I’ll need my purse from upstairs.”

He got her situated in his SUV, almost picking her up to place her in the passenger seat, then went to get her purse and lock the house.

Minutes later, he slid behind the wheel. “I left the boys in the yard.”

Lily leaned against the headrest and shut her eyes. Despite the ice, her wrist and ankle both throbbed with pain.

Mac had them at the hospital in minutes and rushed inside, returning with a wheelchair. He lifted her into it and wheeled her through the emergency entrance.

The nurse behind the counter greeted Mac with a cheerful smile. “Hey, Doc. We just need her to fill out some forms, and we’ve got a cubicle ready for her. Doctor Russell is on duty.”

Mac nodded. “Thanks, Jess. How’s Twinkie doing?”

“She’s a troublemaker but doing great, thanks.”

He took the clipboard and returned to Lily’s side. “Dr. Russell is one of the best, so you’re in good hands.” Mac put on his reading glasses and filled out the forms, asking Lily questions and transcribing her information from her insurance card.

She signed them as best she could with her left hand, and he took the clipboard back to Jess.

She glanced over the paperwork and buzzed them through the door to the treatment area.

Jess went about taking her vital signs, and Dr. Russell came into the room and examined her. "Let's get x-rays first, then we'll see what we're dealing with."

It didn't take long for the doctor to return and show Lily and Mac the films. He used his pen to point at the bones. "Good news, I don't see any fractures."

Lily breathed out a sigh of relief.

"Bad news is both of them are severely sprained. You'd have to have an MRI to get an exact diagnosis, but it won't change your treatment." He went through the protocols, which included ice, resting, compression, and elevation of the impacted areas during the first forty-eight hours.

"We'll wrap them for you, and you might want to consider other styles of braces that are easier to use. You'll want to start doing some light exercises after the initial two days. We want to get your range of motion back and increase the blood flow, so always elevate, but you need to move and use your wrist and ankle to get them functional and strong."

He gave her a sheet with exercises, which were more just movements she should be doing at first.

Lily scanned the pages. "How long do you think before they heal and are usable?"

"I'm guessing you have what we call Grade 2 sprains, and those usually run around four weeks. Sometimes longer. Sometimes shorter."

Mac nodded. "We're getting married in June, so I'm sure that's on Lily's mind, along with figuring out how she can run her bed and breakfast."

Dr. Russell grinned and shook Mac's hand. "Congratulations, Mac. That's great news."

He turned his attention to Lily. "You're going to need some help for a few weeks. I'll order some home physical therapy, and that will help you with some hands-on guidance on exercises. If you do them and behave yourself for the next month, I think you should be able to walk down the aisle in June without a problem."

Her throat burned, and tears threatened to spill from her eyes, but she smiled and nodded. She pictured the stairs to the laundry room and those from the deck to the yard. What about Bodie's training? All because she was too impatient or stubborn to wait for help.

Dr. Russell wrote on his prescription pad and handed it and the order for physical therapy to Mac. Lily was too busy worrying about the next month to listen to their conversation.

After signing a few more forms and well wishes from Dr. Russell and Jess, they were headed back to Lily's house. Mac detoured to the café by the library to pick up some lunch for them.

They skipped the pharmacy since Dr. Russell wanted Lily to treat the pain with over the counter medicine unless it became unmanageable. She wasn't a fan of pain medication and assured Mac she could handle it.

Once at the house, Lily eyed the steps. "I think the garage would be the easiest place for me to navigate. It has the least number of steps and sturdy handrails."

Mac parked in front of the garage door and left Lily while he went inside to open the door. As she wondered how she would manage things over the next month, the harsh reality, like a dark cloud, settled over Lily.

How would she ever begin to plan a wedding and take care of the cottages, not to mention handle the dogs and her daily chores? The timing couldn't be worse.

9

When Mel and Wendy arrived home from their workday, Lily was just waking from a nap. Mac had her installed in the recliner with everything she could possibly need at her fingertips.

The dogs were out in the backyard, and Mac was in the kitchen, cooking dinner. Mel greeted him with her usual exuberance, asking why the garage was open. Lily shut her eyes and listened to the hushed tones as Mac explained her fall from the ladder and the resulting injuries.

Mel tiptoed into the living room and knelt next to Lily's chair. Lily opened her eyes and summoned a smile, with the hope of easing the concern on her face. She gave Mel's hand a reassuring squeeze.

"How are you?" asked Mel, her eyes serious as she glanced at Lily's wrist and ankle, both wrapped and resting on pillows.

Lily shook her head. "I've had better days. I'm so upset with myself."

Mac came into the room, wearing an apron and carrying a cup of hot tea. He added it to the side table and kissed the top of Lily's head. "Dinner's in the oven."

Lily smiled at him. "Thank you. I'm not sure what I would have done without you today."

The door to downstairs banged close, announcing Wendy's arrival. She came through the archway looking confused. "What's happened?"

Mac explained things to her, since as usual, she had made a beeline for her bedroom as soon as she came into the house. She had changed into one of her trendy exercise outfits. Lily hadn't ever seen Wendy exercise, but she'd be dressed to the nines if she ever did.

Wendy moved closer to examine Lily's wrist and ankle. As she swept her eyes over her, she gasped and pointed at her hand. "That ring is new. Is that an engagement ring?"

Lily glanced at her hand and smiled. "We planned to tell you when you got home from work, but it's been a bit chaotic. Mac proposed last night, and I accepted. We're getting married in June when Kevin comes to visit."

Wendy's eyes widened and mouth gaped. She looked from Mac to Lily. "Wow, that's unexpected and fast."

An awkward silence fell over the room.

Mel piped up and said, "Well, I think it's wonderful. You're two of the nicest and best people I know. I'm excited for you and can't wait."

Lily's eyes met Mac's, then she turned to face Wendy. "We decided life was too short to wait any longer. It's going to be a simple ceremony. Just down on the beach, nothing too elaborate."

Wendy's eyes shimmered. "Well, you'll need a dress. If we were in Texas, I'd take you to the perfect upscale bridal shop."

Lily waved with her good hand. "Really, I'm not planning on an actual wedding dress. Just something special, but simple."

Mac took a seat on the couch. "When we got home from the hospital this afternoon, Lily and I talked about possible solutions here at the cottages. How she might manage things while she's recuperating and unable to do all her normal activities."

Mel nodded and sat next to Mac. "I get out of school in a few weeks but could help on Fridays until then, and I'll adjust my schedule at the coffee shop so I work in the evenings."

Lily smiled. "That's so nice of you, Mel. The problem is after this week, we're booked solid, so it's a ton of daily work."

Mac caught Wendy's eye. "Lily said your job at Marla's won't be full time, only weekends, so we thought you might want to work here full time during the week. Lily would be on hand to answer all your questions, but you could handle the physical work."

A flash of uncertainty or maybe even fear flashed in Wendy's eyes. Her nose wrinkled, as if she smelled something foul. She looked out the window, over the yard, and down to the cottages.

She sighed and said, "What's involved?"

Lily reached for her cup of tea, and Wendy helped her. "Well, I help the guests with their luggage, get them checked in, and make sure they get a folio with all the information for the property and the area. If they stay for three days or more, we do some housekeeping and change their linens and towels. Shorter stays, we just change them when they leave. So, lots of laundry more than anything and some light housekeeping. The maid service will come three times a week and do the checkouts, but you would need to do the intermittent service for guests staying longer than three days and any checkouts on other days. You'd need to greet guests and be here to help them with anything they need. I can't go up and down the stairs at all."

Mac nodded. "Lily usually does weekend appetizers and wine by the firepit but could probably get away with delaying that until after Memorial Day." He sighed and added, "If I had a ground-level bedroom, it would work to move Lily to my house while she heals, but she'll need to stay here."

Lily nodded and caught Mel's eye. "We wondered how you

would feel about staying at Mac's place for the next couple of weeks. He could take your bedroom here and take over nursing duties and help with the dogs, if Wendy agrees to take on the cottage work."

Mel nodded. "That works for me. Once school is out, I could move back and help more here."

Mac slipped an arm around Mel's shoulder. "Thanks, Mel. I'll show you how to feed Margo and Coco and Lucy and Ethel, and that's about the only chore you'll need to worry about."

Her eyes sparkled with excitement. "I love those llamas and alpacas, so that won't be a chore at all."

He turned toward Wendy. "So, what do you say? Can you help your sister out for the next month?"

Wendy let out an exasperated breath and shrugged. "I don't know. I mean, cleaning up after people and carrying bags isn't what I'm looking for, but I'm not sure I have much choice."

Lily's head throbbed. The pain in her wrist and ankle had eroded her patience. "Here's the deal, Wendy. You've stayed here rent free in the past and are here again, rent free. Never offering a thin dime and contributing nothing to help. Had I not fallen, I wouldn't be in this horrible position to have to ask you, but at this point, *I* don't have much choice. You, on the other hand, could move out and live elsewhere, if it's too much of a bother for you to lift a finger. Along with living here, I'm happy to pay you wages to take over my duties for the next month. If that's too much to ask, I need to know right now."

Nobody said a word.

Even the dogs were quiet and didn't move from their positions.

Lily's tone was sharper than she intended, but she'd had enough of the whining and complaining. When she and Mac talked about it earlier, and he suggested it, Lily agreed but didn't hold out much hope. She'd never been able to rely on Wendy.

She wasn't convinced Wendy wanted to work at all, but she

needed to know so she could make a new plan. Her only other alternative would be to cancel the upcoming reservations, until Mel could help. She wanted to give her guests as much notice as possible.

Lily closed her eyes, wishing it were all a bad dream. She wanted, more than anything, to leave and take the dogs on a long walk. Clear her head and sit on her favorite piece of driftwood. Breathe in the fresh air and think of something happier.

But she was stuck in the chair and dependent on others for the foreseeable future.

Upon opening her eyes, she repositioned her ankle and winced, prompting Mac to deliver a fresh ice pack and a couple of tablets from her medicine cabinet, along with a glass of water. "Try to get some rest," he said, placing his hand on her shoulder.

Mel stood and volunteered to take the dogs for a walk. Once she had them leashed, Mac invited Wendy to join him in the backyard.

Unsure of Wendy's decision and not thrilled at the prospect of having her interact with her guests, Lily pondered other solutions as her eyes grew heavier. It wouldn't be easy to find a temporary worker, especially one she trusted in her home, to take over managing things for a month. Mac couldn't afford to be away from the clinic, and everyone she could think of had a job or responsibilities.

If all else failed, she could give guests the option of coming but communicating with her via phone or text and making sure they paid for their entire stay via her online reservation program. Between Mel and Mac, they would figure out a way to help as much as possible. The maid service was booked and couldn't provide more than the three days a week they had already scheduled. Maybe she could find someone to handle the cleaning and laundry but not on short notice.

Exhaustion settled over her like a heavy blanket, and Lily couldn't keep her eyes from closing.

~

The aroma of roasted chicken woke her. Lily opened her eyes and blinked several times, disoriented until she moved her wrist and remembered what had happened. Part of her thought maybe it wasn't real, but the wrapping on her wrist and ankle told her otherwise.

The dogs, including Sherlock, kept watch over her, all of them stretched out next to the recliner.

It was time for a trip to the bathroom. She used the remote and retracted the footrest. Mac had brought her a cane to use, just to steady herself, and she used her left hand to grip it and leaned on it to lift herself out of the chair.

She made her way as quietly as possible, not wanting to disturb Mac. It was a bit of a struggle, but she succeeded and returned to the kitchen as a fresh worry nagged at her. Mac was at the stovetop.

"Mac, I just remembered I was supposed to volunteer at the arts center tonight. I can't believe I forgot until now."

He smiled as he stirred the gravy. "I already called them, not to worry. Marcia said she hopes you feel better and not to worry about anything."

Lily blew out a breath and eyed the dinner preparations. "Oh, that's a relief. That all looks so yummy."

"It's almost ready. Are you hungry?"

She nodded. "Yes, the delicious aroma roused me from my nap."

"I'll bring you a tray. We need to keep you off your foot. I'll get some fresh ice packs for you, too."

She hobbled back to her appointed perch and settled into the chair, thankful she had splurged on the electric reclining option.

Mac was there in moments to help her get situated with a pillow under her wrist and cool ice packs for both of her injuries. With her settled, he went back to the kitchen to finish dinner.

Bored, Lily tuned the television to the streaming service she liked and scrolled through the offerings.

Before she had chosen something, Mac returned with a plate of roast chicken, mashed potatoes and gravy, plus roasted veggies. Lily's mouth watered as the scent of the fresh herbs and savory chicken wafting from it.

After letting the dogs out in the yard, he joined her with a tray of his own and settled on the couch. "Mel said to let her know if you need anything, she'd pick it up while she's in town. She works until closing tonight."

Lily nodded as she used her left hand and a spoon to eat the chicken Mac had thoughtfully cut up for her. It was beyond awkward, but she stuck with it. The food was delicious and comforting.

Without the use of her dominant hand, eating took forever. While she took her time, Mac finished his meal and reached for the remote to find something to watch.

As she spooned the last bit of mashed potatoes from her plate, Lily said, "Where's Wendy?"

"Downstairs. I offered her dinner, but she made herself a smoothie and had leftovers from her lunch."

Lily nodded. "I've been thinking, I might just need to cancel some reservations, rather than deal with her and subject my guests to her attitude. I don't know what to do."

"We had a long chat, and she said she'd decide by tomorrow. She's got to work at Marla's again in the morning. Her last full day of work. The boutique is opening this week, which means her hours will be cut back, and her job prospects are slim."

Lily rolled her eyes. "Not that she's been looking much."

"She reminds me of Missy as a teenager." He chuckled. "Actually, not much has changed since then."

"I'm just not sure I want my reputation to suffer at her hands. I've got great reviews and lots of positive comments online. I don't want to risk the future of the cottages."

"I'm hopeful that she'll consider our discussion. Part of me wonders if nothing has ever been expected of Wendy. Maybe she needs some responsibility to prove she can succeed."

Lily nodded. "She probably needs to prove that to herself more than anyone else. Her life as a kept woman didn't do her any favors. Especially when it was all a façade. Chad had to know it would crumble eventually."

"I was telling Wendy about one of my vet technicians who is looking for a roommate. I let her know what it would cost just to rent a room. She was shocked. I don't think she has any concept of money, since she never had to consider it."

"I hope you got through to her. If she agrees, I just want her to treat my customers well."

He grinned. "You'll have some free time on your hands. You can always monitor her interactions from up here and even call on your guests to inquire if everything is to their satisfaction. It wouldn't hurt to tell them you're recuperating and have someone helping, so if they have a problem, they'll let you know. That might help you feel better and more in control."

She sighed. "That's a good idea. I'm just so irritated with myself. I could have saved myself all this trouble."

He winked. "You'll be glad to know Mel helped me, and we finished installing the lights across the yard, and the firepit is ready to go anytime you decide to use it."

"I'm not sure what I did to deserve you, or Mel, but I'm thankful."

He collected her tray and bent and kissed her forehead while he was there. "I also need to call Missy and let her know our news. Do you want to join me on a video call?"

She nodded. "I do. Can we tackle it tomorrow when I hope I'm feeling spunkier?"

"That sounds good. I'm going to run home and collect my things and meet Mel out at the house tonight when she gets off work. I want to make sure she's comfortable with everything. Since Mel's off tomorrow, she volunteered to stay with you. I'm going into the clinic to see some patients. I'm trying to free up some blocks of time so I can be here for you."

She reached for his hand. "I'm so lucky to have you."

"I feel the same." He glanced across the room. "Oh, I almost forgot." He walked over near the entry to collected a tote bag.

He placed it in the corner of Lily's chair. "I shared our news with Cyndy, along with the fact that you injured yourself. She sent this over, so you have something to do while you recuperate, and she offered to help with whatever we need for the wedding or reception."

He helped her unearth several bridal magazines and a folder filled with photos Cyndy had put together for themes, colors, and reception ideas.

As she flipped through the pages, she marveled at the ideas, falling in love with several of them. "Cyndy is a gem. It would take me months to come up with any of this stuff. I don't know how she does it. If she's willing, I might just ask her to handle it. I don't know if I have the energy to do all this. I hadn't even thought about a reception."

"For Cyndy, it's not even work. I've seen her put together so many events, and it's effortless. I know she would love to help us." He bent and kissed her lips before passing her cell phone to her. "I'll be back soon, and I'm taking the dogs with me. You enjoy yourself and call Cyndy. She'd love to hear from you."

Minutes later, he locked the front door behind them. With the dogs and Mac gone, the house was quiet. Lily's eyes were drawn to the flowers in Cyndy's folder. The white bouquets were her favorites, and the one with a few blue forget-me-nots and eucalyptus was gorgeous.

The idea of dress shopping with a bum leg and wrist didn't excite her. Maybe she had something in her closet that would work.

She leaned back in the chair and gazed out the window. With the grief of losing Gary so heavy in her heart when she moved here last year, it was hard to believe she was contemplating a wedding and a new life with Mac. She had been blessed with love twice, and the idea of spending the rest of her life with a man like Mac was a dream come true.

On the other hand, the prospect of trusting Wendy with her business was a terrifying nightmare.

10

After a fitful night of sleep, Lily woke up much later than usual. The dogs weren't in her room, which meant Mel was on duty taking care of them. Mac had arranged with Mel to come to the house early and watch all three dogs and keep an eye on Lily until he got home from the clinic.

Mac had borrowed a shower chair from someone he knew and installed it in the master bathroom, which allowed Lily the dignity of showering by herself, albeit clumsily.

Once she accomplished her morning routine, wrapped her ankle, and put on the wrist brace Mac had brought for her, she managed to get dressed. She even remembered their date for tea and put on a dressier blouse with a cardigan instead of her usual t-shirt. Everything took much longer without the use of both hands, and it was mid-morning when she finally hobbled out to the kitchen. Mel was outside with the dogs, exercising them in the yard.

Lily turned on the kettle and wandered out to the deck while she waited for her tea to brew.

Mel spotted her and waved, ushering the dogs up the stairs. "Hey, how are you feeling?" she asked, smiling and out of breath.

Lily shrugged. "About the same. I can tell I need to get back in the chair with some ice. I'm just having some tea."

"I'll fix it and bring it to you. How about a breakfast sandwich? I was going to make one for me."

Lily nodded. "That sounds great, thanks." She lumbered inside and made her way to the recliner, with the three dogs following.

It didn't take Mel long to appear with ice packs, hot tea, and a tray with a breakfast sandwich and fruit. Once she had Lily settled, she returned with her own tray. "I checked the reservations this morning, and we have two guests arriving tomorrow, both will check out on Wednesday. Rebecca leaves on Friday, but then three guests come for the weekend."

Lily's brows arched. "Normally, I'd be ecstatic that the season is picking up a bit early, but…" She gestured toward her ankle as she picked up half of her sandwich with her left hand.

"Mac went into the clinic early this morning, so I gave Wendy a ride to the boutique. She didn't come right out and say it, but I got the feeling she's going to help manage the cottages. She asked a few questions and seemed less irritated."

Lily took another bite of the cheesy egg inside the fluffy croissant. "I hope we can make it work without driving away the guests."

Mel giggled. "Yeah, she needs to work on her facial expressions."

"Well, if she agrees, she's going to have a busier first week than I thought. I guess it will be trial by fire."

"Oh, I forgot to tell you, Cyndy texted and is bringing dinner tonight. I talked to Rebecca this morning and thought we could have tea on the deck. I'll take care of everything, so you don't need to worry about it. We settled on three o'clock, and Mac is picking up Wendy on his way home tonight."

"Aww, Cyndy is a sweetheart and the best cook. Tea sounds fun. I was looking forward to it and making some cookies together."

"I'll just go by the bakery and get some treats for us."

"Wendy is going to have to bake some cookies and brownies for the guests arriving this week." Lily rolled her eyes. "That should be exciting. Maybe you could get my recipes out for her and make sure we have everything for them. It's easier to make a double or triple batch and freeze them."

Mel nodded, then collected their dishes and took them to the kitchen. Lily readjusted her ice packs and leaned back into the chair. She loved to make lists and with her right hand out of commission, it was too difficult. She had to use her mind, instead of paper.

First, she contacted the maid service and confirmed they would start next week on Monday. That meant Wendy would have to ready the cottages this week.

Next, she called Muffins & More and the Busy Bee Café to see if the breakfast vouchers she purchased for the season were ready. She let them know Mel or Mac would be by to pick them up for her.

Thankfully, her folios were ready with all the local information for guests, so all Wendy would need to do is add the breakfast vouchers.

She made a mental note to show Wendy how to change the security code on the gate, since she liked to do that each week. Empty vases were stored in the cupboards downstairs, and she'd have to make sure Wendy cut some fresh flowers from the garden to put in the cottages. She would also need to get the beverage station ready downstairs in the common area. Lily liked to make sure the guests had access to iced water and iced tea, along with cookies. She remembered her phone had an app for notes and used voice to text to add the to-do list to it.

She sighed. This was all contingent on Wendy agreeing to

the job. If she didn't, Lily wasn't sure what she would do. Relying on her sister was unexpected and on her cold-day-in-hell list.

"Mel," she hollered out. "Could you add lemons to the grocery list, please?"

"Will do," she said, coming around the corner. "We do need some baking supplies. I've got a list made and can run to get them."

"That would be great, and could you stop by to pick up the breakfast vouchers while you're downtown?"

Mel nodded and handed Lily the grocery list. After a couple of trips back and forth to the kitchen to check on other staples, Lily had her add a few more things and gave her cash from her purse.

"The vouchers are paid for, so this should cover groceries and treats from the bakery for our tea."

Mel nodded and slipped the cash into the pocket of her jeans. "The dogs are tired out from running around, so they should take a nap while I'm gone. Will you be okay with them?"

"Sure, we'll be fine."

With a quick wave and a promise to be back soon, Mel was out the front door.

Despite doing almost nothing, it didn't take long for the soft snores coming from the dogs to lull Lily into joining them for a quick nap.

An hour later, the dogs stirred when Mel returned, prompting Lily to open her eyes. Mel hauled in the groceries and placed the vouchers in the desk drawer where Lily always kept them.

Lily got out of the chair for a bathroom break and placed the warm ice packs in the freezer before retrieving cold ones and settling at the island counter, making sure she put her leg up on an adjacent chair. She provided a bit of moral support and advice for Mel as she readied things for their tea.

Mel shooed the dogs outside while she put some eggs on to boil. While they wouldn't be able to offer fancy sandwiches, egg salad was easy and would suffice for the sandwich offering for their tea with Rebecca.

Mel unboxed the bakery treats, arranged them on a glass platter, and retrieved a fancy teapot and matching teacups from Aunt Maggie's collection. After she covered the pastries and cookies with plastic wrap, she took the kitchen shears outside in search of some flowers for the table.

Mel returned with some colorful blooms, and Lily worked on arranging them in a vase while Mel removed the eggs from the stovetop to let them cool. Mel filled the kettle with water and readied the Earl Grey teabags to brew in the pot. She also added a selection of other tea choices in case Rebecca preferred something else.

Lily pointed to a drawer where she kept cloth napkins, and Mel chose the ones in a pretty aqua color and added them to a tray with the cutlery she had prepared. With everything set, Mel sighed. "I brought a nicer shirt, so I'll go change into that. Then you can help me make the egg salad, and I think we'll be ready."

"How did you do staying at Mac's?"

"Oh, it was fine. His place is like right out of a magazine. I missed having the dogs around. It's quiet there at night."

"Maybe you could bring in one of the alpacas. I'm sure Mac wouldn't mind."

They both laughed, and Mel retrieved her shirt.

Lily smiled as Mel hurried to the powder room. It was wonderful to see how much she had blossomed over the last year. She loved seeing her happy and excited. Going to school, along with working as a barista, had been a turning point for her. Her confidence level had increased, and she had made some friends. Now, instead of escaping between the pages of a book, she was willing to put herself out in the world.

All the reservations Lily had when she first met Mel had vanished and replaced with gratitude. Mel was a huge help and now, more than ever, she was grateful she was here.

When Mel emerged wearing a purple shirt that she favored for special occasions, Lily made sure she protected it with an apron before mixing the dressing for the egg salad. With great care, Mel spooned the egg filling onto the mini croissants she had picked up at the bakery. Once she had them finished, she placed them on a cranberry glass plate and put them in the fridge to keep them cool.

Lily pointed out the kitchen window. "Looks like Rebecca is on her way. Maybe help her navigate the dogs, then you can put the gate on the deck entrance, so we keep them in the yard and away from pestering her."

Mel slipped out of the apron and hurried outside to corral the dogs. While she did that, Lily moved from the island and started the kettle. By the time Rebecca and Mel were on the deck, the water was ready to pour, but Lily didn't trust herself with her left hand and her lack of balance.

Instead, she made her way to the deck to say hello to Rebecca and whispered to Mel to brew the tea. A huge smile filled Mel's face as she held up a stack of books. "Rebecca brought me these. She even signed them to me."

"That's fantastic. Few people have signed copies of books."

Mel promised to be right back and disappeared into the house.

Rebecca pointed at Lily's ankle and said, "How are you feeling? Better, I hope."

"Not bad, just frustrated and slow. I start exercises tomorrow but am supposed to keep it elevated until then. Thank you again for coming to my rescue."

"Hopefully, it heals quickly. I'm glad it wasn't more serious."

Lily pointed at a chair. "Please sit. Mel is so excited about this and has everything ready. Thank you for making time for us today. I'm just going to prop my leg on a spare chair."

Rebecca took a chair overlooking the yard and sighed. "Believe me, it's my pleasure. I could use a break. You've got a lovely place here. It's been perfect for writing."

"Next week, we've got more guests arriving, so it won't be as quiet, but I hope you're still able to work."

Rebecca smiled at Mel, coming through the door with a tray of food. "I've taken advantage of the solitude and am way ahead on my word count, so I think I'll be fine."

Mel set the tray on the table and hurried back inside for the tea service. Along with tea, Mel delivered new ice packs and looked delighted at learning Rebecca loved Earl Grey. Mel poured tea for all of them before she took her seat.

After Rebecca filled a plate with a croissant sandwich and pastries, she glanced over at Mel. "This is just lovely. It's the perfect way to spend a relaxing afternoon."

As she watched Mel's face beam with pride, Lily's heart warmed.

Between bites of the delicious baked goods and not-too-shabby egg salad, Mel peppered Rebecca with questions about her writing career. Rebecca wrote mystery and suspense for a large publisher and explained the entire process to Mel, patiently answering every question.

Rebecca's voice was lovely and full of emotion as she explained her writing process and publishing her first book. It was no surprise to Lily that she even narrated some of her own audiobooks. She had a voice that begged to be listened to, and Lily thought she could sit with her for hours and never be bored.

Two hours and two pots of tea went by in the blink of an eye, before Rebecca leaned back in her chair. "This has been such a fun afternoon, but I need to get back to work. I appreciate you going to all this trouble for me."

She stood and put her hand on Mel's shoulder. "Be sure and let me know what you think of those books. I left you my email in the inscription."

The smile on Mel's face that Lily thought couldn't get any larger, widened. "I will. I can't wait to read them. Thank you again for your generous gifts."

Lily moved her leg from the chair, and Rebecca said, "No, don't get up. You take care and thank you again for a wonderful stay. I'm sure I'll be back and can't wait to tell my author friends about it. You may get an influx of those of us who need the quiet escape."

"I'm so happy you've enjoyed it, and we love referrals. I'm sure we'll see you this week. You'll have some neighbors starting tomorrow. Our early season is proving to be busy."

"I'm still probably the only guest who spends all her time in the cottage, so I'm sure it will work for me." She gave a wave as she walked toward the gate.

The dogs, sensing action and the possibility of pets, hurried up the stairs. Mel removed the gate and ushered them inside, but not before Rebecca bent and gave them all a quick scratch on the head.

Mel gathered the tea service and took it inside while Lily stacked the dirty plates and utensils. Mel returned and collected everything from the table, and Lily carried her ice packs and followed her into the kitchen.

As soon as they had the kitchen tidied and things put away, the doorbell rang. Mel rushed to answer it and returned toting a huge quilted carrier and a tote bag, followed by Cyndy and more tote bags.

The dogs' noses went crazy sniffing at everything, and Mel ushered them outside, then changed clothes for her closing shift at the coffee shop and hurried to her car.

Cyndy's cheerful voice and laughter filled the kitchen as she unearthed all the deliciousness she brought with her. She slipped the baking pan Mel had carried into the oven and put a salad in the fridge.

She showed Lily a freezer bag. "You can freeze this and just pop it in your slow cooker, and you'll have sesame chicken ready to go."

She patted the top of a foil-covered pan. "This is a chicken enchilada casserole. I'll put it in the freezer." She laughed and added, "Almost forgot. Mini meatloaves in these." Two more freezer bags went into Lily's freezer.

"Wow, I won't have to cook for a month. You're way too good to us." Lily hugged her friend.

Cyndy smiled and waved away the compliment. "I love to cook, and it's how I show people how much they mean to me. Mac is quite capable in the kitchen, but I want him to concentrate all his time on caring for you and helping you with the wedding plans. Not to mention, I know how tired he is after spending all day at the clinic."

"You're quite possibly the best sister in the world. I'm so lucky to get to be your sister-in-law."

Cyndy's eyes sparkled. "You know, Mac and I have a long-standing tradition for Sunday dinners. I hope we can keep that going, whether it be at your house or mine. I love that time with family."

"I'd like nothing more."

Cyndy hugged her again. "Well, until you're mobile, I'll be bringing dinner here on Sundays."

"Speaking of Mac, he should be here soon. He's picking up Wendy from work. I've got to get a firm answer from her if she's willing to take on managing the cottages for the next month. While I'm worried she'll say no, part of me is scared she'll say yes."

Cyndy chuckled as she took a loaf of bread from one of the

tote bags. "That, my friend, is completely understandable. I wish I could think of someone who could fill in for you, but I haven't come up with anyone."

"Wendy makes the most sense. She's here and needs a job. Her attitude just needs to improve. She needs to be nice and hospitable to my guests."

Cyndy gritted her teeth. "You've got things organized and running smoothly, so hopefully, she can just keep things going and with you right here, you can direct her and let her know how to handle anything that comes up."

Lily nodded and retrieved two fresh ice packs. "Mac and I are going to call Missy tonight and break our good news to her. I'm nervous about that and suspect it will be stressful, especially for Mac. I'm going to put my leg up in the recliner."

Cyndy followed and helped her get situated under a throw blanket. "Missy is a master manipulator. Just remember that and don't let her attitude stifle your happiness. I'll join you in a few minutes. I just want to get everything organized, then I'll pour a glass of wine. Would you like one?"

"Nah, I think I'll stick with tea."

Lily's phone pinged with a motion alert, letting her know Mac and Wendy had arrived. "They're here," she said to Cyndy.

"Wendy and Missy in one night. You sure you don't want to reconsider that glass of wine?" Cyndy laughed as she hurried back to the kitchen.

11

Mac and Wendy came through the front door and with a quick nod to Cyndy's greeting, Wendy disappeared downstairs.

Lily shook her head as Mac placed a hand on her shoulder. "How was your day?" he asked.

"It was a good one. Mel and I had a nice time visiting with Rebecca at our tea. We just finished up when Cyndy arrived with dinner and filled my freezer, so we won't have to cook for weeks." She nodded toward the kitchen. "How's Wendy?"

"Pretty quiet on the ride home." He sighed and took a seat on the couch.

"You sound tired."

"It was a long day but will give me some freedom this week, so I can come home and check on you. I also decided I'll take the three dogs to work with me, so you don't have to worry about them this week, and I'll take Bodie to his training sessions on Tuesdays."

"I feel so bad that you have to disrupt your work with all of this." She shook her head and rubbed her hand across the buttery-soft throw.

"Don't give it a moment of worry. We're used to having Sherlock at work and between everyone, we can handle two more. It'll be good for Bodie's training and interactions. I should be able to manage to take off at lunch and spend the afternoon here all week. I figure that way, if things go sideways with Wendy, I'll be around for the check-ins."

Lily smiled at him. "I'm going to owe you big time. Thank you." She leaned her head against the back of the chair and watched as Cyndy flitted in and out of the dining area, adjacent to the living room, and set the dining room table. Lily hadn't used it much since she moved in, preferring to eat in the kitchen at the large island counter.

"It's hard to describe, but I know you'll understand when I tell you I think the worst part of losing Gary has been that feeling of being on my own. Not having someone to tell my good news or share the burden of the bad news. Not having a true partner to rely on when I need help. Having the stress of having to figure everything out, especially when you're not feeling one hundred percent is tough. So, having you here for me does mean the world."

He nodded as he listened and then added, "I know exactly what you mean. I miss that part of being a team, and I want nothing more than to be there for you when you need me. I don't ever want you to feel alone again."

His kind words and gentle eyes made Lily's heart skip a beat. "Gary was my rock during some of the worst times of my life. I don't think I would have survived the death of my parents without him. I can't imagine facing that on my own. When I would dwell on a future without him, the fear of the unknown, on my own, was debilitating. Now, with us getting married, having you next to me and knowing I won't have to face everything alone, is such a gift."

He smiled at her. "I feel the same way. Cyndy has been the blessing in my life and has helped me through so many of those hard times you talk about. The times you need someone, even if it's just to listen, but I've missed that special emotional connection between a husband and wife. It's part of why I proposed to you. I've felt that since the day we met. Not only was I attracted to you, but I felt like I knew you forever, and I know I can count on you to be there for me when I need it."

"Shall we make that video call to Missy now before it gets too late in Georgia? At least I'm dressed up a bit today and look more presentable."

He nodded. "Let's go into your bedroom, just so it's quiet, and we have some privacy." He helped her out of the recliner, and they sat in the huge window seat in her bedroom.

The view helped calm her nerves, but Lily's stomach was still in knots as Mac punched the button on his phone. She snuggled closer to him so they would both be in the video screen.

Missy's image popped up when the call connected. Lily had only seen older photos of her. She was a beauty, with shoulder-length dark hair and brown eyes. "Hey, Missy, is it a good time to chat?" asked Mac.

With a less than enthused look, she shrugged. "As good as any, I guess."

Mac squeezed Lily's good hand and turned toward her. "This is Lily. I wanted you to meet her, and we wanted to share some good news with you. I proposed to Lily, and she's agreed to marry me."

Missy didn't say a word.

Mac continued, "We're going to have a simple ceremony on the beach. Nothing fancy."

Lily smiled. "I'm so happy to meet you Missy and hope you can come to celebrate with us. We're planning for late June, when my son Kevin will be here. We can arrange a ticket for you to fly here."

Missy shook her head. "I don't think June will work for me. That's short notice, don't you think?"

Mac nodded. "Yes, it's not much notice, but it's a simple ceremony and frankly, Missy, I've finally realized life is too short to keep waiting to be happy again. Lily and I love each other and want to make our life together. I hope you'll look at your calendar and see if you can make something work."

Lily nodded. "Yes, we can make any day work, really. We haven't nailed it down yet, so if there is a specific day that works for you, we can do it then."

"Right, see what you can do. It would mean the world to have you there." Mac squeezed Lily's hand again.

Missy shook her head as she looked down and then faced the camera, her eyes narrowed. "I can't believe you're doing this, Dad. How could you disrespect Mom and marry some lady you barely know? Let me guess, she saw your house and knows you're a veterinarian, and she's looking for someone to take care of her? You better get a prenup."

Mac's face reddened. "That's enough, Missy. Lily is a wonderful woman, and I love her very much. She owns a business and supports herself without any trouble. We're getting married because we love each other and want to make a life together. I won't sit here and listen to you disparage Lily. You don't even know her."

She smiled and nodded. "That's right, Dad. I don't even know her. Once again, you've proven I don't really matter, do I?

Lily scooted away from Mac. She wanted to disappear and not be part of the disagreement. How could Missy be so hateful? Her heart broke as she watched Mac try to reason with her."

After a few minutes of their back and forth, Mac said, "Cyndy's here for dinner, so we need to go, but I hope you'll reconsider."

"Don't hold your breath," she said, right before her video link went black.

Mac disconnected and shoved the phone back in his pocket. "I'm sorry, Lily. This is how it works with her. I was hoping she'd be nicer with you here, but obviously, that didn't work."

Lily's heart raced, and she took a deep breath. "I can't believe it. I mean, you and Cyndy both have talked about how unreasonable she is and how hurtful she can be to you, but wow. Just wow."

Mac stood and said, "I'd like to think I'm immune to her antics by now, but she has a way of shaking me up, and I'm so sorry she was rude to you."

"I thought I had braced myself for it, but she's something else. I hate to see you suffering."

He smiled and put his arm around her to help her up. "Missy is like a black cloud that is always over my head. I can't seem to do anything that pleases her. Let's not dwell on it and have some dinner. I'll call her again this week and see if she's calmed down any."

She leaned her head on his shoulder. She loved him so much, and he was such a good man. The last thing she wanted to do was be a wedge between him and Missy. Her head throbbed with worry as she stepped toward the door. What should be such a happy occasion was turning into turmoil. This wouldn't be easy.

Mac squeezed her shoulder. "Try to put it out of your mind. I know this isn't what you want, and I'm sure you're hurt and feeling horrible about this, but it changes nothing. We'll talk more later tonight."

He opened the door and as they walked into the living room, Cyndy came around the corner with her arm around Wendy. "Dinner's ready, and I assured Wendy I used all organic ingredients in the chicken and wild rice casserole, so she'll be joining us. Everything is ready, so come and have a seat. Mac can make sure you have a chair to rest your leg upon, Lily. Will that work or would you rather stay in your recliner?"

Lily pushed her worries to the back of her mind and tried to contain her surprise at seeing Wendy almost smile. "That would work. Honestly, getting out of the chair would be wonderful. It's getting old quickly."

Cyndy turned toward Wendy, "How about you pour drinks. I've got a pitcher of iced tea and water ready."

Lily's brows rose as she marveled at Wendy helping Cyndy without a snarly attitude. As Mac helped Lily into her chair, he whispered in her ear. "My sister has a way about her. She's the same with Missy. Sort of like a horse whisperer for angry young women."

Lily nodded and stifled a laugh. "You aren't kidding. I wonder if she could convince Missy to come to the wedding."

He shrugged, and she noticed the sparkle had left his eyes.

Within minutes, Cyndy had everything on the table and sat across from her brother, with Wendy across from Lily. Mac pointed at the huge casserole dish in the middle of the table. "That smells wonderful, Cyn. Thanks for cooking dinner."

"My pleasure." She spooned out the casserole and filled plates for the others. "There's a fruit salad there next to you, Wendy, so pass it around, and Mac, you've got the green salad there by you."

Cyndy took a piece of fresh bread and added it to her plate before passing it to Mac. Lily was useless when it came to passing the serving dishes and let Mac fill her plate for her.

She was getting better using her left hand and savored every bite of the delicious casserole. "This is so good, Cyndy."

Wendy nodded. "Yes, it's all delicious."

As they ate, Mac entertained them with a few pet stories from the clinic. When everyone except Lily had cleaned their plates, she glanced across the table at her sister. "So, Wendy, have you decided what you want to do? Are you going to be able to run the cottages for the next month?"

She sighed and said, "I'll do it, but I'm going to keep looking for a job, so if something comes up that works, I'll have to bail on you, and I can't do the weekends. Marla wants me to work on Saturdays, and I'll need a day off to rest."

Confident that her sister finding a new job anytime soon was a longshot, Lily nodded. "Understood. Just give me a head's up if you have a lead, so I can work on another solution. Mac and Mel can handle the weekends. I appreciate you doing it and will be around to help answer questions, I just can't do much, physically."

Mac put an arm around her shoulder. "I'll be around in afternoons this week for sure and can help out, too."

Lily turned her eyes back on Wendy. "The first thing you'll need to do is bake some cookies and brownies for the guests. I usually make huge batches and put them in the freezer, so I don't have to bake each week. Mel set out the recipes and all the supplies earlier today."

Cyndy smiled as she sipped her iced tea. "Oh, I love to bake. Wendy and I will get this dinner mess cleaned up, and I'll stick around to help her on the first batches." She reached out and touched Wendy on the arm. "Are you much of a baker?"

Wendy laughed. "No, as in I don't bake anything, and I don't eat sugar." She glanced across the table. "I probably haven't baked since we lived at home with Mom and Dad." Her smile faded.

"Both recipes are straightforward and easy to make. I like to have a tray of homemade goodies downstairs so the guests can help themselves. We have guests arriving tomorrow and more on Friday."

Cyndy reassured Wendy with a smile. "Well, we better get busy then, so you can be ready for tomorrow and if you don't eat sugar, I'll need to help you sample."

Mac tried to help clear the table, but Cyndy encouraged him to sit and relax with Lily. She and Wendy disappeared around the corner in the kitchen.

Mac made sure Lily had fresh ice packs on her injuries and

then took a seat on the couch nearest her recliner. He leaned closer to her and whispered, "Cyndy has such natural maternal instincts. Wendy was even smiling in there." He pointed to the kitchen. "Her ability to turn Missy around was something I never understood but was so thankful for, especially during her teen years."

Lily lowered her voice. "Our mother had those natural instincts. I'm not sure I possess them, and Kevin was an easy child. Plus, boys, I think, are easier for mothers. Whatever it is, I hope she can leave me some of her magic to sprinkle around for the next month."

Mac grinned. "I've asked for her secret countless times, but it's unique to her. I'm going to see if she'll give Missy a call about the wedding."

Lily cringed when he mentioned her name. She needed time to figure out what to do about having the daughter of the man she loved hate her.

She pointed at the paperwork on the side table. "The physical therapist comes tomorrow at nine in the morning, which will be good. It won't interfere with the busy check-in or check-out times." She sighed and picked up the exercise flyer. "I've been doing these easy ones today, basically just moving my ankle, hoping I can cut down on the recovery time."

"She'll probably have you doing something more now that the initial swelling is gone. I'm not an expert on humans, but that seems to be the modern medical approach."

"I'm for anything that speeds up the process."

Cyndy poked her head around the corner. "Lily, I meant to tell you, I've got an acquaintance that owns a bridal boutique over in Port Angeles. She said she'd be happy to work with you on the phone or video chat to help you find a dress. She can ship them to you or drive over one evening for you to try them."

"Ah, that is so sweet of you and of her. I was hoping to find something that wasn't too bride-like or poofy. I want it to be special, but casual. I don't want her to go to so much trouble for what likely won't be a big sale with lots of bridesmaids and all that."

Cyndy nodded. "I explained all that to Paula. She loves Driftwood Bay and is a wonderful person who genuinely enjoys helping brides. We share a love of wine, and I may have suggested we could enjoy some together, and she could stay over at my place, especially if she comes on a weekend, since her shop is closed on Sunday and Monday." She glanced at her brother. "You remember Paula?"

Mac nodded and chuckled. "Yes, I remember picking you two up from that winery a couple of years ago, when you'd spent a few too many hours there."

She smiled and shrugged, a look of mischief in her eyes.

"Well, that sounds like fun. If Mel is interested, I could treat her to a new dress for the occasion, so she might like to be involved and choose a dress." Lily pulled up the reservation system on her phone. "Any Saturday would work since we don't have any check-ins or outs for the next month. All the guests typically arrive on Thursday or Friday and leave on Sunday or Monday."

"Perfect, I'll let her know and will get back to you when she picks a date. I'll give her your cell number so she can call and chat with you first."

"Thank you, Cyndy. You're so good at all this. I appreciate your help."

Mac nodded. "I told you she'd have it all figured out before we could even think about it."

"I did look at your magazines and your wedding idea book you put together, Cyndy. I love so many things in there, especially all the sea glass colors. I think that's fitting."

"I figured you would. You two should think about a reception and what you want to do. Have it here or at Mac's or at a restaurant? I know you're keeping it small, but we'll need to book somewhere soon."

Mac cleared his throat. "We haven't picked a date yet. We called Miss today to tell her the news and invite her, hoping to choose a date that works for her."

Cyndy frowned. "I take it from the look on your face, it didn't go well."

Mac nodded. "That's putting it mildly. I don't have much hope that she'll come."

Cyndy responded to Wendy, calling her name from the kitchen, and held up a finger to Mac. "Let me get this sorted, and then we'll talk."

Lily reached for the binder of wedding ideas and flipped to the pages she had marked with sticky notes. She turned to the page with a wedding arch crafted from driftwood and showed it to Mac.

"I like this idea. It's simple and incorporates my love of the driftwood along the beach. Just a few flowers and some gauzy fabric add just the right touch, don't you think?"

He nodded. "It looks great. Andy and Wade could put that together lickety-split."

She grinned. "That's what I thought." She sighed and added, "I hadn't given much thought to a reception."

He drummed his finger on the page. "What do you think about a sunset wedding? We could make a pathway with some lanterns that lead to the archway."

She arched her brows. "Oh, I love that. That reminds me of the lanterns on the water."

"Sounds like you're getting some help with a dress. What do you think I should wear?"

"Keep flipping in the book. There are some ideas for men in there. I think you should wear what makes you comfortable. Tie or no tie. Jacket or no jacket. Maybe a vest as a compromise. You could even wear khakis."

"Maybe I'll let you pick your dress and then decide based on it. I'm not much of a fashion-forward guy."

She looked at her phone again. "I have one Wednesday that isn't booked in late June. That would let us have the reception in the backyard, since we wouldn't have any guests. Maybe I should block it out, and that would give us our date, unless you think we should choose a weekend to make it easier for Missy?"

"Let's do Wednesday. I doubt Missy will come, and it would be nice to have the cottages empty."

She poked a button on her phone and said, "Done."

Excitement mixed with a bit of worry swirled in her. Imagining a sunset and the archway made her smile but thinking about Missy boycotting their nuptials made her stomach lurch. She wanted to embrace the happiness and thrill of it all, but uneasiness nagged at her.

She wasn't sure she could enjoy it all knowing what Missy's disapproval did to Mac. Were they setting themselves up for a horrible disaster?

12

Monday morning, Mac kissed Lily goodbye before he left with the three dogs in tow, for an early start at the clinic. He left her instructions to text him if she needed anything or wanted him to bring her lunch but planned to be back at the house by one o'clock.

Lily sat in her recliner, enjoying the scent of freshly baked cookies that lingered in the air from last night's kitchen activities. She sipped the tea Mac had made her and let her thoughts wander to the wedding plans while she waited for her first therapy appointment.

She had texted Kevin the date, so he would know the plan. He was due to arrive about ten days before the wedding and would fly out the Saturday after it. She could hardly wait to see him and treasured the time he was there. The idea of Brooke coming with him changed things.

The days where she and Kevin would be each other's world were disappearing.

Too soon. Too quickly.

Lily hoped she would genuinely love Brooke, especially after dealing with Missy and her disdain. No matter what, she would never do to Kevin what Missy was doing to Mac. She trusted Kevin and while part of her was sad to see her son grow up, the larger part of her was so proud of him and wanted nothing more than for him to make a happy life for himself. If Brooke was part of that happiness, Lily would love her.

She couldn't help but think of Gary. She wondered what his take on all this would be. Deep in her heart, she knew he would want her to be happy, so marrying Mac would be something he would support. That didn't stop the red flag of worry waving when it came to Missy.

She closed her eyes and wished her mother were here to talk to about it. She had a way of listening and giving advice that always made Lily feel better. Missy, living in Georgia, wouldn't be involved in their daily lives, but the weight of her disapproval hanging over them would be a heavy load.

The idea of a prenup was a good one. They needed to see an attorney and think about the future and how to handle their respective estates once they were married. Izzy popped into her mind, being a lawyer and a friend. She hoped she might agree to handle that piece for them. She sent a quick text to Mac with the idea of asking Izzy to see if he agreed. The thought of all of it made her head spin. She wanted nothing from Mac, except his love and presence but wasn't sure how to convince Missy of that.

Her phone alarm sounded, and she took her time getting out of the recliner. She waited by the door for her therapist, hoping not to disturb Wendy. Her sister wasn't a morning person, and Lily wanted her in the best mood possible when the guests arrived in the afternoon.

Angie, a young woman with fiery red curls contained in a ponytail, arrived right on time and after asking some medical history questions, looked at Lily's injuries. Lily had been doing some of the range of motion exercises the doctor had given her, and Angie had her demonstrate them.

The young woman provided more pieces of paper with additional exercises. "So, with this type of ankle injury, I will only see you once a week for a maximum of four weeks and as your healing improves, we'll increase the types of exercises you can do. The important thing is to keep icing and elevating, especially after your exercises."

She demonstrated some additional range of motion exercises, using a towel, and added some new stretching exercises to Lily's routine. She also gave her a small ball to use when doing the grip exercises with her wrist. She had Lily do several repetitions, guiding her through the routine. "Okay, so do these routines three or four times a day and then ice and elevate. When you can stand on it without pain or swelling, we'll add some strengthening exercises, and then we'll add balance."

As Lily continued to work, Angie tapped on her laptop. "Oh, I see there's a note here that you're getting married in June, so you have a great goal ahead of you. I always like patients to have something to strive for, so that's terrific. Congratulations."

"Thanks," said Lily, as she concentrated on her last movement. "We've got a date now; it's June twenty-ninth."

Angie waved her hand. "No sweat. We'll have you ready to go in plenty of time. Who's the lucky guy?"

"Mac, uh, Jack MacMillan, he's got the veterinary clinic."

"Oh, yes, I take my dog to him. He's wonderful. I'm happy for both of you."

She helped Lily rewrap her wrist and fetched the fresh ice packs for her before she packed up her backpack and headed for the door. "I'll be here next week, same day, same time. Just give me a call if it doesn't work and be sure to call me with any problems or questions."

Lily thanked her and stayed in her chair with her ice packs while the cheerful young woman saw herself out. She rested against the back of the chair and let the magic of the cool ice do its job for the next twenty minutes.

She already missed Fritz and Bodie. The house was quiet and still without them. As she contemplated another cup of tea, the door to downstairs opened, and Wendy came in from the kitchen.

Lily studied her sister's face, trying to gauge her mood. At least she was dressed and ready for the day. Lily waved at her. "Good morning. Would you mind popping the kettle on while you're there?"

Lily heard the flick of the power switch.

She excavated herself from the recliner and hobbled into the kitchen. "Thank you again, Wendy, for helping me out with the cottages this month. We've got two guests arriving today. Both single women here for just two nights."

The kettle boiled, and Lily scooted over to it and poured it with her left hand, taking extra care so as not to splash the hot water out of the cup. "Would you like a cup of tea?"

Wendy was glancing out the window to the yard below. "Yeah, I'll take one. The organic, please."

Lily found the special organic tea bags Wendy favored and tossed one in a cup, steadying the kettle as she poured a second cup, while balancing on her good leg. Sometimes she wondered if Wendy was capable of empathy.

Lily carried her cup to the island counter and sat, leaving Wendy to retrieve her own. "You and Cyndy did a great job on the treats last night. That should get you through the next couple of weeks."

Wendy plucked her tea from the counter and joined her sister. "I hope so. That was a ton of work."

"Speaking of work. I've got the folios ready to go that should get you through the month. You'll just need to add the breakfast vouchers. I keep them locked in the filing cabinet next to the desk. They get a voucher for each night they stay and if they stay more than one night, I mix up the vouchers so they can try both cafes. Go get them, and I'll show you what I do." She pointed to the office area off the kitchen and handed her a key ring made from a piece of sea glass. "This is the master key to the cottages and the filing cabinet."

With little enthusiasm, Wendy trudged over to the desk and came back with two folios and the stack of breakfast vouchers.

Lily showed her how she liked to label the folio on the front with the guest's name and cottage number and get them ready in advance. She included the security code inside the folio and showed Wendy the drawer with the cottage keys. She had a chart she updated each week with the cottages and when they would need housekeeping services and sent a copy to the maid service, so they knew the checkouts on the days they serviced the cottages.

Lily made sure Wendy knew how to use the email system and gave her a quick overview of the reservation system, since Lily would be able to handle that herself for the most part. By lunchtime, they had things organized and ready for the two guests who would be arriving in a few hours.

Lily's stomach reminded her she hadn't eaten all day. She made her way to the fridge and selected leftover egg salad sandwiches and some cookies from their tea party. She made another cup of tea and sat to eat, while Wendy pulled out a quinoa bowl meal from the cupboard.

She watched as her sister opened it and stirred the contents, surprised it wasn't refrigerated. Lily pointed at it. "That's interesting, I would have thought that would have to be kept in the fridge."

Wendy wrinkled her nose. "I haven't tried these before but found them online and ordered them. Your market doesn't have much in the way of what I eat. These had good reviews and if you don't finish it, you need to refrigerate the leftovers."

Lily's brows rose as she watched Wendy mix the basil pesto into the quinoa. It didn't look very appetizing, but she was glad Wendy found something to eat. She finished her sandwich and another cookie and carried her tea into the living room.

She was just about to sit and remembered she forgot ice packs, so she made her way back to get those from the freezer. She'd been up long enough that her ankle was bothering her.

Once she had those, she reclined and added the packs to her ankle and wrist, tugging the throw blanket over her. When Mac got home, she'd do another round of her exercises and then do one more set before she went to bed. Her phone chimed with a reply to her earlier text. Mac thought Izzy was a great idea and encouraged Lily to email her the particulars.

She used her phone to compose a voice to text message, outlining the major points of the prenuptial agreement that she and Mac would retain their separate property acquired before marriage, and that Kevin would inherit her estate, and Missy would inherit Mac's.

She hated thinking about losing Mac. She wasn't sure she could handle burying two husbands but tried to remove her emotions and think logically. If Mac died, she would move out of the house and back to her property. Missy could have it all. She didn't need Mac's money and wanted to keep things separate, so there was no chance of Missy infringing on the cottage property. Money seemed to be her main concern, and Lily didn't want Kevin's future jeopardized.

With that task done, she settled back into her recliner to rest. No sooner had she closed her eyes, Mac and the dogs came bounding through the door. Her three furry buddies were excited to see her, thwacking their tails against the chair as they vied for her attention.

Mac leaned over the back of the chair and kissed her on the forehead. "So, how was your first day of therapy and being here on your own?"

"Therapy was good. I've got some new exercises and need to do a set this afternoon and another tonight. I showed Wendy how to get things ready for the guests and went over a few things. I had some lunch and was just letting the ice packs do their magic."

Mac took a few steps and craned his neck to look in the kitchen. "Where's Wendy?"

"I don't know. She was finishing her lunch when I came in here."

He glanced again and then said, "Oh, she's outside on the deck, all huddled up in a jacket." He pointed to his shirtsleeve. "It's gorgeous out there today. Almost time for shorts."

Lily chuckled. "I think she's used to the heat of Texas, so this probably seems a bit cool. Most of her clothes are for warmer weather."

Lily's phone chimed with a motion alert. She checked the screen and said, "Looks like one of our guests has arrived early."

Mac headed for the deck off the kitchen. "I'll let Wendy know and go down to help."

"Could you put the gate across the deck, just so the dogs stay up here and out of the way while the guests get settled?"

He hollered out, "Will do."

After the flutter of activity, with Wendy grabbing the folios and keys, along with the tray of cookies before hurrying downstairs, Lily couldn't help herself. She got out of the chair, stowed the ice packs in the freezer, and went out to the deck. She moved a chair, hoping to stay incognito but close to the edge of the deck to hear the conversation below.

She heard Mac's voice first, chatting with the woman, Claudia, who was apologizing for her early arrival.

Mac assured her it wasn't a problem and offered to put her bags in the cottage while Wendy went over her paperwork. "You're in number three, the one with the turquoise door," he said.

"That would be great, thank you so much. I received the

email from the owner about her injuries, I hope she's doing okay."

"Lily's doing well, thank you. I'm Mac, her fiancé, and Wendy is her sister. We're helping while she recuperates, but I'm sure you'll see her out on the deck from time to time."

"Oh, that's good news. Pass along my best wishes to her. I was in Driftwood Bay many years ago and sadly, I'm back with my sister's ashes." She paused as her voice broke. "Bonnie loved it here and wished to have them spread here in the bay. She used to come and visit often and stayed here at the cottages, so I thought it was fitting that I stay here to say my final goodbye."

Lily's throat went dry as she listened to the obvious strain in the woman's voice.

"I'm sorry you're back for such a sad occasion. You have my sincere condolences," said Mac. Lily watched as he set out with her bags and carried them into the cottage for her.

Claudia and Wendy were inside, and Lily could only hear muffled conversation. As Mac returned from the cottage, he waved and shouted out a greeting to the other guest, who had just arrived and was coming through the side gate.

He went through the same routine, helping the young woman, Shelly, with her bags. She was in a hurry to get the keys and information, as she was in town for a friend's birthday and was heading out to visit.

Mac made quick work of getting her settled and once she had her keys and folio, she left the property, and he and Wendy came up the deck stairs.

Mac did his best to keep the dogs from bothering Wendy, who still hadn't warmed to them and flinched each time they got close to her. Lily smiled at her. "Well, how was it with your first two guests?"

She shrugged. "Pretty easy. You've got a good system set up, and they were both nice."

"Most of our guests are easy going and nice, but we've had a few that tested our patience. One of my favorite groups that came and stayed in all three cottages was a group of widows from Vermont. They called themselves the Winey Widows and loved to visit and drink wine."

Mac laughed. "Yes, they were quite the characters. It's one of my favorite things about the weekends during the summer. Sitting out here around the firepit and meeting new people."

Although not yet summer on the calendar, the afternoon was idyllic with a gorgeous blue sky and sunshine. Lily sighed at the beauty.

Lily noticed Claudia wandering outside in the yard, taking in the view. She understood the sadness that had to be weighing on the woman and raised her hand, waving from the deck. "Hello, Claudia. It's Lily up here on the deck."

Claudia looked up and waved and took a few steps closer to the house.

"Would you like to join us for a cup of tea? I was just about to have some."

"That sounds lovely, but I don't want to intrude."

"Not at all, I'd love the company. I've got three dogs up here, though. Fair warning."

Claudia laughed. "I love dogs and miss my own, so that would be even better. I'll be up in a few minutes."

She turned to Mac. "Now, that I've volunteered tea, would you mind filling the kettle and getting it ready? I'm useless at this point. Will you stay and visit with us, Wendy?"

She almost smiled. "I could use a cup of tea. I'll help Mac."

Lily almost fell off her chair. It was the first time Wendy had willingly offered to help. Maybe Mac was right about responsibility and expectations.

By the time Claudia was heading across the yard, Mac was coming out of the kitchen with a tray loaded down with tea and cookies. Lily pointed toward the yard. "Claudia is on her way.

Maybe you could put the dogs in the yard after they greet her. You know how they are with new friends."

He chuckled. "Right, they aren't big on respecting personal space. I'll take care of it."

Wendy came through the door with nice cloth napkins and her special box of organic tea.

Once Mac introduced all the dogs to Claudia, who took the time to talk and pet each of them, he ushered them to the stairs and secured the gate. "I'm going to take these three for a walk on the beach while you ladies enjoy your tea."

Lily's heart melted as he grinned at her. Having him in her life made everything so much better, even when things around her were going wrong.

Claudia chose a bag of the organic tea and once they all had their cups in front of them and cookies, Lily guided the conversation toward Claudia. "I overheard you're here to say goodbye to your sister. I'm so sorry."

"Thank you. I've been nervous about coming here. We lived here for a short time as children. I'm younger than Bonnie, so I don't remember it like she did. I think she left part of her heart here when we moved, and she was specific in that she wanted me to bring her back here, just me."

As they chatted, Claudia shared that she lived in a suburb of Dallas. That piqued Wendy's interest and the two of them talked about places they knew and liked to eat and shop. They had similar tastes in restaurants and knew the best coffee places.

Lily took a bite of her cookie and asked, "You mentioned Bonnie wanted you to come back with her. Did she have children or a husband?"

"No husband. He had passed away several years ago. She has one son, and he lives in Pennsylvania. Bonnie passed away a few months ago, and we had a memorial for her, but she was specific about her remains." Claudia's voice wobbled. "Part of them went to her son, but she wanted me to bring her back here."

Lily nodded. "You mentioned she came back here and visited over the years. My aunt and uncle owned the cottages, and I have many of their old records. I bet she's in their registration books. I just took over last year when my uncle passed away."

Claudia's eyes widened. "Oh, I bet she is in their records. Bonnie Perry was her name. She was a regular for years." Tears dotted her cheeks, and she sniffed. "She invited me to join her so many times, but I was always too busy." She shook her head. "Or so I thought."

Lily resisted the urge to reach across the table and pat the woman's hand. "Time has a habit of going by too quickly and drifting away, doesn't it? We always think we'll have more, but it doesn't always work that way."

Claudia nodded and took a sip from her cup. "I'm ashamed to say I hadn't even talked to Bonnie in over a year when she died. I was too wrapped up in my own life. We had always been close growing up, but once my parents passed away, we drifted apart."

She reached for a brownie. "That's not fair. Bonnie extended invitations to me and tried to keep in touch. I was the one who let our relationship fade. Truth is, I was more focused on impressing my circle of friends and entertaining in our lovely home. My husband worked in the energy sector and made a good living."

Claudia shook her head, and her shoulders slumped. "Bonnie lived in a small town in Wyoming. She invited me dozens and dozens of times, but I was always too busy. If it was winter, I had the excuse it was too cold and during the summer, I was busy hosting parties and attending gatherings with all the other wives in the company. We went on extravagant trips and cruises. I never once invited Bonnie to go with me. Now, it's too late."

She reached for another sip of tea. "My husband passed away and at the end of the day, I found out all those friends I had entertained and gone to lunch with weren't really my friends. They were acquaintances, at best. I'm ashamed to say, they were like me. In the group for business reasons, to get ahead, to be with the popular crowd, eat at the right places, wear clothes to impress them. It was just like high school. After Darrin died, they disappeared, and I was left with nobody."

She dabbed at her eyes with a tissue and glanced at Wendy and then Lily. "You two are so lucky to be able to be here together. You must be thrilled to have Wendy here to help you while you let your wrist and ankle heal."

Lily smiled and took a sip of hot tea to try to dislodge the lump that had formed in her throat. Listening to Claudia talk about her life and her sister was difficult, and Lily's heart ached. It was eerily similar to the relationship she shared with Wendy. Lily glanced over at Wendy and saw tears gliding down her face and plopping onto her linen napkin.

"I'm very thankful to have Wendy here. I don't know what I would have done without her." Lily smiled and reached with her good hand to grab Wendy's.

Claudia smiled at them. "Well, you're much smarter than I was. Cherish your connection and bond. Nobody can replace a sister, and I now realize how sad Bonnie must have been to have me rebuff her and regrettably, I didn't take much interest in her son's life either. I don't have any children, and I can tell you it's lonely when you're the only one left, and you have no family. I made so many mistakes." She reached for her tea and added, "Mistakes that are no longer fixable."

13

By the time Mac returned from the beach, Claudia had gone back to her cottage and without asking, Wendy collected the tea dishes and washed them all. Lily set about doing her exercises she had meant to do before the guests arrived.

Lily consulted her paperwork to make sure she was doing them properly, while Mac stood by and watched, offering pointers here and there. With that done, she was ready for ice packs and a nap.

Mel was coming over for dinner after her group study session, and they were having Cyndy's leftovers, so with little to do, Mac stretched out on the couch, surrounded by the three goldens, who looked to be settling in to join the two for a nap.

Lily's eyes had been closed for what seemed like only a few moments before the doorbell rang out and startled her, along with the dogs and Mac.

He and the dogs made their way to the door and welcomed Jeff and Donna with a hearty greeting. The chief of police and his wife, the town librarian, came bearing gifts. Jeff balanced two huge disposable trays and carried a large tote, while Donna carried a bakery box and a bag from the café across the street from the library.

Donna smiled and said, "We didn't want to disturb Lily, but we put together some food for you. I know her busy season is just beginning and the last thing you need to worry about is your meals."

Mac took the trays from Jeff's hand and carried them through to the kitchen, while Jeff and Donna stopped at Lily's recliner. "Oh, my goodness," she said. "You brought enough food to feed us for the month. That's so kind of you."

The sting of tears threatened Lily's eyes as Donna explained how to bake the chicken enchiladas. "I made a huge macaroni salad, and we picked up some meats and cheese and that yummy soup I know you love from the café. That way, you can have easy lunches, too."

Lily reached for Donna's hand. "I can't believe you did all that. I appreciate it. You two are such good friends."

Donna handed Mac the bag and box she still held before retrieving two books from her bag. "I snagged these new releases for you, so you have something exciting to read. Keep them as long as you need them, and I can pick them up when you're done."

Jeff put his hand on Lily's shoulder. "We just want you to rest and recuperate so you're ready for your wedding. We heard the news and couldn't be happier for both of you."

Mac came from the kitchen smiling and retrieved the other bags and containers. "Lily's worried about planning things, but Cyndy is helping, and we're keeping it small."

Lily nodded. "But, of course, we want you two there. We're just doing a ceremony on the beach and then a reception here in the yard." She gave Donna the date and promised an actual invitation would be forthcoming. "It's a Wednesday, but in the evening, so hopefully, it works with your schedule."

"We'll make it work. Two of our favorite people getting

married is something we wouldn't miss. If Cyndy needs help, just let me know."

The door to downstairs clicked open, and Wendy came into the living room. Lily motioned to her. "Donna, do you remember my sister Wendy? She's come back to help while I'm dealing with my injuries and will be running the cottages for me."

Donna nodded. "Yes, you were working at Poppy's last time you were here. Welcome back, and that's so nice of you to come to help Lily. There's nothing like sisters, is there?"

Jeff clapped Mac on the back. "We need to get home and get out of your hair but let us know if you need anything at all." They said their goodbyes and headed for the door.

"Hon," Mac hollered from the kitchen, "I'm going to put these enchiladas in the oven for tonight. We can have leftovers another day, but these are calling my name."

Lily chuckled. "Works for me, and the timing should be just right for when Mel gets home."

Wendy took a seat on the couch and turned to her sister. "That was nice of you."

Lily frowned. "What do you mean?"

She shrugged. "The way you introduced me and said I came to help you. You didn't say I'm homeless, and my husband is in prison, and I had nowhere else to turn. You made it seem like I came here for you."

"I'm grateful you're here, Wendy. It's a huge relief to have you around to help with the cottages. Listening to Claudia talk about her regrets with her sister made me realize I'm lucky to have you." She paused and added, "Jeff and Donna are great, and it wouldn't matter to them about your situation. Donna is the one who introduced me to Mel and encouraged me to take her in. She's continued to help Mel get a scholarship and is a wonderful person."

Wendy nodded, and tears fell from her eyes. "What Claudia

said really hit home with me. I've neglected you and Kevin and put my friends, who turned out to be anything but, at the top of the list. I worried about all the wrong things, and now I have nothing."

For the first time in years, Lily saw sincerity in Wendy's eyes. Her heart broke for her sister, who was facing a dark valley in her life without so much as a pen light.

"Well, you've got us, and you'll get through this."

Wendy's lip quivered. "I just want my old life back. I didn't have to worry about anything, and I liked it. It's all too much now."

"When Gary died, I went through a period of intense anxiety. I was worried about the future and the unknown. I was trying to think ahead way too far, giving myself too many variables and possibilities. It's easier if you just take a smaller chunk of time and figure out what you will do this week or this month, as opposed to thinking too far ahead. Wait until you're stronger and after you figure out a few weeks, it will be easier to look ahead without fear."

Wendy nodded. "I don't know how you did that, Lily. You're so strong and capable. I never realized until now. I was awful to you and Kevin and didn't do enough for you when Gary died. I'm so sorry."

"Thank you for saying that. It was the worst time of my life. I felt very lost and alone, but things are much better now. If I can get through that, you can get through this bump in the road. I think your life was always defined by Chad, and now you have an opportunity to make your own choices and figure out what you want. Try to look at the positive side, and we can try to put all the other stuff behind us and focus on the future and do a better job as sisters. Agree?"

Wendy nodded as the flow of tears increased. "Thanks, Lily," she whispered.

By Saturday, the household had settled into a new routine. Mac treated Lily to an early morning coffee or tea and visit before leaving early with the dogs during the work week. Lily took advantage of the quiet time to concentrate on doing her exercises and getting ready for the day before Wendy was up and about.

Thanks to Cyndy and Donna, they hadn't had to cook a meal all week. Lily missed her morning walks on the beach with the dogs, but Mac made sure they got their walk in the afternoon when he got home.

Wendy's attitude, while not stellar, had improved from when she had first arrived. She sometimes got huffy when Lily explained how she wanted things done but complied. Wednesday, Claudia, along with the other guest, checked out, which meant Wendy had to do the housekeeping and launder all the linens and towels.

It had been a struggle, and Mel had helped her finish the cottages when she got home from school. Thankfully, no new guests were checking in, so the extra time didn't pose a problem. It bugged Lily to no end that she couldn't go downstairs and watch over Wendy.

It was clear her sister hadn't done housework in a long time, and Lily had to go over things several times to explain the cleaning routine and even how to do the laundry. Wendy bristled each time Lily gave her instructions or had her do something over because she hadn't done it correctly.

Rebecca was due to leave, and another couple was checking in this afternoon, so Mel and Mac would tackle the housekeeping in the first cottage.

With it being Saturday, Wendy had to be at work at Marla's by nine o'clock, and Mac had offered to drive her and do some shopping at the market while he was downtown. He was a saint on both accounts.

Lily stayed up late reading one of the new books Donna had brought her and slept later than usual. She took her time getting up, doing her exercises, and showering, with Mac slipping in her bedroom with a delivery of toast and tea before he left to take Wendy downtown.

He left her with a quick kiss. "Rebecca isn't leaving until eleven, so I'll be back in plenty of time to help her with her bags. You relax and enjoy the morning with the dogs."

The gorgeous morning enticed her outside to the deck, where she managed to carry her fresh cup of tea and get situated with ice packs on her injuries. Wendy had been taking care of watering the flowers, and they were in good shape, soaking up the gentle morning sunshine.

She was enjoying the view and the soft chirps of the birds in the nearby trees, when Rebecca came around the side of the house and waved. "Good morning. I was hoping you'd be out and about. I just went to the bakery to get some treats for the road. I'll trade you a pastry for a cup of tea and a quick chat."

Lily laughed. "That's an offer I can't refuse. Please come on up. Just be aware of the dogs."

Rebecca insisted on Lily staying put, and she went into the kitchen to put the kettle on and brewed their tea. Lily told her where to find plates and napkins, and she returned with all the makings for an al fresco breakfast.

Lily took her first bite of an almond croissant and moaned. "These are so yummy. Thanks for sharing."

"I've got a long drive ahead of me today, so I wanted to have some comfort food for the road. I should have planned to leave earlier, but I finished my manuscript, so I'm delighted."

"Congratulations, that's terrific."

"I'm serious that I'm going to share this place with my author friends, and I'm sure I'll be back next year or maybe even this fall. It would be the perfect place for a writing retreat. Four or five of us get together each year for a week and do lots of writing, brainstorming, and drink our weight in wine."

"We'd love to have you."

"If we rent all the cottages and are the only guests here, it would be perfect, giving us a wonderful setting and a common area but privacy. I already sent photos to my friends, and they're working on dates."

"I'm delighted you enjoyed your stay. We love it when guests tell others about us. It's quite busy during the summer, starting now. Mac and I were choosing a date for the wedding, and I found one Wednesday in June when we didn't have guests, so that's our date. We want to have a small ceremony down on the beach and then a reception here in the yard."

"That sounds perfect and no matter what day you do it, I'm sure it will be wonderful."

"We've both lost our spouses, so it's not our first rodeo. Mac and I decided life is too short, too unpredictable, to wait around for the right time. Plus, my son will be visiting in June, and I wanted him here for the wedding. I'm not sure I've ever done anything so impulsive except decide to move out here."

Rebecca took a sip from her cup and smiled. "Well, I'm no expert, but from what I've seen, you've got yourself a good man in Mac. You two seem to fit together perfectly."

Lily smiled. "I think so. Mac's grown daughter, on the other hand, isn't too happy with the news. She lives in Georgia and hasn't made Mac's life easy since losing her mom."

"I'm sure that makes things challenging, but I think you have to live for yourself, not to please your kids, especially if they're grown and out of the house. You and Mac deserve to be happy and live the life you want." She laughed and added, "I have the opposite problem. I'm divorced, and my daughter is always trying to set me up with eligible men and worries that I'm on my own. I enjoy my solitary life, but she doesn't understand."

"Life is interesting, isn't it?" Lily took another sip from her cup.

"You're getting better at using your left hand, I see. Are your sprains feeling a bit better?"

"I think so. I'm doing my exercises and will get more on Monday, but it seems like the pain is diminishing, except for after exercising. I just try to keep them elevated and iced as much as possible. I want to speed up the healing process and get this wedding planned."

Rebecca finished her tea and checked her watch. "I better get a move on and get packed so I can hit the road."

"Mac just ran to the market, but he'll be here to help you with your bags."

Rebecca stood and took her bakery box. "Thanks again for your hospitality, and I wish you and Mac all the happiness in the world. I'll be in touch for a reservation soon." She turned to go down the stairs and then stopped. "Tell Mel I'm going to send her a copy of this new book as soon as I get my copies."

"She'll be over the moon. She loves books and was so thrilled you took the time to chat with her. It was a real treat."

Rebecca talked to the dogs and waved at Lily as she set out to her cottage.

Lily finished her last sip of tea as she contemplated Rebecca's words. As much as she tried to push the worry over Missy to the back of her mind, it was always there, like a dark cloud of doom, hanging over her as she tried to choose flowers and colors.

Cyndy's friend Paula was driving over with dresses on Saturday night and would be coming over on Sunday morning. She wanted to enjoy the experience, especially with Cyndy and Mel and maybe even Wendy. She hoped Rebecca was right and that she and Mac could live their lives without Missy's blessing.

14

Mel worked all day Saturday so she could have Sunday off and spend the day with Lily helping her choose bridal dresses. With her living out at Mac's, Lily realized how much she missed Mel and was thrilled to have her back in the house, even if only for a day.

Lily was up early, completed her exercises, showered, and dressed in loose-fitting clothes that were among her easiest to manage. Mel arrived first thing in the morning, loaded down with fancy coffee drinks, followed by Cyndy minutes later. Mac joined them for a coffee and visit but set out to spend part of the day at the clinic and the rest of it and the night at his house with the dogs, taking care of some outdoor chores.

Mel was taking possession of her old room for the night, since Cyndy promised an all-day affair of wedding planning. There were no guest arrivals or departures to deal with, so they had the entire day to spend on wedding tasks.

Mel offered to do some light housekeeping and ran the vacuum and dusted the upstairs and cleaned Lily's bathroom for her, while she put her laundry in the wash. Lily cringed at the sound of the vacuum, hoping it wouldn't wake Wendy. With her guest bedroom not being under the carpeted areas, she accepted the risk since the house could use a bit of sprucing before Cyndy and Paula arrived.

Without the use of her arm and hobbling on one leg, Lily hadn't been able to keep up with much. She hated being so helpless and propped herself at the kitchen counter to peruse the wedding binder Cyndy had prepared.

As Mel came from putting Lily's laundry away, the front doorbell rang. She hurried to answer, and Lily came from the kitchen to welcome Cyndy and her friend Paula.

With their arms loaded with dress bags and totes, Cyndy introduced Lily and Mel to Paula. She smiled at her soon to be sister-in-law. "This is going to be such a fun day, and Paula is staying over with me, so we've got the entire day and night to get everything done."

Mel led them into the living room and helped hang the dresses in Lily's closet, so they wouldn't get rumpled. Cyndy dashed out the door to retrieve a few more things, and Mel went with her to help.

Paula, tall and willowy, stood and looked out over the backyard. "You've got a gorgeous view here. Cyndy tells me you're doing a beach wedding, which will be lovely."

Lily nodded. "Yes, we're keeping it small and simple, and I love the beach, so it's the perfect spot. Come on in and have some tea." She led her into the kitchen and flicked the button on the kettle.

Mel had set out the tea and cups, so they just had to wait for the water. "It's so kind of you to take the time to put all this together and drive down here. I can't tell you how helpful it is." She lifted her injured wrist. "This fall couldn't have come at a worse time."

Lily admired Paula's chic hair, frosted and short, as she waved away Lily's concern. "Oh, I love coming to Driftwood Bay. I've done this for other people who have far less reason to need a home visit than you. Sometimes, people don't want to bother with coming to the shop. Not to mention the bonus of seeing Cyndy."

At the mention of her name, Cyndy and Mel came into the kitchen and unpacked more totes, filling Lily's fridge. Mel poured the tea, and Cyndy added a plate of fruit and pastries to the counter. She winked at Lily and said, "We need sustenance."

Lily patted the binder. "Good news is I found a wedding invitation online that matches the driftwood arbor I want to use on the beach. I can personalize them, and they'll be here in a matter of a few days. I don't need many, so that should work."

Cyndy smiled and picked up a pen, putting a checkmark on her wedding to-do list. "In other good news, I talked to Tides and Bayside Grille. Tides can do the food for the reception, but Bayside is too busy. So, I went ahead and booked Tides, but you can change and choose something else. I just didn't want to lose the spot."

Lily nodded as she popped a berry in her mouth. "That's great. They've got casual food that fits with the whole theme."

Cyndy slid a catering menu across the counter. "You can take a look at this with Mac and decide what you want and how many people." She wiggled in her chair as she put another happy checkmark on her list.

With a smile, she pointed at her notepad. "I think having your wedding on a Wednesday is working in your favor. I talked to Angelica at the flower shop, and she can do it that day. She just needs the order as soon as you can get it together."

Lily flipped the pages in the binder and pointed to the white bouquet with the sprinkling of blue forget-me-nots. "I'm drawn to this one, but we may need to pick the dress before we decide on flowers."

Paula nodded. "That's a gorgeous bouquet, but I think it's wise to choose your dress and build around that. I brought several for you to try with lots of choices in the sea glass colors you like for any attendants or family."

Cyndy nodded. "Before we get to that, the other things we need to settle on are the music and photographer."

Lily wrinkled her nose. "Music is more Mac's department. He's friends with the guys in that band that played at the tavern. I'm not sure if we need a band or should just play something ourselves." She took a sip of tea. "I'll let Mac decide that one." She slid her phone closer to her and poked the button for the microphone to let it do the typing for her and sent Mac a text so he could weigh in on the music.

"Okay, we'll get that sorted, and we need some photos. Do you have a recommendation?" She arched her brows in Cyndy's direction.

"The best one in town is Jeanette. The only slight hiccup is she was close to Jill, so I'm not sure how Mac would feel about her being at the wedding."

Lily frowned. "Oh, that might make it awkward for him. Is there another option?"

Cyndy shrugged. "There's another guy in town who does some and a few hobbyists, but Jeanette does the best work. Maybe just talk to Mac and see what he thinks. I haven't mentioned it to Jeanette but looked at her online calendar, and that day is available. If we want it, we need to grab it."

Lily nodded. "Okay, I'll talk to him tonight and let him decide."

Cyndy glanced at her list. "Okay, I think we've reached the moment for Paula's expertise." She waved her hand in front her, as if inviting her on stage.

"With Lily's mobility hampered, how about we move into the master bedroom. That way she doesn't have to wear herself out going back and forth?" She picked up her notepad and led the way.

Lily and Mel followed, and Cyndy said, "It's almost noon,

and I wanted to make this just like a visit to the boutique, so I've got some bubbly I'll bring in for us to sip while we try on dresses." She glanced at Mel and added, "I brought some sparkling juice for you, and it looks just like champagne."

Lily laughed and said, "I better go with the juice. I'm still taking some over the counter painkillers and don't need any alcohol added to that."

Cyndy promised she'd be right there and went about filling glasses.

Lily chose the window seat since it was the easiest to sit on and watched as Paula brought out the first dress. She placed it across the bed and unzipped the cover. "Cyndy told me you wanted something simple and a shorter length, so let's start with this one."

Cyndy arrived with a tray of champagne flutes and passed them around, setting Lily's on the wide windowsill before taking a seat in a chair.

Mel gasped when Paula revealed the lacy dress. Paula pointed at it and said, "This is a simple V-neck with a lace overlay and lace sleeves. It's timeless and comes in white or ivory or a few other colors."

Lily stood and hobbled into her large master closet with Paula. It took some time to get out of her clothes, and Paula did most of the work of getting her into the dress and pulling the zipper up the back.

Lily looked in the mirror before emerging to let Mel and Cyndy weigh in.

They both complimented her, and Lily turned every which way to take in every angle. She frowned and said, "It's okay but doesn't wow me."

Paula let out a sigh. "Oh, thank goodness. I know you wanted to go short because you were concerned about the dress dragging on the beach, but I have a couple in here that are simply gorgeous and would be perfect for you. Let's try one of them."

When Paula unveiled the next dress, Lily's heart skipped a beat. It was beyond gorgeous with a sleeveless top done in beautiful embroidery and lace. It was lined in all the right spots and when Lily slipped it on, she felt like a princess. The long skirt fell over her hips and while it had a bit of a train, it wasn't elaborate.

Lily glanced in the mirror and smiled at her reflection in the long ivory dress. "This one looks better and hides my hips with the bit of flare in the skirt. I like it."

Paula nodded and smiled, helping her out the doorway.

"Oh, oh, that's so beautiful," said Cyndy, as Lily took a few careful steps toward her. "It's quite stunning on you."

Mel's mouth was open as she stared at Lily. "I've never seen anything so pretty."

Paula smiled and added, "This one is also available in white, if the ivory isn't what you want."

Lily smiled and turned to see Wendy at the bedroom door. "Wow, you look great in that one. It's beautiful."

Cyndy motioned Wendy inside the room. "Will you join us in a glass of bubbly and watch the fashion show?" She stood, took Wendy by the arm, and introduced her to Paula.

"Paula brought some other dresses for all of us to try on in case you'd like a new dress for the wedding. First, we're helping Lily pick her dress."

Wendy smiled and sat on the edge of the bed. "Have I missed any other dresses?"

Cyndy wrinkled her nose. "Only one, and it's not the one, so it doesn't matter. It was short and didn't look that great." She stepped toward the door. "I'll be right back with your glass. Anybody need anything else?"

Everyone else was fine, and Cyndy promised to be right back.

Wendy made Lily turn a few times and nodded her head. "That fits you well. What shoes are you going to wear?"

Lily shrugged. "I hadn't even thought of shoes. Nothing high heeled for sure, I need to be steady on the uneven surface."

Paula nodded. "Many times, beach brides go barefoot or choose a simple flip-flop style of sandal. I've even had brides choose tennis shoes."

Lily nodded. "Yes, I like the flip-flop idea."

Paula made a note on her notepad. "They make some pretty ones with sparkles and rhinestones." She gazed at Lily. "Shall we try the next dress and see what they think?"

Cyndy returned with a glass of champagne for Wendy and the bottle to top off the other glasses, along with the sparkling juice bottle. She set them on the bathroom counter and went back to her chair. "I'm ready for the next one."

Lily disappeared into the master closet with Paula following. She unzipped another protective cover and removed a chiffon dress in ivory. "This one is very simple." She helped Lily into it and noted the beading along the empire waist below the halter-style neckline.

Lily turned and looked in the mirror. "I like this one, too. It's much less weddingy."

She stepped into the bedroom so the others could weigh in and help her decide.

Paula, much like a host of a fashion show, explained the fabric and style. "There is no train on this one, so it fits with Lily's original specifications and doesn't scream bridal dress. It comes in several colors."

Lily stood in front of the other three women. "What do you think?"

Mel smiled. "It's also very pretty, but I like the other one better."

Cyndy nodded. "I agree, Mel. That dress with the lace is magical. I know it has a longer train than you wanted, but we could work on some sort of walkway to protect it from getting dirty."

Lily shrugged. "That's an idea. I just don't want to have someone put too much work into this. Simple, remember?" She smiled at the woman she already thought of as a sister.

"I bet Andy and his dad could come up with something." Cyndy smiled back at her.

Paula guided Lily back to the closet. "I've still got a couple of other dresses for Lily to try, then some for the rest of you."

Lily was getting used to Paula helping her, and their system for changing her dress was getting quicker. Minutes later, she emerged in another long gown with a short train, like the one they all liked.

This one had a V-neck and instead of just lace and embroidery on the bodice, it had a whole layer of lace and embroidered flowers over the entire dress. Wendy was the first to comment. "This one seems too girly girl for you. It's gorgeous but seems a bit too young for you."

Nobody could accuse Wendy of sugar-coating her words. Lily took a few more steps closer to the other two women. Cyndy nodded. "It's beyond gorgeous, but I do like the other one with the higher neck. It's more elegant."

Lily twirled, the best she could with one ankle out of commission, and nodded. "I agree. It's like a fairy tale dress, but that other one feels more like me."

Paula helped Lily out of it and said, "One more for you, and then you'll have to make a choice." She winked as she unzipped another cover. She lowered her voice to a whisper, "This one is a little bit of a trick. I brought it in a beautiful sea glass blue to have the other ladies try it, but I thought you could also try it in white, if you like it for a bridal dress."

Lily watched in the mirror as the chiffon layers fell over her. It was another V-neck style, with a bit of ruching across the bodice. The long dress had a simple skirt, but the added drama of several sheer panels flowed over and around it. It was flowy and gorgeous, and the gossamer fabric that floated around it gave it the illusion of a small train.

Lily smiled. "I can't wait to see this in the sea glass colors. It's gorgeous."

She stepped out of the closet, and all three women gasped. "Wowza," said Cyndy.

Lily took a few steps around the bedroom, letting them see it from all angles. The weightless fabric floated around her and reminded her of a waterfall. She turned and caught Paula's eye and winked.

Paula took a sip from her champagne flute and said, "Ladies, the good news is, this is not a bridal dress, per se, but can be used for bridesmaids or attendants. I brought it in a subtle sea glass blue color that I thought you could try. Of course, Lily could choose it for her dress, but I like to think the bride should stand out in something spectacular of her own."

Cyndy's mouth gaped open. "That would be gorgeous in the blue you mentioned. In their desire to keep the wedding small, Lily and Mac aren't having attendants, but I'd love to wear something in the colors of the wedding. What about you, Wendy?"

She nodded and stood next to her sister, running her hand over the whisper-thin chiffon. "This is beyond gorgeous."

"I brought some different sizes, so you can all try it on and see what you think. We'll let Lily take a rest, and she can weigh in on your dresses."

Lily nodded. "I've about had it and need to get some ice on my ankle, so watching the rest of the fashion show sounds good to me." She hobbled into the closet and slipped on her robe, not sure if she'd need to try anything on again.

By the time she emerged, Cyndy had ice packs and a fresh cup of hot tea, plus her sparkling juice ready for her in the window seat. She helped her get settled before she hurried to the closet to change into her dress.

Mel was the first to emerge, and her smile brought tears to Lily's eyes. "Aw, Mel, you look like a beautiful mermaid." The color was somewhere between that soft blue and subtle aqua she had loved and reminded her of so much of the sea glass her aunt had collected. It was simply perfect.

Mel twirled and smiled, and the dress swirled around her, giving Lily the full impact of the fluid-like way the fabric floated when she moved. It was like the ocean itself had been transformed into a dress.

Next, came Wendy, who looked striking and for once sported a huge smile. She, too, posed, although more expertly, much like the fashion models Lily was sure Wendy had observed in person. The dress looked picture perfect on her.

Cyndy was the last to emerge and sported a grin from ear to ear. "I've never had anything so decadent. I love it." She held the sheer panels between her fingers and turned in front of Lily and turned toward the mirror. She grimaced. "I never go sleeveless. I think my arms are a little out of shape for this."

"You look wonderful. All of you do. It's such a beautiful dress, and the color is perfect." Lily glanced at Wendy and Mel. "You don't all have to get the same dress. Like Cyndy said, I decided not to have actual bridesmaids. I want the wedding to be simple. Kevin is going to walk me down the aisle, but then it will just be Mac and me. I don't need a long, drawn-out ceremony."

Paula cleared her throat. "I did bring another style that has a sheer jacket over it, that Cyndy might like. It's the same designer, so the same color." She motioned Cyndy over to the closet.

Minutes later, she came out the door in a shorter style that hit at the knee. The dress itself was a simple sheath with wide straps and a sweetheart neckline, but over it was a layer of sheer fabric adorned with glitter and fabric stitching that gave it a very up-market and polished look. To top it off was a sheer elbow-length jacket with the same flowy hem of the other dress.

Cyndy took in her silhouette in the mirror and smiled. "I think I like this much better on me. It hides my flabby arms."

"You've got killer legs, and this dress shows them off. You look fabulous," said Lily, smiling and sipping her tea.

Paula had the other two women join Cyndy, putting her in the middle, and Lily gasped. "Oh, that is perfect. All of you look magnificent."

Paula nodded. "I agree. I'm not sure what the three of you think, but I think those styles are perfect on you."

Mel bobbed her head. "I love it. I've never seen anything so beautiful."

Wendy smiled and said, "I agree. I think they're beautiful and as much as I love this style, I think Cyndy looks magnificent in this shorter one."

Paula clapped her hands together. "Okay, that just leaves our bride. Did you make a final decision?"

"I love this dress," she said, pointing at Mel, "but, I agree about the bride having something unique, so I'm going to go with the one with the lace embroidery bodice. I thought it looked the best, and I liked the ivory, especially for a second marriage."

Cyndy smiled. "I think you made the right choice. It was perfect on you and in ivory, it will be easy to choose something for Mac to wear that complements it."

Wendy nodded. "I agree. It's elegant but still has the beach vibe that makes it work for the casual atmosphere you have planned. I can see Mac in a beige linen that would be perfect with it."

"Okay, ladies, let me get my pin cushion and notepad, so we can make any alterations to these dresses. Then we'll get the bride to try hers on one more time and do the same."

She dug into her tote bag and handed Lily a catalog. "Here's some shoe choices, if you need something, or if any of the other ladies need shoes."

Mel dashed over to Lily's window seat and lowered her voice, "I don't have any shoes that would work for something this nice."

Lily reached for her arm. "Well, look through this and pick out something you'd like to wear, and we'll get them ordered. The dress and shoes are my treat, so don't worry about the price."

Tears filled the young woman's eyes as she reached out and hugged Lily. The feel of the young woman, who when Lily met her was more like an abused puppy and wouldn't let anyone near her, made her heart swell. Despite her efforts to maintain composure, tears dotted Lily's cheeks.

So many emotions swirled inside her. Lily wasn't sure how she would get through the ceremony without shedding more tears.

15

The next weeks flew by, with Mac and Mel handling the dogs and everything else Lily needed done around the house. Memorial Day weekend was upon them, with the cottages full of guests and the town bustling with activity.

Even Wendy was pitching in and had settled into her new routine as innkeeper. She still needed guidance and encouragement to be patient with the guests, but she had come a long way in just a matter of weeks. It didn't hurt that they had received a card from Claudia. She had written a lovely thank-you note to them and included a photo she had taken the day she had spread her sister's ashes in the bay.

She promised to be back for a visit next year and told them how wonderful it had been to spend time at Glass Beach Cottage and to talk with them. She felt it was a true gift that she had connected with sisters at a time when she needed her sister more than ever.

The card and sentiment had touched Wendy, who had teared up when she read it and held it close to her chest. Claudia's visit and her words were a good reminder of the importance of cherishing their relationship, no matter how fragile it became.

Mel had addressed all the wedding invitations, taking great care to do so with perfect penmanship. She and Mac had worked together to include close friends, which was more difficult for him, since he had so many connections in Driftwood Bay.

Lily limited her list of out-of-town guests to Kate and Spence, along with Izzy and Colin. They promised to be there and looked forward to Mac and Lily visiting the island for a combination honeymoon and Fourth of July celebration the following week.

Jeff and Donna and Andy and his family were the other close friends Lily added to her list. She couldn't forget Nora and Bree, who were among her first guests and now lived in Driftwood Bay. With Bree being such a good friend of Mel's, she couldn't leave them out. When Lily envisioned a small wedding, she had envisioned only Kevin, Wendy, Cyndy, and Missy joining them, but as she and Mac worked on it, they both realized they had to include others.

Mac kept his close friends list small, since space on the beach was limited. He compromised by inviting more of them to the reception. They had ordered two batches of invitations, with the majority printed with the reception information only.

Lily had been diligent about her exercises and therapy, and her healing was ahead of schedule. Her ankle and wrist were greatly improved, and she was able to stand on her ankle and put weight on it. She no longer needed the cane. While neither injury was completely healed, her physical therapist assured her the next week would bring about positive changes with her increased exercise regime.

Lily pondered the wedding list Cyndy had copied for her. She was thrilled to see so many items checked off and completed and could even use her right hand to add notes.

Paula had delivered the altered dresses and shoes, all beaded flip-flops in solidarity with Lily, and they were safely tucked away in Lily's master closet. Between Paula, Wendy, and Cyndy, they had outfitted Mac in casual linen pants and an ivory shirt that matched Lily's dress. After making him try vests and jackets, they all agreed he looked perfect in just a short-sleeve shirt. Mac was thrilled not to have to wear a jacket or tie.

The florist was set on using white and subtle sea glass colors in the flowers that would be on the tables for the reception, as well as the archway they would use on the beach. Andy and Wade were building it out of driftwood and would have it ready well in advance of the ceremony.

Cyndy had found a bamboo runner and several photos of wooden ones that would serve as a walkway on the beach and protect the gorgeous wedding dress. With the help of his friends who had a band, Mac had the music handled and together, they had picked the menu from Tides.

Lily took a sip from her cup of tea and looked across the yard from her perch on the deck. It was a lovely Saturday morning, and Mac had taken the dogs for a walk along the beach. He was so good about making sure they got in their beach time, even if Lily couldn't. He looked forward to three days off from work, as he had been juggling his clinic hours and helping Lily and hadn't had a true day off in a month.

Wendy came through the door carrying a cup of tea, dressed and ready for her day at Marla's. Lily smiled at her. "You look beautiful in that dress."

Wendy did a quick twirl before she sat. "That's the best part about working there. Dressing up and being surrounded by all the pretty things."

"Have you had any luck finding something else that's full time?"

She shook her head. "Nothing has worked out. Most of the jobs are retail or restaurants, and Marla's is the only store I'd like to work in. I was sort of hoping she'd get so busy, she could bring me on full time, but her daughter is here for the summer, so that idea went out the window."

"Oh, that's a shame. I'm sorry, I know you like it there."

Wendy shrugged and took another sip. "Running the cottages isn't too bad. I thought I'd hate it, but it's been okay."

"I'm so glad to hear that. Mac and I have been talking about our living arrangements. After the wedding, we need to decide where to live. As much as I love being here and all the memories, we've decided to make Mac's house our home."

Lily drummed her fingers on the table. "That leaves this place vacant, and I wanted to ask you if you would be interested in taking over the management of the cottages, full time. Live here, upstairs, and handle everything related to the cottages. You'd get to live here rent free and get a salary. I'd still be on hand to help whenever you needed it."

Wendy's eyes widened. "Wow, I need to think about it. I must admit, I wondered how it would all work when you got married."

Lily laughed. "I know, I didn't think it all the way through when I said yes. Now, we need to figure out the practical side of everything. Also, I want to talk to Mel and see what she wants to do. Mac is open to having her live with us at his place, but I also want her to be able to stay here if she wants. She's much closer to town here, and it might be better for her. Plus, she's quite capable of helping with the cottages."

Wendy nodded. "Oh, yes. She knows how to do everything and is so good at it." She paused and added, "If I do this, I would like her to stay here. I'd feel better having her here. Not so lonely."

Lily couldn't believe her ears. "I think you should tell Mel that. She's a lovely young woman, who has come so far from where she was. I think that would make her feel good to know."

Wendy hung her head. "I misjudged her and wasn't kind. As

snippy as I was with her, she was always sweet to me." She glanced at the fashionable watch on her wrist. "In fact, she should be here in a few minutes to take me to work. She's been awesome about that, too."

"Yes, she's got a kind heart. You think about the idea of taking over here and let me know as soon as you can."

Wendy stood and nodded. "What will you do if I say no?"

"I'd just have to do it until I could find a manager or maybe see if Mel wanted to do it part time and split it with me. I don't like the idea of a stranger living here but would have to deal with it if it came to that."

"So, where would I live if that happened?"

Lily shrugged. "I'm sure you could stay here until you figure out your next move."

Mel came through the door. "Ready to go, Wendy?"

"Yeah, I'll be right there." She turned back to Lily. "I'll give it some thought today, and we can talk tonight when I get home."

Lily nodded and smiled at Mel. "Have a good day at work. We'll see you tonight for dinner."

She watched as the two of them went through the door, both more relaxed together. Hearing Wendy say she was enjoying managing things at the cottages surprised her but also made her hopeful that she would agree to stay on. Even with Wendy earning a salary and working at Marla's, it would be a long time before she could afford to move and get a place on her own.

It warmed her heart to listen to Wendy speak about the transformation of her thoughts about Mel. As much as she would miss seeing Mel each day, Lily hoped it worked out that Mel would stay at the cottages with Wendy.

Mac and Lily had an appointment at the bakery, and he convinced her to head downtown early and have lunch before they commenced with cake tasting and meeting with Sonja, the wedding cake designer at the bakery.

She even managed to climb the stairs to the upper deck of the restaurant without any pain. The small ankle support brace she wore now was all she needed. While enjoying a leisurely lunch on the deck overlooking the bay, Lily told Mac about her conversation with Wendy.

He popped a tortilla chip in his mouth. "Do you think she'll agree to stay on at the cottages?"

She shrugged. "I think so, at least for the short term. I don't see that she has many options and with her admitting she likes it, that works in our favor."

Mac nodded. "I'm curious what Mel will decide to do."

"I hope she'll stay with Wendy. Honestly, it would make me feel better to know she's around to help, and I think it would be nice for them to have each other. Mel could still come out and visit whenever she wanted or even stay over. I think she'd feel more independent staying at the cottages, instead of with us."

"True, I just know she loves Margo and Coco and Lucy and Ethel so much; they might be a big draw."

"She'll miss the dogs for sure, too." She sighed. "I'm not sure we thought all this through when we decided to marry and complicate everyone's lives." She laughed, but part of her worried about Mel and Wendy. Their relationship was still fragile, and she didn't want to be the cause of a derailment.

Mac reached for her good hand and squeezed it tight. "I can see you're worrying. They'll be okay. You'll only be a few miles away."

She nodded. "Have you heard from Missy?" Might as well pour all her worries out on the table at once.

He shook his head. "I emailed her but didn't get a reply. Of course, the invitation went out to her a couple of weeks ago. Nothing."

She squeezed back and added, "I'm so sorry. Are you sure you want to do this without her?"

He looked across the water and sighed. "I'd love her to be here and be happy for us, but I've resigned myself to the reality that she probably won't come and honestly, it will be less stressful without her. She leaves a wake of turmoil when she comes, and we don't need that."

"You're probably right. I just worry that you'll regret it later."

He brought her hand to his lips and brushed her knuckles with a kiss. "Try not to worry. We've done all we can do to include her and reach out to her. I know it seems harsh, but I've been dealing with this for years, and there is nothing I can do about it. I've tried, and it always ends the same way."

She nodded. "I'll try. Maybe Cyndy can work some of her magic."

He grinned. "I'll ask her to give it another try. Missy was pretty closed off about it, even to her, the last time Cyndy talked to her."

"Okay, I'll quit nagging you. It just makes me feel horrible."

The waitress brought the check and brought an end to their conversation.

After Mac paid the bill, they strolled down the sidewalk to the bakery and were shown to a small backroom where they found Sonja standing next to a table set with two place settings.

The short woman, with shocking white hair, smiled as she rested her hands atop her round midsection, draped by a white apron. "Welcome, come in and let's get to the best part of the wedding." She chuckled, "Well, at least I think it's the best part. I've got some samples for you to try."

She disappeared behind a large counter and returned with two plates. "First up, I've got a lemon lavender. It's a vanilla cake with zesty lemon filling and a very subtle hint of lavender in the buttercream."

Lily's eyebrows arched as she took in the pretty slice.

Sonya smiled and said, "I'll leave you to it and get the next candidate."

Mac frowned and said, "Lavender, like the plant?"

Lily took a bite and said, "Yum and yes, it's the plant."

Mac took a hesitant bite and then nodded. "Okay, not as bad as I expected. I thought it might taste like soap."

She giggled and took another bite. "I like it. It's quite good and different."

Mac made a note on the paper Sonja had left next to each place setting.

Sonja returned with a chocolate raspberry. The aroma of it made Lily's mouth water. The combo was delicious, and there wasn't much in the chocolate family that she didn't like.

She smiled as she noticed Mac taking several bites after his initial taste. "Good one, huh?" he said.

She laughed and nodded. "Yes, it's yummy."

Sonja came from behind the counter with a pretty slice of white cake filled with fresh strawberries and cream. "This is a wonderful cake for a summer wedding."

Lily took her first bite and shut her eyes. "It tastes just like I remember. My mom always made a similar cake, and I loved it."

Mac smiled as he licked his fork and took another huge bite. "From the look on your face, I think this is the one. It's delicious and if it reminds you of your mom, that's even better."

A lump formed in Lily's throat, and she took a sip of water. "I wish she were here, and Dad, too. You would have loved them, and they would have loved you."

He reached for her hand and lowered his voice. "Let's not tell Sonja it's the one. I want to keep tasting them all."

Lily burst out laughing, her temptation at sadness thwarted once again by the man she loved. "Deal," she said.

16

With the holiday weekend ending, Mac and Lily sat outside next to the firepit on Monday evening. All the guests were out, Mel was at work, and Wendy had gone to Marla's house for a barbeque to celebrate the holiday and the new store.

Sunday, Wendy talked to Lily and agreed to stay on and manage the cottages. Her spirits were low, since on Saturday, Marla let her know her daughter would be working Saturdays, which meant Wendy was out of a job. Not that it was a huge moneymaker, only working one day a week, but it was something she enjoyed.

Marla was happy with Wendy, but her daughter needed the work, and there wasn't enough business to keep Wendy on the payroll. Wendy tried to blow it off, but Lily knew she felt rejected, even though Marla promised her the first chance at any position that opened in the future and softened the blow with an invite to her Memorial Day party.

As Lily consoled her sister over a cup of tea, Wendy made it clear, managing the cottages wasn't a forever decision, but she committed to staying for the rest of the season when she and Lily could reevaluate things during the winter months.

It was all Lily could ask for. She didn't imagine it was Wendy's dream to be an innkeeper but knowing she could count on her during these months as she and Mac started their new life together, eased her mind.

With less than a month before the big day, Lily felt more relaxed with all the preparations handled and everything checked off her list. With nowhere to go and Mac staying one more week at the house, until she was released from therapy, she enjoyed a glass of wine, while Mac chose a cold beer.

The flames from the fire danced before them with the last band of light dipping into the sea, leaving way for the stars to fill the dark sky. The solar lights throughout the space and the lights strung across the yard provided a gentle glow and made it easy to navigate the pathways, while providing the perfect ambience. It was a beautiful evening to kick off the official beginning of summer.

Mac took a swallow from his bottle. "I felt for Mel last night when we talked with her about what she wanted to do and where she wanted to live."

Lily nodded. "I know. I could tell she was torn."

He smiled at her. "She's so loyal to you and wants to please you."

Lily frowned. "I know. I wanted her to do what worked best for her. I was hoping not to influence her decision. I think she wants to be around the cottages to help Wendy. I don't think Mel fully trusts Wendy to do everything yet."

Mac chuckled. "She's a smart girl."

"You telling her to keep the key to your house and to come home whenever she wanted, was so sweet."

"Well, I didn't mean to make the poor girl cry. I just wanted her to know she didn't have to give up that option. I never want her to feel alone."

"That's why I love you, Mac. You're a good man."

He wiggled his eyebrows. "I thought it was my irresistible good looks and never-ending charm."

She laughed. "Yes, those too." She took a sip from her glass. "With Wendy moving upstairs, at least Mel will have a semblance of her own space."

"I'm not sure she's too concerned with that. She was more distraught about not seeing the dogs. I imagine she'll be out every weekend to visit them."

"Maybe we ought to rethink our plan to take them on the trip and let her stay with them at your place?"

He nodded. "That would work. It would give us more freedom and not burden Izzy with three more dogs."

"I'll ask Mel and see if it would work. We could pay her to make up for her time away from the coffee shop."

"Sure, and Cyndy would help if need be. Plus, the dogs have a great setup out there and can use the doggy door to come in and out of the fenced yard as they please. They'd be perfectly fine to stay there while she's at work."

"True. I hate leaving them, but they'd have fun together and hopefully, your house will still be standing when we get home."

"Sherlock would make sure they behave, trust me." He laughed and took another sip from his beer.

"Mel's picking up Wendy from the party when she gets off work. I'll ask her tonight and let her give it some thought before we make a change. She'll need to stay with them on the Fourth of July, with the fireworks going off."

Her phone chimed with a message. It was from Jeff. She read it quickly and smiled. "So, Jeff says he heard from his mechanic, and he checked out that used car, and it's in good shape."

"That's great news. It's a good price, and Wendy is going to need transportation to handle getting supplies and shopping. I know you don't want to give up Gary's truck, and we can keep it in the barn at the house. I think buying the car makes sense, and you can write it off."

She gritted her teeth. "It wasn't in my budget, but I agree it makes the most sense. I wish I weren't so attached to that old truck, but I just can't hand it over to her. I'd be gutted if something happened to it."

He winked at her. "You won't have that same attachment to an old Subaru wagon."

She laughed and took another sip from her glass. "You are correct on that point. I know it won't be up to Wendy's standards, but it beats walking."

He reached for her hand. "Things are working out the way they're supposed to, I think."

She smiled. "I think you're right. I'm getting so excited for Kevin to visit. It's going to be a fun few weeks with him and the wedding and our trip to the islands. I just hope Wendy can handle everything."

"Let her take the wheel completely while you're still here, and she can get help. It will be a good practice period for her to be on her own. That way you and Kevin can leave and do whatever you want."

"I feel a smidge guilty that he'll be here and your daughter won't be."

He shook his head. "Don't let Missy dampen your excitement. I'm finally standing up to her tyranny, and she needs to get used to it. There's nothing she can do to ruin this for us."

Lily nodded. "Kevin's bringing Brooke, so I'm sure we'll be exploring the area and maybe take a trip up to Olympic National Park or even over to Victoria. I'm leaving it up to them to decide what they want to do. I just hope I like her."

"I can see the worry on your face. You think she's the one, don't you?"

She shrugged. "I do. I'll love her if Kevin does, but I hope I genuinely like her and enjoy being with her. So many women have a rocky relationship with their daughters-in-law, and I don't want that. Granted, I'm not sure anyone would be good enough for Kevin, at least in my eyes, but I want to like her and for her to like me."

"One time, you mentioned maybe Kevin staying with me, since with Wendy and Mel, you're short on bedrooms. What did you decide?"

She gasped. "Oh, my gosh, I forgot all about that. I'm not sure how to approach that whole issue. Do you think they expect to share a bedroom? Maybe I should see if they both want to stay at your place; that way, I wouldn't have to know."

He laughed. "That's fine with me. There's plenty of room downstairs."

"I hate not to have him here so I can soak up very minute with him, but in reality, it's not going to work."

"Maybe we should move you out to my house earlier and transition Wendy upstairs. You could invite them to stay at my house, and you could also stay there. That way you'd get to see more of him. We could let them have the downstairs and what they choose for bedroom arrangements would be up to them. You can take the guest bedroom upstairs by the master, and that leaves them with two bedrooms downstairs and Mel here in her own room."

She sighed. "I hate that this is so complicated, but I don't want to split them up and have one staying here and one staying with you. That seems overly manipulative."

He nodded. "I would agree."

"And I don't want to shove Mel out of her place here. She's already been inconvenienced. I think your idea is best." Her thoughts shifted to her bedroom furniture and the rest of her things. "I guess it makes sense just to leave the furniture here as is and pack up my personal things. When I know more about Wendy and the future, that will determine what I can do here."

"We can change out any furniture you want, so don't be shy about saying so. I'm not attached to anything."

She reached for his hand. "I appreciate that. There are just a few things I want to be sure to take, but I can wait on the furniture. It's not like Wendy has anything to move in here, so she needs to use it."

"I can organize some help to move what you want, and we can get that done before Kevin arrives." He cleared his throat. "I have a very serious question for you now."

She stared at his serious eyes, her heart pounding in her chest, wondering what could be coming. "Okay, I think."

"How would you feel about adding to our family?"

She smirked. "Uh, safe to say, that's impossible at this point."

He chuckled. "I'm talking goats. I have a line on a doe and two baby goats and thought I could give them a home, but only if you're okay with it."

She laughed. "I can't say no to baby goats. Maybe we could incorporate some goat yoga into our routine."

"That's so crazy and so popular. You might be onto something. Maybe an added service for your cottage guests."

"You know who's going to be over the moon about the idea?"

He nodded. "Mel, I know. I can't wait to tell her. That will give her one more chore to handle when we're away, but I have a feeling she'll be all too happy to take care of them."

"She'll have them wearing pajamas by the time we get back from our trip."

He smiled. "Maybe we could host a small family dinner at the house, our house, when Kevin is here. Include Cyndy, Mel, and Wendy, sort of a non-rehearsal rehearsal dinner." He paused and added, "And we could have Sonja make that chocolate raspberry cake we both loved in a smaller size."

She grinned. "You liked that cake, didn't you?" She nodded. "Dinner sounds like a great idea. It's probably a good thing for Kevin to get acclimated at your place… our place and make him feel at home. Well, Brooke for that matter, too. I have a feeling she'll be with him whenever he comes to visit."

"So, you think we might be headed for a wedding in New Hampshire someday soon?"

Her shoulders sagged. "I think it's a possibility. Just the way he talks about her, I can tell." She sighed. "It's such a bittersweet thing, watching your son grow up and become a man. Part of me is so proud and excited for him to make his own way and succeed, and the other part wants to still be able to rock him to sleep and smell the top of his head."

"It goes by in the blink of an eye, doesn't it?"

Tears burned in her throat, and she reached for her glass. "Too fast," she whispered.

17

Tuesday morning, they were easing back to their old routine, and Lily accompanied Mac and the dogs on their morning beach walk. She was slow and careful, especially on the trail from the house to the beach, but her ankle felt stronger, and she wanted to get back to normal.

They held hands as the dogs romped down the beach, happy to play along the edge of the water. With Lily not needing as much help, Mac was moving back to his house, and Mel was returning to her old room tonight. They decided to tackle moving Lily on a weekend when a couple of Mac's friends could help them.

Mac took Sherlock to work, as he did most days, but Lily kept Bodie and Fritz with her. She had missed them and wanted to take Bodie to his training lesson. She wasn't brave enough to leave Fritz with Wendy, so he was going with them. She still wasn't keen on the dogs and although they were interested in being friends with her, Wendy continued to give them the cold shoulder.

That was one of the best things about moving to Mac's. She wouldn't have to worry about the dogs, and they would have a beautiful and safe place to roam. She would miss the memories of her aunt and uncle that comforted her and reminded her of happier times, but she was determined to make new memories with Mac.

Spending time with their friends on San Juan Island was at the top of her list, and she couldn't wait for their honeymoon trip. Mel liked the idea of staying with the dogs and watching Mac's house while they were away, so that problem was solved. School was over, and there was enough time to make sure her work schedule would allow her to spend most of her time at the house.

Lily's phone pinged with a motion alert, and she saw the used car she purchased in the driveway. She went out to thank the mechanic but was too late, as he was climbing into the shop truck, which had followed him. He waved, and she waved back before going down the steps to inspect it.

Mac had arranged for it to be detailed, and it was shining as only a 2005 model could. She plucked the keys from the visor and took them inside the house.

She was surprised to find Wendy in the kitchen brewing a cup of tea, dressed and ready for the day. "Hey," she said, "I have something to tell you."

Her serious tone made Lily sit.

"Chad's lawyer sent me divorce papers and a letter from him. It sounds like it's the best path legally, and he doesn't want me to wait around for him. The lawyer thinks it's best that we divorce. Then I'm more distanced from whatever repercussions will come. I guess there could be some civil lawsuits. I don't understand it all, but I've gone ahead and signed them."

Lily shook her head. "I'm so sorry, Wendy. I know this isn't the life you had planned."

She shrugged. "It's probably best to put it behind me and make a clean start. I think part of me kept thinking something would change, and things could go back to what they were, but that's not going to happen. Like you said, this is my new reality."

"It's still difficult, I'm sure."

"The upside is there's nothing to fight over. We literally have no assets."

Lily reached across the island counter and patted her sister's hand. "You'll get through this, Wendy. I know you will. You can make a new life."

She sighed and took a sip from her cup. "I hope you're right. Anyway, I don't want to dwell on it but wanted you to know. I didn't see the point of trying to fight it, and I think deep down Chad is trying to do me a favor and let me go and be rid of whatever else awaits him."

"For what it's worth, I think it makes sense, and you made the right decision. He could be facing a lifetime of problems and wants to spare you."

Her sister nodded. "What are you up to today?"

Lily held up the keys. "I've got a little surprise for you."

Wendy frowned and then noticed the keyring and smiled.

"Don't get too excited, but I bought a used car for the cottages. You can use it to run errands and go shopping. It's old, but reliable. I just need to get your driver's license number to add you to the insurance policy."

Wendy's grin widened, and she took the keys from Lily's hand and rushed to the front door. Lily stood at the top of the steps and watched as she danced around it like a teenager getting her first car. She had expected her to turn up her nose at it, but Wendy opened the door and slid behind the wheel, her smile visible as she checked all the features and adjusted the seat.

After a few minutes, she came bounding up the steps and hugged Lily. "Thank you for this. It's been such a drag not to have a car, and this will be a huge help."

Surprised but happy with the reaction, Lily said, "I can't

expect you to manage the place walking to town for supplies, can I?"

Wendy stood next to her and gazed upon the car. "Well, it's no match for my old Cayenne, but it's perfect for Driftwood Bay."

"Speaking of supplies, you'll need to get the things to put together charcuterie boards for this weekend for Friday and Saturday night. I've got plenty of wine, but you'll need to get crackers, cheese, fruit, all of it, and bring the receipt back." She gave her a ballpark budget.

Lily had added Wendy to her business credit card account but had made sure to put restrictions on it, so it couldn't be abused. She wanted to trust Wendy, but it was hard to do. At this point, she needed to earn it. Maybe now, with Chad in the rearview mirror and not waiting and wondering what she would do, Wendy could move forward and figure out her life.

After she emailed Wendy's driver's license number to her insurance agent, it was time to get the boys and go to Bodie's training session.

As she drove from the training center, ideas of what to do when Kevin and Brooke arrived continued to swirl through her mind. Since Brooke was from a rural area in New Hampshire, the idea of a trip to Olympic National Park was at the forefront of her ideas. Whidbey Island was also a fun day excursion and easy to do. Victoria would take more planning and if that was something they wanted to do, she needed to book it soon.

She hadn't planned lunch, so she made a quick stop at the deli and got something to take home, along with a homemade pumpkin dog cookie for each of the boys and one to take home to Sherlock.

As she reached for the door of the deli, she ran into Mel. Her eyes widened. "Hey, are you on your lunch break?

"Yep, just walked down for a sandwich. Mac came out this

morning and told me about the goats. I'm so excited I can hardly wait."

Lily laughed. "I knew you would be. There isn't anything much cuter than a baby goat."

Mel's eyes sparkled. "He told me I could name them. The mom is Marigold, but the two babies need names."

"Oh, I can't wait to hear what you come up with."

Mel's order was ready, and the woman behind the counter held up her bag. Lily waited for Mel to collect it and wandered outside with her. "Did he tell you we're going to transition my stuff out to the house and move Wendy upstairs so you can have the downstairs to yourself again?"

She nodded. "He said you were working on that so Kevin and Brooke could stay out at Mac's house when they come, and you wouldn't have to deal with the hassle of moving right after the wedding, especially with your trip."

"Right and having you there to take care of the dogs will be wonderful. We love having them with us, but honestly, they'll be more comfortable at home, where they can run around all day. I'm so glad you're willing to do that."

"I love taking care of them, along with the alpacas and the llamas. Now, I'll have some goats to play with, too. I've got my things in the car, so I'll be moving back in tonight after work. I'll be there for dinner."

Lily smiled at the young woman she had missed having around the house. "Sounds good. I took out Cyndy's casserole to thaw this morning, so we can have that."

Mel waved as she hurried back down the street, and Lily slid behind the steering wheel, the dogs sniffing at the package she put in the passenger seat. "You need to wait until we get home, so you don't slobber all over my car."

They gave her their saddest eyes, but she didn't budge and turned the car for home. Once in the kitchen, she herded them to the deck and rewarded them with their treats, while she dug into her sandwich.

She loved the turkey and provolone with a bit of tart cranberry sauce and dressing. It was like a Thanksgiving treat in the middle of summer. She scanned her tablet while she ate, checking on reservations and messages, just to make sure there weren't any problems.

As she scrolled her messages, one stood out at her. It was from Missy and was in reply to the message she had sent her last month about the wedding, inviting her to stay and letting her know all the details and how much she was looking forward to meeting her. She had used every ounce of tact and grace she had in her to compose it and seeing the reply made her heart beat quicker.

She knew no matter how much Mac said it didn't bother him, having her at the wedding would mean the world to him. Lily hoped it would be the first step in a journey that would see them reconciled and at least having a semblance of a relationship.

She poked the button and as she read it, her heart sank. Her sadness quickly turned to pure anger as she continued reading what she could only describe as a hateful rant.

Missy hadn't changed her tune; if anything, her written words were filled with even more vitriol than her video chat. Lily's favorite sandwich felt like a heavy ball of lead in her stomach.

She read it again, trying to remove herself emotionally, but it was almost impossible. The gist of it was that Missy let her know if she married Mac, she would never speak to him again, and he would never be involved in her life. The only time she would be in touch would be to collect her inheritance, of which she would make sure Lily received nothing.

She accused her again of being a woman looking for a rich man and making Mac her mark. She said more than once that no woman could ever replace her mother, and Lily would be sorry if she married him because Missy would make her life a living hell. She wouldn't give them a moment of peace and would ruin them.

Her fingers trembled as she poked at the buttons on her tablet. That tiny worry that had been nagging at her ever since Mac proposed had ballooned and was overwhelming every thought she had.

How could she marry Mac knowing his daughter intended to use that to make his life even more miserable? He would tell her it didn't matter, but someday in the future, it would matter and then what?

She swallowed several times and then rushed to her bathroom and wretched into the toilet. She was shaking, and her throat was raw.

She sank to the ground and rested her head on the bathmat. She had no idea what she would do to solve this problem.

18

After spending the rest of the afternoon and evening in bed, feigning sleep whenever anyone dared to open her door to check on her, Lily was up early on Wednesday morning.

She still wasn't sure what to do but knew she had to get away and think. As quietly as possible, she fed the dogs their breakfast, then got ready for the day and packed a small bag.

She could only think of one place to go and had texted Izzy last night. Her sweet friend asked no questions, expecting her on the afternoon ferry.

Lily sipped a cup of tea and penned a quick note to Wendy and Mel, letting them know she needed to be gone for a few days and trusted them to handle the cottages and guests. She told them she just wanted a few days alone.

She added a promise to call soon and loaded the dogs and their gear into her SUV.

She eased out of the garage, cringing at the sound of the door and hoping Mel wouldn't come out to see what was happening. She sped off toward the ferry dock, hoping to be aboard before anyone knew she was gone.

Several hours and many miles later, she drove off the ferry dock at Friday Harbor. She didn't even remember most of the trip. The day had blurred into nothingness.

She hated feeling weak and unsure and couldn't shake either feeling. On the trip across the water, she had tried to concentrate on the beauty around her and petted the dogs to calm her nerves, but her mind kept going back to the hateful words in Missy's email.

Lily liked her life now. She never imagined being so happy, much less finding a second chance at love. She loved Mac with all her heart, but she didn't want any part of a family war and the constant madness Missy promised to deliver. That wasn't the life she envisioned with Mac.

Maybe they could just go back to dating and forget the whole marriage idea. Maybe Missy would calm down, and they could plan a wedding next year.

Before she knew it, she almost passed the turn off the highway into the golf community where Izzy lived.

She shook off the funk she was in and tried to paint a smile on her face. She hadn't divulged anything to Izzy, only told her she needed a few days away and hoped she might be up for a houseguest and her two furry friends.

Before she could get out of the car, Izzy already came down the walkway, a huge smile on her face.

Lily took a deep breath and got out of the car. Izzy engulfed her in a long hug. "I'm so glad you're here."

Izzy kept her arm around Lily's shoulder. "How's your wrist and ankle doing?"

"Much better. I only notice when I overdo it." She sighed. "Sort of like now. It's been a long day, and I didn't sleep well last night."

"Let's get these hooligans out of the car and your stuff inside.

I've got just the cure for you."

Izzy carried the small overnight bag Lily had brought, along with the tote full of dog supplies, while Lily took care of the dogs and gave them a short walk around the yard, letting them explore all the new scents.

After letting them stretch their legs, she ushered them through Izzy's front door. Lily's stomach growled at the inviting aroma of cinnamon and baked sugar. Sunny was there to greet them with nose boops and tail wags. The three of them scampered through the kitchen and into the living area.

Izzy pointed at the countertop. "I've got some tea brewing and made a cinnamon coffee cake. I thought you might be hungry when you got here, and that will tide us over until dinner. Kate is coming over for dinner, and Colin and Spence are going to take the dogs to Colin's house to give us a girl's night."

"That coffee cake smells heavenly. I'd love some. I didn't eat anything today."

"Just sit down and relax." Izzy went about slicing generous chunks from the cake pan and delivered them along with steaming cups of tea to the island counter.

Lily took a bite and moaned. "Ah, that's delicious. Thank you for all this, especially on the spur of the moment."

"I'm always up for a visit, but I get the sense something is wrong. If you want to talk about it, I'm here, but you look like you need some rest. I'll take care of the dogs, and you can take care of yourself and curl up for a nap."

Lily didn't trust her voice and being hungry and tired took their toll on her strength. She simply nodded and reached for Izzy's hand and squeezed it. Izzy topped off Lily's cup with fresh tea, handed her two ice packs, and led the way upstairs to the guest room.

A vase of freesia next to the bed filled the room with the comforting fragrance and once settled onto the bed, the ice packs in position, and the soft throw blanket over her, Lily surrendered to the exhaustion and despair she had been holding at bay.

Several hours later, Lily woke with a start. She took in the light-filled room and blinked several times. She touched the velvety soft throw, and reality set in.

It hadn't been a dream.

The nightmare was real.

She had turned her phone to silent for the trip and dug it out of her purse. She didn't need anyone to worry but wasn't prepared to talk to anyone yet.

She had several missed calls. She had a text from Mel, apologizing for bothering her, linking to a few online review sites that all showed the same horrible one-star review of the cottages that had posted yesterday. The reviewer had said they had stayed at the cottages last week, and they were filthy, and the owner was horrible and did nothing to help with the problem.

Lily's head throbbed, and her heart raced. It had to be Missy. She was making good on her threat to ruin Lily.

Wendy also texted to make sure she was okay. Mac sent a text and wanted to know if she was feeling better or needed anything. He offered to pick up some soup for her and bring it by after work.

Tears fell from her eyes. He was such a good man.

She loved him.

She hated to break his heart.

She sent a quick text back and said she felt a bit better but needed a few days away, alone, and that she would be in touch by the weekend. She stressed not to worry, she was just overwhelmed and needed some space.

She texted Wendy to see if she needed anything and let her know she had gone to see a friend for a few days, and that she was fine but needed some time away.

Moments later, Wendy texted back to let her know everything was okay at the cottages, but that she was worried about her.

Lily scoffed. "That's a first." She tapped a reply and stuffed the phone in the pocket of her jeans.

She had no idea how to deal with the phony reviews. Kevin was good at all the tech stuff, but she didn't want to bother him and get into the whole dysfunctional family saga.

She went into the bathroom and spent some time making herself look a bit less bedraggled and more presentable. Her hair fluffed, her cheeks a bit pinker, and a bit of glossy color on her lips, she took one last look in the mirror and headed downstairs.

She crossed the entry to walk into the kitchen, expecting to see the three dogs, but they were nowhere to be found. A spicy aroma of something cooking tickled her nose. She saw the clock and realized it was past six o'clock.

She was past hungry, but the nasty reviews threatened to derail her appetite. Izzy might have some ideas on how to fix the problem.

She kept walking and through the French doors, saw Izzy and Kate sitting on the patio, and opened the door.

Kate smiled at her and rose from her chair. "Lily, it's so wonderful to see you and have a pre-wedding surprise visit."

They hugged each other, and Izzy poured another glass of iced tea from the pitcher on the table. "We were just visiting and enjoying this lovely evening. Colin and Spence have the dogs and are grilling over at Colin's place."

Lily nodded and slipped into a vacant chair. "That's great. Thank you so much for taking care of them and giving me a chance to rest. I feel much better."

"We've got salsa verde chicken in the oven, whenever we're ready to eat."

"Oh, that sounds yummy," said Lily.

"So, how are your wedding plans coming along?" asked Kate.

Lily took a swallow from her glass. "Everything is organized and handled. Cyndy has been terrific as my unpaid wedding planner. She's got everything under control, and my checklist is complete."

"That's wonderful news. We're looking forward to making the trip over and then having you and Mac here for your honeymoon," said Izzy.

Lily sighed. "I'm in a bit of a crisis mode now. I'm struggling right now and needed a few days away to figure out what to do."

Izzy nodded and rose to collect the pitcher of tea. "Let's go inside and have dinner, and you can tell us what's going on."

The three of them collected their glasses, and Izzy invited them to take a seat at the dining room table, right next to the French doors. "Everything is ready, so it will just take a few minutes to get it on the table."

While Lily sat, thinking, the two of them returned with plates and silverware, a huge dish of salsa verde chicken, a tomato and cucumber salad, and a colorful fruit salad. Izzy also opened a bottle of wine and filled their glasses.

"Nobody's driving tonight, so cheers to us," she said, clinking glasses with them.

As they ate the delicious food, Lily felt stronger. "Everything is great with Mac," she began. "The problem is with his daughter Missy." She slipped her phone out of her pocket and tapped a few buttons. "Here, it's easier to just let you read her email to me."

She passed it first to Kate, whose eyebrows rose several times as she scanned the screen. She said, "Wow," and handed the phone to Izzy.

Izzy reached for her reading glasses and scrolled through the message. She looked up at Lily and said, "Let me read it again."

She retrieved a notepad and pen and scribbled as she scrolled through the message. "Well, I've seen less threatening language be granted in a temporary restraining order. She's beyond unpleasant."

Lily couldn't contain a laugh. "That's such a tactful description. I see why you're a lawyer." Lily scrolled on her phone and found the reviews Mel had sent her. "In addition, I suspect she's behind this review that she has splashed all over the internet. I have no idea what to do about that."

"I can help you with that. We can report the review and then supply facts related to the guests that you had that week and follow up with all of them. You'll need to reply with a professional response, offering to help and asking for more information so the sites see you as helpful and trying to solve the problem." Izzy tapped her pen on her notepad. "So, was she better when Mac told her the news, and she's just treating you like this?"

Lily shook her head. "No, she's been a beast to him. Since her mom died, she's been very manipulative with Mac. And he knows it. She's made sure he never had a chance at a successful relationship after Jill's death. Over the years, Cyndy has tried to help and intervene, but Missy left Driftwood Bay as soon as she graduated and rarely visits."

Lily took another sip of wine. "It's strange. She doesn't appear to want anything to do with her dad's life. She doesn't call and rarely responds to his calls. He tells me it's a no-win situation with her. If he contacts her, she accuses him of butting into her life and if he doesn't, he's labeled as non-caring. He's given up and when we told her about the wedding, she was awful. Mac tells me not to worry about it, but it's been bugging me from the get-go. Now, this is just…"

Izzy shook her head and grinned. "My Mia is also a master

manipulator, so I totally get it. You know some of the hell she's put me through, and Kate knows even more. I understand Mac moving on with his life and wanting to build a life with you and basically leave Missy wherever it is that Missy wants to be."

Lily nodded. "Exactly. He said he's done bowing to her demands and wishes. She's kept him from living a full life for several years, and he doesn't want to give her that control any longer."

Kate nodded as she reached for her wine. "Easier said than done, right?"

Izzy drummed her fingers on the table. "I've already put together a draft prenuptial agreement that spells out the separation of your property and the beneficiary process for each of you. I've given each party ninety days to vacate before the house would pass to the heir. For example, if Mac were to die, you would have ninety days to remove yourself and your personal belongings from the house, then it would go to Missy to dispose of as she wishes. The only complication will come if in the future, you make a purchase of something together. So, say you buy a vacation home together. The way I've accounted for that is all jointly acquired property after marriage will pass to the surviving spouse and then upon the death of that person, the property would be split between the heirs, Missy and Kevin or their respective offspring."

Lily nodded. "That makes sense. And you accounted for the animals, right?"

Izzy bobbed her head. "Oh, yes. Your animals would go to Mac and Mac's to you. If you both die, the animals and a provision for their care will go to Mel first, and then Andy, if Mel is unable. I know you didn't want Missy involved with the animals and didn't want to burden Kevin with them."

Lily ran her finger along the edge of her plate. "We thought if we presented the prenup to Missy, she would understand I'm not after Mac's money and be more accepting."

Izzy wrinkled her nose. "Maybe, but it may take more than that. I think she's maneuvered and controlled Mac and fully expects to continue to do so. She's a grown woman but is behaving like a spoiled child. I can relate because Mia is quite similar."

She paused for a long swallow of wine and continued, "I think Mac is taking the right approach to this, albeit a few years too late. Missy will probably continue to act out and because she didn't get the response she wanted—for Mac to acquiesce and call off the wedding, she's targeted you."

Kate nodded as she listened. "I don't have the same experience with children like Mia or Missy, but I agree with Izzy's assessment. I can see her turning her nastiness on you, since Mac didn't respond like she thought he would. Over the years, he's sort of trained her that if she makes a big enough fuss, he'll comply. This is probably the first time he hasn't."

Lily let their words sink in as she finished another bite of the fruit salad. "That does make sense. I'm just not sure I'm up for dealing with all this hatred and chaos. I didn't picture my life like this. I love Mac, and I know he loves me. We just want to be happy and have a quiet life together."

She finished off the wine in her glass. "As much as I hate to, I think I need to call off the wedding."

19

Wet tongues licking her fingers woke Lily on Thursday morning. Fritz and Bodie stood next to the bed, their gentle brown eyes filled with concern as they stared at Lily.

She reached out to pet their heads. "I'm okay, boys. I promise."

Having confessed her intention to Kate and Izzy last night, she felt better. They were both supportive, telling her they understood why she was considering calling things off, but they encouraged her to think it through. She had stayed up late to post the responses to the fake reviews, hoping to stem the bleeding from any potential guests reading them.

She also checked her reservation system on her phone and sent an email to Rebecca and asked if she had time to post a review. Most of the advice on the review sites recommended getting as many positive reviews as possible. She also put together a generic email and targeted a few other guests asking them to do the same and saying she had a malicious reviewer and could use the help.

She hated begging for reviews and resented Missy for

making her jump through hoops when she had better things to do.

She got up and dressed in her exercise clothes. She and Izzy made a pact to take the dogs to the beach for an early morning walk. She found Izzy and Sunny downstairs and ready to go.

They loaded the dogs into Izzy's SUV and set out for Cattle Point. Lily took in the beauty of the water and the pink layers in the sky as the sun rose from the sea. The dogs weren't impressed with the stunning beauty of the sunrise but enjoyed frolicking along the beach and exploring the grass along the trails.

The view from the base of the lighthouse was breathtaking. Nature had a way of grounding Lily, making her troubles seem smaller as she marveled at the power and beauty before her.

Focusing on the ebb and flow of the water along the shore calmed her mind and her fragile heart. She breathed in and out with the water, letting her worries escape with each exhalation. She visualized the fear and worry she harbored falling into the tide and getting carried out to sea.

Izzy was the perfect companion in that she was quiet and spoke only to the dogs. She didn't prod or pry into Lily's thoughts about their late-night conversation. She and Kate were terrific listeners and offered wise advice. They had the unique ability to do so without pushing her in one direction or the other.

With Izzy's daughter sharing so many traits with Missy, she understood the heartbreak Mac had suffered and what all the current strife was likely doing to him. She had moved to Friday Harbor, in a large part, to put some distance between her and Mia.

Izzy had sworn off any chance of a new relationship after her divorce, and her choice stemmed from the way Mia reacted. Now, with Mia grown, she had found a second chance with

Colin and while they had no plans to marry, she was content and happier than she had been in a long time.

She had confessed that she had resolved herself to a fractured or even non-existent relationship with Mia. She had decided to build her new life without her daughter since each time she had tried to appease her, Izzy hadn't been happy, and her acquiescence to Mia had done nothing to improve their connection. It was purely a method Mia used to control, and Izzy was done doing that.

Listening to her heartfelt struggles helped Lily understand Mac's perspective and his decision to move forward despite Missy and her outrage.

She followed Izzy as she turned to walk back toward the car, leaving the dogs between them.

Kate's loss of her precious daughter gave her a perspective nobody else had or wanted. Her strength and determination to overcome such a loss and endure what she did with her ex-husband were inspiring and made Lily's problem pale in comparison.

Last night, she had asked Lily an important question, and Lily was still trying to come to grips with the answer. *Are you so afraid of another loss that you'd rather leave behind a second chance at the full life you clearly desire?*

She had a point. Lily was beyond worried that Missy would eventually tear them apart, and the idea of losing Mac was worse than never having a life together as husband and wife. They could keep things the way they were and wait for the right time.

When she said it aloud to Kate and Izzy, she remembered Mac's words when he proposed. He was done waiting for the perfect moment and didn't want to let time slip away from them.

She wasn't sure they could remain as they were if she called off the wedding. The thought of not having Mac in her life shook her to her core. She was a problem solver by nature and hated the helpless feeling of being stuck between two equally risky choices.

Over an hour had passed when they reached the SUV, where she and Izzy wiped the dogs' paws before loading them into the back of it.

Izzy steered the car to the highway. "If you're up to it, I was going to ask Colin to join us for dinner tonight, along with Kate and Spence. Not to worry if you'd rather just have another girl's night. It's up to you."

Lily smiled. "I'd love to see them. That sounds great. I need to decide if I'm leaving tomorrow or Saturday."

"Stay as long as you like. You're facing a huge decision and need the time to relax and think."

"Thank you for being such a good friend. I had to get away, and coming here was the first place I thought of. I appreciate it so much."

Izzy chuckled. "That's why I moved here. I came here to get away and decided it was perfect, and I never wanted to leave."

She drove into the driveway, and they unloaded the dogs. Once inside, the dogs hurried to the mud room and looked at their empty bowls.

Lily laughed. "Okay, guys. Breakfast will be ready in a few minutes." She went about dispensing kibble and added some berries to each of their bowls.

Lily left the dogs to eat and found Izzy in the kitchen, brewing tea and slicing more of the coffee cake. "After all that food last night, I shouldn't be hungry, but can't resist more of that sinful cake for breakfast."

Izzy laughed. "I normally don't have such treats, but with you visiting, it's a perfect excuse." She slid a plate across the island to Lily. "Come to think of it, Colin does pop by with bakery treats more often than I like to admit."

"Mac's the same."

"Not sure if you're up to it, but I thought it might be fun to go into town and look around. Maybe stop by Sam's coffee shop for a latte and have lunch along the waterfront."

"That sounds like a perfect day. I just hate to leave the dogs in your house, alone. Fritz isn't a problem, but Bodie can still find trouble."

Izzy laughed and took a sip from her tea. "Colin volunteered to take them if we go to town. His dog Jethro loves the company. He and Sunny spend lots of time together."

"That would be great. I hate for him to interrupt his work day."

She waved her hand in the air. "Not to worry. He's got a very flexible schedule and puts in a ton of time off hours, so he often slips away during the day. He'll entertain them and take them on a long trail walk."

Lily nodded as she took her last bite of coffee cake. "I'll get a move on and jump in the shower."

~

After a carefree afternoon spent window shopping along the harbor, and a bite to eat at the Front Street Café, they stopped to linger over a latte and visit with Kate, Sam, and Linda. Lily's spirits had lifted during the day, and she felt much better.

They sat on the deck, drenched in afternoon sunshine and sheltered under a bright-red umbrella. As she listened to the four of them banter and laugh with each other and greet other customers as they wandered in and out of the coffee shop, stopping to say hello or chat, she understood what drew Izzy to this place. Lily envied the close friendship the women enjoyed on their tiny island.

Never having had many close friends, she was always guarded when it came to sharing or trusting, but the wonderful group of women had welcomed her and made her feel like she belonged from the first time they met. Sam and Linda were so excited to see her and talked about the upcoming Fourth of July celebration and her honeymoon. Then, they peppered her with ideas of having a spontaneous bride-to-be party before she headed back to Driftwood Bay.

Lily didn't have to say a word. At the suggestion and the talk of her honeymoon, the angst and nerves she thought she had banished at the beach, came rushing back.

Sam's face fell, and Linda's filled with worry. Sam reached across the table and patted Lily's hand. "I'm so sorry. We've upset you and didn't mean to." She looked from Kate to Izzy.

Izzy gave Lily a questioning look, her brows raised high. Lily couldn't find her voice but nodded at her, giving her permission to tell the other two women why she'd made an impromptu trip to the island.

In what Lily imagined was Izzy's detached lawyer-like tone, she explained the situation with Mac's daughter in a succinct manner.

Linda and Sam looked at Lily with such kindness and concern in their eyes, it made Lily cry. Sam squeezed Lily's hand. "We've all had our ups and downs with dealing with new relationships, losses, divorce, second marriages, stepchildren who aren't our biggest fans, or even our own children who like to cause grief. We understand, believe me."

Linda smiled. "That's part of how we all bonded, including Regi and Ellie. Life can throw some real curve balls at you, and it helps to have friends to lean on when you need help."

Sam left the table and returned with a plate of warm brownies, a pot of tea, and clean cups. "I think we'll need chocolate to get through this, and I propose we all go online right now and leave glowing reviews for Lily's cottages."

At the suggestion, they all pulled out their phones and did so, hoping to make the wretched one-star invisible. Their camaraderie brought tears to Lily's eyes.

Lily longed for the closeness she felt to these women. She wished she had that kind of relationship with Wendy. Maybe in the future, but right now, she couldn't open up to her, not like this. Mel was too young to burden with such problems, and Cyndy was probably her closest friend, but it was awkward with her being Mac's sister.

The women sitting around the table didn't rush Lily or pry her for more information. They let her tell her story without judgment or interruption. When the brownies were gone, and another pot of tea had been drunk, Lily looked around the table.

She asked each one of them to weigh in with what they would do if faced with the same situation. She listened as each of the women she respected offered her best advice, with all of them stressing that Lily had to make the choice that would make her happy and not worry about what others would or wouldn't do.

The afternoon had evaporated, and it was nearing the dinner hour. Lily hugged each of them goodbye and walked to the car with Izzy and Kate. Colin and Spence were in charge of cooking and dog handling and would have dinner ready for the ladies in a matter of minutes.

Colin and Spence, both wearing aprons and finishing up in the kitchen, greeted Lily with hugs and smiles. Izzy retrieved wine and added it to the table while Colin retrieved the salmon from the outdoor grill.

They had just sat when the doorbell rang.

Izzy frowned, and Spence motioned to her. "I'll get it."

Moments later, he returned with Mac behind him and the dogs following them. Colin got up and shook Mac's hand, welcoming him, while he ushered the dogs outside and into the fenced area of the yard.

Lily's mouth gaped open as she stared at Mac. She had purposely ignored her phone, not wanting to talk to Mac until she was prepared. Now, here he was and amid the embarrassment she felt at dragging her problems out in front of Spence and Colin, all she wanted to do was rush over to him and hug him close.

She took in his tired eyes and slumping shoulders. His normal smile wasn't there, and he looked as if he'd aged ten years in the last few days. She hated that he was worried and upset.

Mac hugged Izzy and Kate and rested his hands on Lily's shoulders as he stood behind her chair. "I'm sorry to arrive right at dinner and equally sorry to show up out of the blue. I was worried about Lily and figured she was here, which Spence confirmed when I broke down and called him this morning."

Spence shrugged and caught Lily's eye. "Sorry to divulge you were here, but Mac was very worried, and I wanted to ease his mind."

Lily smiled. "It's not a problem at all." She reached to her shoulder and placed her hand on top of Mac's.

Izzy appeared with another place setting and shifted her chair to give Mac the chair next to Lily. "Sit down and enjoy dinner with us, then you two can talk."

Mac slid into the chair and glanced at Lily, squeezing her knee as he waited for the serving bowl to reach him. He leaned over and whispered, "I'm sorry to show up like this. I didn't expect everyone to be here."

Tears burned in her throat. "It's okay. We need to talk, and I'm glad you're here. I've missed you."

Lily went through the motions of eating, or at least picking at the food on her plate. She smiled and nodded, but her mind was elsewhere. The conversation she had to have with Mac couldn't be postponed any longer.

20

Everyone rushed through dinner, and Kate and Izzy had the table cleared and the dishes done in record time. As soon as they were done, Kate and Spence said their goodbyes, and Colin and Izzy left to take a walk, taking all the dogs with them.

Mac and Lily sat at the kitchen counter in a much too silent house.

He turned to her. "Wendy was checking your emails for the cottages and saw what Missy sent you. She called me, and I went over and read it. I'm so sorry, Lily."

He shook his head with tears in his eyes. "I knew something must have happened but had no idea she would stoop to that level. I am heartbroken that she would set her sights on you and hurt you like that."

Lily swallowed the lump in her throat. "Have you talked to her?"

He shook his head. "No, I'm too angry to talk to her. I talked to Cyndy about it last night." He sighed. "Missy is out of control. I don't want you to worry about it. She's just trying to ruin things. She's determined that I can never be happy again."

Lily let out a long breath. "That's the thing, though. I do worry. I am hurt. I can't do this, Mac. I can't be the one who makes things worse. Missy will always be there. She's your daughter, and I know you love her. I don't want to be part of this and have her hatred poured over us for the rest of our lives."

She found the malicious reviews and handed her phone to him. "I suspect this is also her doing. It's a farce because we had no problems last week. I'm hoping the sites will take them down."

He scanned the phone, and his already weary face drooped. With crestfallen eyes, he shook his head. "I'm so sorry, Lily. Your business should not be in jeopardy because of Missy. This is beyond uncalled for."

He put both hands on the side of his head and rubbed his temples. "This is my fault, Lily. I've let Missy sabotage every chance of a relationship I've ever had since Jill died. I allowed her to rule my life, bowing to her every whim, not wanting to upset her or cause her any more pain. That desire of mine, to protect her and keep her insulated and happy, it's been weaponized. I'm ashamed to say she learned to manipulate me early on, and I should have anticipated when I didn't cave, she'd up her game."

Lily had never seen Mac so flustered and upset. Amid turmoil, he was calm and measured, with a plan to solve a problem, whether it be figuring out what to do about Wendy or helping a dog who had been injured. This impossible conflict was eating him alive.

She wanted to reach out and shake Missy. How could she be so hateful and terrible to her father? He was loved by everyone, and Lily knew in her heart he could never have done anything to warrant this treatment.

It was clear Missy needed counseling, at a minimum. Like Izzy had told her, once a child was of age, a parent could do nothing to help them get treatment, beyond suggesting it, encouraging it, and offering to pay for it.

One night, over a bottle of wine, Cyndy had shared Mac's journey with his daughter. She had recounted all of Mac's efforts when Missy was living at home. Initially, he coddled her and tried to comfort her with attention and material things. A new house, a decorated room, a horse, anything she desired to make up for the loss of her mother. Nothing worked. He took her to counselors and therapists, and she would go to the appointments, but he saw no improvement.

Once she was out of school and left town without much of a chance for him to question the decision, the clock ran out, and any attempts to bring up further counseling were met with a chilly response. After listening to Izzy's struggles with Mia, Lily could understand Mac's desire and ability to wall her off and carry on with his life.

He'd had time, lots of time, and countless drama over the years, to come to that decision. She had not.

"It's not your fault, Mac. As a parent, I understand all the regrets we have, that we could have done better, but this is bigger than all of that. Missy is an adult and has no right to treat me or you like she has been. It's wrong and frankly borders on harassment. If she weren't related, it wouldn't be tolerated."

He nodded. "I agree. My problem is, I can't control her. Like I told you, I'm done giving her power over me. I just didn't think she'd shift her focus to you. I figured she would be angry when I didn't react like she wanted, and I assumed she would just add another lock on the door that she enjoys slamming in my face. We have a non-existent relationship now. I honestly thought I'd never hear from her again, unless I was dying, and she came to check on getting my money."

He chuckled, but Lily could see he was serious. "I finally made the decision that I could live with that. My suffering all these years hadn't been enough and hadn't made her happy. I don't have the luxury of having my daughter in my life now, and I know having you as my wife would bring me all the joy I need. If I do as Missy wants, she'll make me think she'll be in my life, but I know she won't. It's a false promise. Choosing marriage and a life with you, choosing happiness is a decision I didn't make lightly, but I finally decided it's my life and whatever time I have left, I want to be happy and spend it with the woman I love. I'm done waiting for the daughter I'll always love to come back. I think that little girl is gone forever, and I've accepted that."

Tears leaked down Lily's cheeks as she watched Mac swipe a finger under his eyes. She reached for his hand. "I understood that when I accepted your proposal and believe me, I want nothing more than to make a future with you and work to make our dreams come true. I'm just not sure I can do it. Maybe we could just keep things the way they are, let everything calm down a little. We did move quickly, which I know we understand, but maybe that set her off. I don't want you to wake up one day and regret this and blame me for being the one who made it impossible for you and Missy to ever reconnect. I don't want to live dreading the next call, the next email, or heaven forbid a visit. I don't want to lose you, Mac."

He reached for her and brought her close to him, embracing her. As he clung to her, he sobbed into her shoulder. "That won't happen. Believe me, I would never blame you for anything." He squeezed her tighter. "I can't lose you, Lily," he whispered.

~

The soft morning light woke Lily, who had finally gotten some much-needed sleep. Colin and Izzy stayed out late last night, affording Lily and Mac all the time and privacy they needed. Lily was wrung out and exhausted after talking to Mac. He understood her concerns and reluctance to enter a marriage destined for strife and hostile attacks from Missy.

At the same time, she wanted to make a life with Mac. He thought Missy's attitude would fade and over time, she'd go back to her old ways of not communicating. He understood how upsetting it was but was convinced it didn't warrant them giving up their life with each other.

Lily had been prepared to call it all off but promised Mac she would think about it and wait until next week to decide. She had tossed and turned all night, going through the pros and cons of the choice before her.

When she emerged from the guest room, she saw Mac's bedroom door was open and the room empty. She took her time getting ready, standing under the cascade of hot water longer than normal, letting it loosen the muscles in her neck and shoulders and wash away her tears.

She didn't want to be a buzzkill for Izzy and promised herself she'd try to put aside her worries and enjoy the beautiful scenery and Izzy's hospitality. The whole trip needn't be about her and Mac's problem.

She went downstairs and found Mac and Izzy at the island countertop, sipping coffee and talking. The dogs rushed from their pile in the corner and greeted her with tails in full motion and lots of kisses and attention.

"Good morning," said Izzy, sliding from her chair. "Coffee or tea for you?"

"Tea, please." She noticed the legal pad and pen next to Izzy's cup.

"I just put a breakfast casserole in when I heard you up and about. It should be ready in about fifteen minutes."

Lily took the chair next to Mac, and he reached for her hand. "Did you get some sleep?"

She smiled and took the cup of tea Izzy offered. "Some, but not as much as I hoped. How about you?"

He shrugged. "Same."

Izzy cleared her throat. "We've been talking a bit about Missy. I don't want to overstep but wanted to make an offer to you and see if I can help." She laid out an idea for her to contact Missy, as their attorney. She would go over the prenup with her, so Missy understood that Lily wasn't a threat to her future financial security.

"Then, if you both approve, once I've done that, I could also explain to her that she cannot harass you with threatening calls and emails. I would make a record of the request, acting on your behalf, that she must cease and desist those actions, including the fake reviews she has posted. I will demand she remove them and do a bit of sleuthing and some bluffing that we've traced them to her. If she pushes back at all, I'll let her know about restraining orders and that I will be filing one and taking whatever steps necessary, legally, to make sure she discontinues her behavior."

She paused and looked at them. "I can be quite convincing and tough, and it's clear any intervention from Mac wouldn't have any impact. She, like Mia, has been manipulating for far too long. Lily, you're the wild card here. She doesn't know you, and this approach would let her know you're not going to sit idly by and let her bully you or control your life."

Mac's shoulders slumped, and Lily squeezed his hand tighter.

Lily took a sip from her cup and sighed. "I like this idea much better than throwing in the towel and letting her win. I think it's worth a try. Sometimes bullies need a strong dose of their own medicine. Or at least a slap with reality."

Mac nodded. "I'm so embarrassed to be in this position. Having my own daughter act like a terrorist with her demands. Trying to ruin and undermine Lily's livelihood. I never imagined this could happen."

The timer went off, and Izzy stepped to the oven and took

out the bubbling egg casserole. "Don't feel bad, Mac. I suspect Mia would be doing the same thing to me, should I decide to marry. In our efforts to try to make our children happy and save them from disappointment and sadness, we sometimes sacrifice too much of ourselves. Like you're doing, I've now built my own life without Mia, because I just couldn't take it anymore. I fully expect we'll never have a strong relationship, and it breaks my heart, but I would be in the same situation if I were living near her and doing everything she wanted me to do, or if living here and being happy, having my own life. On the plus side, she still has her dad, so she can play us against each other, and he's a softer touch." Izzy winked as she dished up their breakfast.

Mac smiled. "It's hard for dads not to indulge our daughters, and I've been trying for years to make up for the loss of my wife. I know it's impossible, but it was what I hoped to do." He sighed and took the plate Izzy handed him.

Izzy brought her plate and Lily's to the counter, along with English muffins dripping with butter. "Don't beat yourself up. I think this approach, for me to be the bad guy, via Lily, could work. Missy will know that Lily isn't someone she can roll over, and it could set the stage for a new beginning as you build your life together."

Lily took her first bite and nodded. "I think it's worth a try. I hate feeling helpless and like you say, it sends a signal that what has worked in the past, won't work this time."

Izzy smiled. "Remember, Missy has no idea she has caused all this angst and that you're so upset, Lily. If she tries to make contact again, don't reply and if she ends up calling you, just remain cool or let it go to voicemail. I hope it doesn't come to going to court, but if it does, we want the evidence of her threats and you being the calm one. I'll advise her she is to communicate through me, so hopefully, that will thwart any issues."

Mac set his fork down. "I suspect she'll have no problem contacting me to express her dismay."

Izzy nodded. "You're probably right. Don't take her call, don't let her catch you off guard and respond. Let her leave a message and call her back when you're ready. We need to disrupt her normal pattern. Again, just be calm and reiterate you're not going to tolerate her threats and harassment. It's unusual but not unheard of for family members to file restraining orders." She took a sip from her cup and added, "I have a feeling after we talk and if I must, follow up with a written letter, she'll dial it down. She may not be happy and approve and come rushing back to you, but I think she'll think twice and leave you alone."

Lily looked at Mac and nodded. "That's all we can hope for right now. Maybe someday, she'll figure out what she's been missing and reconcile, but right now, I'd be satisfied if she left us alone."

Mac slipped his arm around Lily. "Me, too. I have no illusions about a happy future with Missy. I say we try it."

Izzy looked between them. "Okay, then. I'll get on it. I'll contact her Monday to go over the prenup issues and have a chat. I'll let you know how it goes the moment I'm done."

She refilled their cups and addressed Lily. "Shall we enjoy the rest of the weekend? Colin snagged us dinner reservations down at the clubhouse. Mac says Mel and Cyndy are taking care of his place and Sherlock. You can check in with your sister and if things are okay, you can both stay and relax and go home Sunday."

Lily rested her head on Mac's shoulder. "That sounds lovely. Thank you for the offer and for your idea. It helps to have a third party involved."

Mac smiled. "Especially a skilled lawyer."

Izzy nodded. "Let's keep our fingers crossed."

21

The rest of the weekend, Lily and Mac didn't discuss Missy or the wedding. They enjoyed walking with the dogs on the beach and going for long drives to take in the scenery. Mac made sure Lily rested her ankle and wrist and applied ice to them whenever she could.

Mac surprised Lily with a romantic sunset picnic on the beach, complete with a beautiful bouquet of flowers and candles. She rested against his chest as they enjoyed the show nature put on over the water while nibbling on fruit and cheese.

Colin and Max booked a game of golf for Mac while Linda, Izzy, and Lily binged on a British series they enjoyed, followed by pizza and wine on Izzy's deck.

Sam and Kate organized a group get-together, and Sam and Jeff hosted it at their place. In addition to Mac and Linda, Lily and Mac got to visit with Regi and Nate, along with Blake and Ellie. Lily's heart felt lighter as she watched Mac and Spence laugh with each other and soaked in the friendship among the six couples.

If not for the underlying worry, it would have been a perfect long weekend escape. Mac hadn't brought his car on the trip. It had been a spur of the moment idea to travel to the islands, and Cyndy had driven him to the ferry terminal.

Sunday morning, he offered to drive Lily's car to the harbor, and she was more than happy to let him. Part of her never wanted to leave the island. She and Mac could run away and escape the reality that awaited once they returned to Driftwood Bay.

After a tearful goodbye on Lily's part, which embarrassed her, but she chalked it up to the emotions of the trip and the fragility she felt at the prospect of losing Mac, they headed to the harbor.

The two of them made a pact not to discuss Missy and enjoy the trip home. Instead, they held hands, while they stood at the railing with the dogs and soaked in the sheer beauty of the lush islands as the ferry churned through the water.

They let the dogs out at the park by Deception Pass, where the views never failed to impress. Mac suggested a late lunch at The Point in Coupeville, where they had eaten before and knew dogs were welcome at the outdoor tables.

Lily suspected, like her, he wanted to prolong the lazy day and not step back into real life until they had to. Over soup and sandwiches, they chatted about the upcoming work week. Mac was working lots of hours so he could take time off for the wedding and honeymoon without feeling guilty.

They lingered over their meal. Neither anxious to get home. Lily sighed as she looked at the vista before them. "I haven't breathed a word of this to Kevin or anyone outside of our Friday Harbor friends. From the email, Wendy knows, but I'll talk to her when I get back and make sure she keeps it to herself. I don't want to be the subject of gossip."

Mac nodded. "Same here. Just Cyndy knows on my end. Oh, I guess Mel knows a bit, too. I made an excuse at work and said a friend was ill, and I needed to help the family and had to leave. They don't need to know anything else."

"Cyndy and Mel won't say anything, and Wendy doesn't have any friends to tell, so hopefully, we can carry on like nothing has changed."

"We should know more tomorrow after Izzy talks to Missy." He chuckled. "I'd like to be a fly on the wall and listen to that."

"I just want this nightmare to be over."

Mac reached for her hand. "No matter what happens, Lily, I'll never stop loving you. Like I told you, I want the rest of my life to be the best of my life and that only happens with you by my side."

Mac drove to his house and after collecting his overnight bag from the back of the car, he kissed Lily goodbye before she slid into the driver's seat. "Let's get together tomorrow night. I'll get takeout and meet you here after work. We should know something by then."

She agreed and waved goodbye as she headed back to the highway.

She pulled into the garage, the house still standing and quiet. The dogs were happy to get out of the car and scampered into the house. She found Wendy sitting on the deck, flipping through a magazine.

"Hey," said Lily. "How'd things go?"

"No problems. Mel helped me with the snacks on Friday and Saturday. The guests seemed happy, and everything has been quiet. I'm just waiting for a guest to arrive now. They called and said they'd be late. How about you? I couldn't believe that email from Mac's daughter."

Lily shrugged. "Yeah, it threw me for a real loop. Sorry I disappeared, but I had to get away and went to visit friends. I didn't intend to throw you in the deep end here in managing the cottages, but it looks like you did a great job."

Wendy beamed at the compliment. Relieved to not discuss Mac or Missy, Lily poured it on a little thicker. "It's great to know I can count on you, especially with it being so busy now. I really appreciate it."

"Honestly," said Wendy, "If Mel hadn't been around, it would have been much harder. She knows how to do everything and is helpful. I've never interacted much with someone so much younger, but like you told me, she's nice and kind."

"It's interesting. When I met her and agreed to have her stay here, my heart ached for her. I thought I would be the one helping her, but it turns out she's been the one to help me so many times."

"She sure missed your dogs while you were away and loved taking care of Mac's place and Sherlock. She's very responsible."

Lily smiled. "Yes, she is. Sometimes I forget how young she is, but then she gets so excited over the smallest thing, and I'm reminded she didn't have much of a childhood."

"That girl loves her books, right?" Wendy shook her head. "I don't read at all, so I'm lost in those conversations, but she keeps telling me about certain books and even offered to pick some up at the library for me."

"You should take her up on it. She's very well read and volunteered at the library when I first met her."

The motion sensor alert chimed on Lily's phone. "I think the late arrival is here."

Wendy rose and walked to the stairs. "I've got their folio ready. Be back in a minute."

Lily put up the gate across the stairway and let the dogs onto the deck while she brewed a cup of tea and checked the reviews online. They hadn't been removed, and she hadn't received anything but an automated reply for the website administrators of each. Izzy had warned her it was a long process, and they often didn't take action.

Deflated, she returned to sit on the deck, listening as Wendy helped the couple who had arrived. Her tone had improved since the first guest, and she was polite and answered their questions about breakfast and pointed out things on the map they might want to visit. She even offered to take their luggage, but the husband said he could handle it.

She walked them to the cottage with the turquoise door and led them inside, where her voice was more muffled, but Lily knew she would be showing them the amenities.

Rather than deal with Wendy's aversion to the dogs, Lily elected to take them on a short walk down to the beach. She scribbled a quick note to Wendy and hurried them through the yard and down the trail.

Thankful her ankle was feeling stronger but still careful, she took her time and let the dogs run ahead of her. The sun was low on the horizon, creating a brilliance of gold and orange across the sky. While the sunrise from her beach was always stunning with the view of the eastern sky, the sunset wasn't near as breathtaking. Tonight was an exception, though.

Being on the periphery of the main event, the colors were usually softer, but tonight, the fiery colors were on full display. She made her way to the driftwood log and sat, watching the ebb and flow of the tide along the beach.

Thoughts about the wedding and moving to Mac's flooded her mind. She wanted to enjoy her time with Kevin and focus on him and not worry about the wedding and Missy. The idea of calling it off or postponing it made her stomach ache. She'd suffer through the embarrassment of it, if it were the right thing to do but hated what it could do to Mac. He had so many friends in Driftwood Bay, and it would be hard for him to explain his daughter was the cause.

Not only would his heart be broken, but he'd also be the subject of gossip. All his patients would know, and it would be so awkward for him. He was so excited about the wedding and despite keeping it small, everyone in town knew about it.

Lily was most concerned about telling Kevin. She hoped they would have everything figured out before he arrived. They only had this coming weekend to move her and get situated before Kevin arrived.

That was, if she moved at all.

She thought she was ahead of the game with all the details done, the cake ordered, the flowers chosen, the dress hanging in her closet. She never imagined she'd be sitting here, mere weeks out from the day, and unsure if it would happen.

She didn't want the visit with Kevin and Brooke to be overshadowed by her worries. Whatever happened, she wanted to savor that time with him. Mac offered to drive her to the airport to pick them up and planned a stop for dinner on the way home. It had sounded perfect when they planned it, but now it was just one more complication if things fell through.

She hoped Izzy could get through to Missy and things could move forward. Even if they married as planned, a fragment of worry would always remain, like a tiny splinter in her heart. Unless Missy elected to cut herself off from them, her threats would always be there, under the surface. In targeting Lily's business, she had shown her true colors and capabilities.

Lily suspected Missy liked the power it gave her over Mac and wondered if she would cut off all ties with him, or if the pull to stir things up and antagonize him would be too great. She knew plenty of people in second marriages who didn't exactly hit it off with their spouse's children or other family members. For most, they tried to initiate a relationship, got rebuffed, and did their best to tolerate interactions at holidays and other family events but didn't engage much beyond that.

From what Cyndy and Mac said, Missy never visited, which would make things easier. Mac never expected her to be involved in their life or take an interest. Technically, she wasn't interested, just bent on destruction.

If Lily thought about her for too long, it made her head hurt.

It was horrible that she had lost her mother and at a crucial time when a young girl would need a mother in her life, but Mac was a good man and from all accounts, a good father.

Lily had hoped Missy would come around and re-establish a relationship with Mac, but at this point, having her thousands of miles away sounded like the perfect solution.

Grandchildren though could complicate things even more. Missy shared nothing of her life with Mac but through Cyndy, they knew she had a boyfriend. There was no indication it was serious, so leaping to grandchildren was overthinking it a bit.

Lily wanted more than anything for Mac to be happy.

She also longed to be happy, and he was the man who held the key to her heart.

Their whole future and all their dreams hung in the balance.

If Izzy's idea didn't work with Missy, she wasn't sure they'd have one.

22

Monday, Lily could barely concentrate on anything. If she checked her phone once, she checked it a hundred times.

She put in her earbuds and listened to music, hoping to distract herself. She brought out the cleaning supplies and tried to scrub her way out of her worries. Still mindful of her wrist and her ankle, she didn't put as much effort into it as she could have, but by the afternoon, every surface in the house gleamed, as did the outdoor living space.

With all the chores she could think of, even the pesky ones like baseboards done, she poured herself a tall glass of iced tea and settled into her chair on the deck. Once positioned, she added an ice pack to her wrist and ankle, just to keep any swelling at bay.

Wendy had kept busy with checkouts and preparing things for new arrivals, which was ideal since Lily didn't feel like talking. She checked the time again and after finishing her tea, she rounded up the dogs.

She had a key to Mac's house and would rather brood there alone than risk getting a call and have Wendy or the guests overhear it. He'd be home in an hour or so and by then, they should know something from Izzy.

The dogs, always happy for an adventure, wagged their tails as they got situated in the back of Lily's car. On the drive out, her phone pinged, and she resisted the urge to pick it up and check it.

Once she turned off the highway and onto Mac's property, she stopped and checked. It was a text from Izzy saying she'd video call them at a six o'clock with an update.

Lily sent a reply letting her know that time would be perfect.

She parked and let the dogs out and into the pasture where Sherlock greeted them at the gate, wiggling and wagging, excited to see his friends.

She let herself in and took in the lovely home that was both cozy and modern, with views she could enjoy for the rest of her days. Tears stung her eyes as she contemplated the future. It had taken her time to get used to the idea of giving up living at her uncle's home, but the expanse at Mac's and the stunning views looking out and down to the sea had helped ease the pain of leaving the place she had grown to love even more since settling at the cottages.

Depending on what Izzy had to report, she might have to deal with losing what could have been. After the excitement of Mac's romantic proposal, they had discussed practicalities and logistics, and Lily was thankful she never even considered selling the cottages and that property.

She and Mac were more than aware of the unpredictable nature of the future, and neither of them wanted the other to be without a place to go or their children to have as their own, should the unthinkable happen.

She chuckled as she considered this unthinkable event hadn't been on their radar.

She didn't have to wait long before the dogs alerted her to Mac's arrival. While he parked, she collected the dogs and let them inside. He came in through the side door of the kitchen and placed the bags from Noni's on the counter. The enticing aroma that never failed to satisfy Lily wafted from the bags.

Mac greeted her with a kiss and a hint of a smile, but tired eyes and dark circles under them betrayed his exhaustion. She went about filling the dogs' bowls with their dinner. "Izzy is going to call at six o'clock with an update."

He nodded and tossed his phone on the counter. "My phone has been blowing up most of the afternoon. I had it on silent but felt it vibrating in my pocket and checked before I left for the day. Twenty-six text messages from Missy."

Lily's eyes widened. "Wow, that can't be good."

He shook his head. "More text messages than she has sent me in her life, I think." He pointed at the phone. "I read a couple of them and stopped. Go ahead."

She shook her head. "Give me the short version."

He retrieved some plates and silverware, and they unpacked their dinner. "She can't believe we would sic a lawyer on her and how we had no right to do that. She's not happy, which may mean Izzy has good news for us. Have you checked your email for anything further?"

She shook her head and slipped her phone out of her pocket, tapping a few buttons. "Nothing."

"That's progress," he said, carrying their plates to the table. "I haven't eaten all day, so I'm famished. Let's try to enjoy dinner."

Lily tried to push her worry aside and dug into one of her favorite dishes but couldn't eat much. Mac, on the other hand, cleaned his plate.

With only a few minutes before Izzy was due to call, Lily put her leftovers in a box, hoping she'd be able to finish after hearing what Izzy had to say. She left her phone on the counter, waiting for the chime of a video call.

Right on time, Izzy appeared on the small screen, and Mac and Lily crowded together to fit in the camera view. Izzy smiled at them. "Hey, guys, I'm sorry it's taken me all day. I'm sure you've been worrying."

"We just hope you have some good news," said Mac.

She nodded. "First off, I think we took Missy by surprise, for sure. She was cordial at first, when I went over the prenuptial agreement and made sure she understood the terms and that both of you were making sure she and Kevin were protected financially and would retain your respective property. I couldn't see her, so I could only judge by what she said, but I think the terms surprised her. I made sure she knew that had been in the works since your plan to marry. I didn't want her to think she pushed that point."

Mac nodded, and Izzy looked down at her notepad. "Part of what took some time this morning was my investigator that I use, checked out Missy's digital presence and linked the IP address she used for her social media posts with the bogus reviews. So, I didn't even have to bluff on that point."

Lily's bottom lip disappeared as a new wave of anger rippled through her. She suspected it was Missy and part of her was relieved to know it was, but the other part of her was upset that she would threaten her livelihood. She was old enough to know that was wrong.

Izzy consulted her notepad. "To say she was caught off guard would be a huge understatement. I think she was ready to end the call after I explained the prenup. Once I had her attention on the bogus reviews, I let her know I would be following up with a formal cease and desist letter and sending that to the administrators of all the review sites. She was clearly shaken at that, and I think surprised that she would face a consequence. She had no room to deny it and verbally agreed she would take the reviews down."

"Well, that's a bit of progress," said Mac, squeezing Lily's hand in his.

"Then, I moved right into the harassing email she sent Lily.

She hemmed and hawed a bit and tried to tell me she had every right to express her thoughts." Izzy shook her head. "She reminded me so much of trying to talk with my own Mia. I let her know she didn't have the right to harass or threaten and that as your lawyer, I was demanding she cease and desist and would be following up with a written letter to that end. I let her know further actions on her part would result in legal action, including a restraining order and any other legal remedies at my disposal."

Mac blew out a breath. "I can imagine that went over well."

"Like we discussed in planning, I think she was stunned. She was quiet for several minutes, so much so that I asked if she was still on the line. She became short and clipped with me, but I pressed her to make sure she understood the severity and ramifications and that both of you were united in making sure she stopped with her harassing communications."

Lily entwined her fingers in Mac's grip.

Izzy continued, "I took the liberty of letting her know you would both be thrilled if she would stop all this nonsense and come to the wedding and get to know Lily. I reiterated that you will be starting a new life together and would love for her to be part of that and have a relationship with you, especially Mac. Nobody expected her to automatically embrace Lily, but that her behaviors and actions were quite juvenile in nature and that she had to understand she had no right to judge Lily without even knowing her. I encouraged her to reach out to Cyndy, who knew Lily quite well. I tried to add a bit of a human element to the conversation but made it clear that any more threats or harassment to Lily would be dealt with in a swift and legal manner."

Mac took a deep breath and sighed. "Well, the good news is she hasn't contacted Lily at all. The bad news is, she has sent me a couple of dozen ranting texts."

Izzy nodded. "She obviously took to heart what I had to say

regarding Lily. You, as her dad, are fair game in her eyes. Like we talked about, she's had years to perfect her skills in manipulating you and getting you to do what she wants. I can intervene on your behalf, if you would like, but she will need to hear from you at some point. The risk of her cutting all contact with you is probably quite high at this point."

Mac nodded as his shoulders slumped forward. "I agree, and I understand. I knew that when I proposed to Lily and expected that to happen. Honestly, that beats all this drama and madness."

Lily cleared her throat and took a sip of water. "So, do you have any suggestions on where we go from here?"

Izzy took off her reading glasses. "Honestly, I think Mac will need to be very firm with Missy. I know how hard this is, believe me. I think she's tested the waters with Lily and got bit. The threat of legal action was sufficient to make Missy understand that but now, Mac needs to do the same, only perhaps not legally. I know Missy communicates with Cyndy, and she might be another one who needs to be firm with her on this issue."

She shook her head. "I'm not saying it will work. Trust me, I still don't have it figured out with Mia, but if you two want a life of your own, it's going to require much more than tough love." She paused and added, "We can go the legal route with her, if necessary, at some point, but Mac will need to draw his line in the sand. The sooner, the better."

Mac nodded. "Understood. It's something I should have done long before now."

Lily glanced at Mac and then back at the phone. "Thank you for your help, Izzy. I don't think we could have made any progress without your intervention."

"I'm glad I could help. I'm sorry this is so stressful. I understand how heartbreaking it is. If you need anything else, let me know. We're looking forward to seeing you soon."

Mac nodded. "Thanks again and send along your bill."

She shook her head. "No charge. I'm happy to help. Consider it an early wedding gift." She waved and signed off.

Lily poked the button on her phone and leaned back in the chair. "Well, now what?"

Mac took his phone and said, "Now, it's time I have a serious conversation with Missy. Most likely an email, since I doubt she'll do anything but hang up on me like usual. I'm done being a puppet on a string to her stunts. I'm done being afraid of losing her or causing her pain. It's past time she grew up and way past time I had a life."

23

Tuesday morning, Lily was up early, having gone to bed as soon as she got home from Mac's last night. She fell asleep from the sheer exhaustion of the last few days, with a promise from Mac that he would stop by on his way to work and update her this morning.

He wanted to spend the evening crafting the right message to his daughter. Listening to him, she understood he had no reservations about getting married. He was convinced Izzy's intervention would keep Missy from doing anything further to harm Lily. He was willing to put up with whatever hostility she elected to send his way. He had been doing it for years.

As they talked, he made notes and assured Lily he would let Missy know she was welcome to visit or attend the wedding but only if her intentions were born out of a sincere respect and in the spirit of celebrating their new life together. Like Izzy had said, he needed to draw a line in the sand and was firm on letting her know he intended to make a life with Lily and while he didn't need her approval or blessing, he hoped, if not now, in time, she would come to recognize and know Lily as he did.

He was more resolute than Lily had ever seen him.

She wished she felt as confident.

She took the dogs for their customary walk to the beach and let the calmness and quiet wash over her. The sunrise was her daily reminder that there was always hope and another chance.

After letting the dogs romp, she led them home, fed them their breakfast, and got ready for the day.

As she filled the kettle, her phone chimed, and she hurried to the door, so as not to let the bell disturb Wendy.

Mac's smile, along with a hint of sparkle in his eyes, had returned. He held up a box from the bakery. "I come bearing gifts." Sherlock wiggled past him and rushed to find Bodie and Fritz.

She ushered the dogs outside and led Mac into the kitchen and flipped on the kettle. "So, did you hear back from Missy yet?"

He shook his head. "Not yet, which might be a good sign. She likes to lash out, and I'm hoping she's actually thinking. I talked to Cyndy last night, and she read it over before I sent it off and helped me fine tune it. She's planning to call Missy later today and check on her."

She handed him plates and then carried their mugs of tea to the counter. He pointed at the box. "I brought enough for Mel and even picked out a gluten-free one for Wendy, if she'll eat it."

Having not eaten much dinner, Lily was hungry and dug into a chocolate croissant. "So, from what you said last night, I take it there's nothing Missy can say that will dissuade you from getting married in a couple of weeks?"

He smiled and nodded. "That's right. I've made my position clear, and it's the first time I've stood up to her and told her I'm going to do what I want and need to do, regardless of her feelings. She's an adult, not to mention, she has zero involvement in my life. The prenup secures her financial future, so there's nothing left for her to object to. Well, nothing that has any validity."

He grazed the top of her hand with his fingers. "What about you? How are you feeling? I know you don't want to have strife and have Missy upset about our marriage, but I can't make that happen. It's up to her now. I've said my piece. I've told her what's going to happen, and it will happen with her or without her."

Lily nodded. "I do feel a bit better just having Izzy confront her, and I checked this morning, the reviews are down from those online sites, so Missy did as she promised. I'm sure she thinks I'm a wicked witch, but I suspect that will be the end of her threatening me."

She paused and took a sip of tea. "I'm just trying to rationalize it all in my mind. I keep thinking if Kevin didn't want me to marry you, I probably would consider calling it off." She shook her head and added, "But I know that's not a fair comparison, since he and I have a very different relationship."

"I know it's not how you imagined starting our life together, but I promise you, I will never leave you, I'll never stop loving you, and I will do everything in my power to make your life happy. I think we met each other for a reason, and I'm not about to let my dreams of living out the rest of my days with a woman I love slip through my fingers."

His words made Lily's heart flutter. "I can't imagine my life without you, and I think that's what scared me most. I don't want to lose you, and the threat of that hanging over us was overwhelming."

He put an arm around her and leaned closer to her. "You'll never lose me, Lily. I'm willing to wait, if you think that's best, but I can tell you from my experience with Missy, most likely time won't change her. I'm convinced we need to move forward as planned, mostly for us, for the plans we've made, for Kevin, and partly so Missy understands her reign is over."

She smiled. "I'm not crazy about the idea of your daughter hating me, but I agree with you about making our life and with what you've told her, you've made it clear she's welcome in your life and our life. I was just worried I'd become the roadblock to you having a relationship with her, and that would end up jeopardizing our marriage."

He kissed her cheek. "That won't happen. I know it sounds trite, but it won't. I've let Missy be that barrier for all these years. She'd put up a fuss, and I'd always cave, not wanting to hurt her or heaven forbid, have her do something unthinkable. I can't keep living like that, since it's not living. I offered to pay for her to go back to counseling. Everything is there for her taking. She just has to want to do it."

"You're a good man, Mac, and a good father. I would love nothing more than to marry you and carry on as we planned."

He smiled wider and kissed her with a fervor she didn't expect. "That's what I've been waiting to hear. I know this has been hard, but trust me, Lily, together we can get through anything."

The door to downstairs opened, and Mel came through with the dogs running to greet her. She glanced between Mac and Lily, still locked in an embrace. "You two look happy."

Mac kept his arm around Lily. "We're just excited to get married." Mac pointed at the bakery box. "I brought some pastries and an important update for you… the goats are arriving on Friday."

She beamed at both pieces of news, grabbed a plate, and sat across from them. "I've been giving it some thought and think I have the perfect names. Nibbles and Sweet Pea."

Mac smiled. "Those sound perfect and with the doe being called Marigold, they fit."

Mel got up, fixed herself a cup of tea, and said, "I've got to work Friday but will be off around the dinner hour, so I can come out and meet them, if it works."

"Sounds perfect," said Mac.

Lily pointed at her phone. "Oh, those bogus reviews you sent me got taken down, so everything is good on that front. Thanks for alerting me."

Mel nodded. "I figured it was some prankster. I'm so sorry." She downed the rest of her tea and collected her dishes. "I need to get going. See you tonight."

Mac checked the clock and said, "Me, too. I need to get moving. I'll call you later with any updates." He kissed Lily, reminding her to be gentle with her ankle, collected Sherlock, and headed for the door.

Lily spent the rest of the day packing up the things she wanted to take to Mac's and cleaning out her drawers and closet, so Wendy could move into her bedroom. As she lifted Gary's urn from the shelf, she sat on the edge of the bed and held it.

She hoped Mac wouldn't think it too strange, but she wanted Gary with her. She had felt his presence when she moved here, especially at the beach each morning. Even with him physically gone, she had relied on him to give her the strength to move here and then to tackle the renovations and everything that went with her new role as an innkeeper.

She still remembered the last time she had felt him, heard the whisper of his voice, and knew that he was there. It had been that night at Mac's house when she first held his hand and they walked along the cliff. She believed it was a sign from Gary that he knew she was safe and would be okay and didn't need him anymore.

In her heart, she knew Gary would like Mac.

He would approve of him.

He would want her to be happy and live her life to the fullest.

She was lucky to have found two men she loved. It had taken her some time, but she finally understood by loving Mac, she wasn't replacing Gary. A part of her heart would also belong to him, her first love and the man she never imagined being without. His loss, after time, allowed her heart to grow bigger and make room for Mac.

Mac reminded her of Gary in so many ways. His quick humor, his calm demeanor, his ability to solve problems, and his deep and loyal love. The only thing to give her pause was his daughter. After listening to him today, she felt more secure. Like Izzy had said, he was the one who had to set a boundary and enforce it.

She added the urn to a box and made sure it was protected before labeling the outside of it and stacking it with the others.

Cyndy sent her a text in the late afternoon and invited her to join her for dinner. After confirming Mel would be home and able to watch over her dogs, she replied and let her know she'd be there.

Lily put one of Cyndy's meals in the oven for Mel and Wendy, who had been eating dinner more and more with them, instead of making her own. Lily never knew if what she was making would meet Wendy's standards, but her sister wasn't much of a cook. As time went on, Wendy's objections waned. Lily suspected it was more the matter of Wendy not being interested in putting forth the effort required to make her special meals.

Things were better with Wendy… not perfect, but better. Like Mac, Lily had established a clear boundary with her sister and wasn't giving in. She hoped Mac and Missy would get to a point where they talked more and had a connection, even if Missy never accepted the marriage.

It was easy for Lily to go down the rabbit hole when she thought about the future and how they would handle it if Missy were to marry. Would it be too awkward for Lily to go? Would she even invite them? What if she had children?

She shook her head and forced herself to deal with the

present, like her dogs taught her. Those things were out of her control and like Mac said, together they could get through anything.

~

As usual, Cyndy's meal didn't disappoint. She had put together a crunchy cabbage salad with lots of chicken and a flavor-filled dressing and paired it with fresh bread from the bakery and some fruit.

As they ate and enjoyed the wonderful evening from Cyndy's back porch, she brought up her niece. "I know Mac told you I helped him edit his email to Missy, and I called her this morning. I've always been the one to bridge their communications, and Missy, thank goodness, has maintained a relationship with me, even when she refuses to do that with her dad."

Lily nodded. "I know Mac relies on your ability to talk with her and keep those lines of communication open. He has said more than once, he would be lost without you and your almost magical way of engaging her."

Cyndy laughed. "It's just easier when you're not the parent, and we've always had a special connection. I've tried hard not to alienate her, even when her behavior has been abysmal. Mac and I never wanted to lose touch with her, and he liked knowing she was safe and what she was doing, even if it was second-hand information. We talked at length and thought it best that while Missy knows I am always going to be there for her, she also needs to know I fully support you and Mac marrying and don't approve of what she did."

Lily took a sip of her iced tea. "We talked about the importance of a united front when we were at Izzy's."

Cyndy nodded. "Exactly, so it was a tense conversation. She was honestly shocked and taken aback that you engaged a lawyer about her threatening email and the phony reviews. I think that was smart to set the tone with her that you won't put up with her bullying. She's been doing it to Mac for so long, I'm sure she expected it to work again. I divulged your background in law enforcement. That took her by surprise, and I suspect she's rethinking her tactics."

Cyndy sighed and looked out over her yard. "I tried to appeal to her heart and dig into why she didn't think her dad deserved to have a happy life. We talked at length about her mom and how there's some part of her deep inside that blames Mac for Jill's death. It makes no sense whatsoever, but it's clear that is some of her reasoning for wanting to punish him. I think it might stem from the fact that she held Mac in such high regard, as we all do, for his abilities to heal animals and while he's lost his share of them, he always goes the extra mile and will take what others think of as lost causes and end up curing them."

"So, she expected him to be able to figure out how to save her mother?"

Cyndy shrugged. "I'm no psychologist, but that's my take. We talked at length about her antics in the past and how she was determined never to let her dad get involved with another woman. I was much more insistent than I had been in the past and pushed her, asking her how she could justify doing that, especially now, when she expressed almost no interest in her dad or even called to check in with him."

Lily gritted her teeth as she listened to the tenseness in Cyndy's voice.

"I'm not sure what will come of our long conversation, but I've made it clear that you are a lovely woman, and you and Mac are perfectly matched, and I am wholeheartedly in support of your marriage. I left the door wide open should she want to come and be part of the celebration, letting her know she could stay with me, or if she wants to come later when it's quieter, my door would always be open."

Cyndy took a long swallow from her glass. "She did finally admit that she resented her dad and acknowledged what she had done in the past. I think I made a bit of an inroad with her, but it's hard to say. She's been so volatile, and Mac and I have both treated her with kid gloves. It's past time she grows up and faces reality, and I tried to tell her that in a gentle way."

Lily reached for Cyndy's hand. "I appreciate that. This has been weighing on me so much, and I know even though Mac says he's done worrying about Missy and what she thinks, it eats at him." She paused and added, "I'd like your honest opinion. Do you think I should go ahead and get married as we planned, or would it be better to postpone and wait for Missy to be more accepting?"

Cyndy smiled. "I have dreamed of Mac meeting the right woman and getting a second chance at love, at life. You, my friend, are exactly that. I love you both so much and speaking from experience, giving into Missy and postponing things won't help. It will just reinforce her bad behaviors, like we've been doing for the last umpteen years. Izzy was right about setting a firm boundary and sticking to it. Maybe this will jar Missy from her fog and set her on a path that leads to some type of reconciliation."

Cyndy drummed her fingers on the glass-topped table. "And maybe not. But that doesn't change what I see as your true love for Mac. I won't sugar coat things and make you think it will all be rosy from here forward, but I think you both deserve the happiness I know you can give each other. Missy can be part of that or not but don't let her keep you from your dreams."

Cyndy stood and put her arms around Lily's shoulders. "I'm so excited to have you as a part of the family. A sister if you will. From the moment you walked into my shop, I've felt a connection with you and love you like a sister."

Lily let out a long breath. She admired Cyndy so much and took her words to heart. She knew what it was like to lose a mother, although not as young as Missy, and it broke her heart that Missy was in such pain and that she had transferred all of that to Mac. He didn't deserve it and after talking to Cyndy, she had an even deeper understanding of their past. Calling off the wedding would only embolden Missy and destroy Mac.

For the first time in the last week, Lily felt confident that starting a new life together with Mac was worth whatever risk there was. They loved each other, and that was all that mattered.

24

By the time Friday night arrived, Lily had everything packed and ready to move to Mac's. She had spent the week moving some things herself, including her clothes and the contents of her bathroom. She set up her temporary quarters in Mac's guest room, just down the hall from the master, where she'd be moving in a matter of weeks.

Mac was a more talented cook than she was, and his kitchen was outfitted with every possible pan and accessory she could dream of needing. The only things she took from her kitchen were her tea kettle she loved and her aunt's collection of teacups, saucers, and teapots that held such good memories of her childhood.

Books, family photos, and other treasured memories had been removed from the living room shelves. All her aunt's sea glass had been boxed, along with Lily's supplies for making mosaics from them. Mac had suggested she set up a room downstairs where she could keep her supplies at the ready and use it for her projects.

Mac and his friends were coming to transport the rest of her things in the morning. The only cumbersome items would be the living room set, including Gary's old recliner and the TV Lily had mounted to the wall, which she and Mac decided would be a nice upgrade in his downstairs area. He and his friends would move his old downstairs furniture and older television back to the cottages so Wendy would have a living room set.

They had all morning to get things moved and organized, then she and Mac would drive to Seattle to pick up Kevin and Brooke at the airport. Lily had made sure the downstairs bedrooms at Mac's were outfitted with fresh linens and added flowers to each of them. The guest bathroom was set with fresh towels and toiletries and by tomorrow, the living area would be spruced and ready.

Wendy was excited about moving upstairs and was adjusting to her innkeeper role with surprising ease. After her initial reluctance, Lily noticed she was happier and not so negative about everything.

The schedule and the freedom the role offered worked for her. Wendy wasn't an early riser and had a hard time conforming to standard rules, so managing the cottages fit her needs. She still wasn't a fan of cleaning and doing laundry but complained less and less.

Having the use of the car had been a bit of a turning point with her, and Lily recognized it represented freedom. As much as Wendy irritated her and could be so arrogant, she understood how hard it must be to go from having the best money could buy and a home and cars envied by many, to having almost nothing and having to rely on her big sister for food and shelter.

Mac had been onto something when he recognized Wendy needed a purpose, responsibilities, and expectations, much like a child did.

Lily gazed out at the deck, and a pang of sadness hit her heart. She would miss her time on the deck and the views it afforded. She loved the plants she had added and the twinkly lights throughout the yard. Mac assured her she could add anything she wanted to his deck and yard, but there was something here she would always miss.

Mac's deck and acreage provided for stunning views and in time, Lily was sure it would feel like home, but there was a tiny part of her that would miss living at the cottages. More than anything, it was the memories she held from childhood and all the things that reminded her of spending her summers with her aunt and uncle. Not to mention, the sweat equity she had poured into all the renovations and putting her stamp on the property.

She especially hated the idea of leaving the lovely dog house Andy had gifted her, but it matched the cottages and was such a cute addition, she didn't want to remove it. Besides, she and the dogs would spend time here, and they could still get use out of it. Mac had the perfect yard for the dogs, including a house big enough for all of them, so there was no need to take it with her.

Tears dotted her cheeks and surprised her. She didn't think it would be that hard to leave.

Mac had invited Mel out for pizza and an introduction to the goats, but Lily had begged off. She wanted to spend her last night at the house, reminiscing and visiting with the guests around the fire pit. This place had been her refuge, her haven, and it wasn't easy to leave it.

After losing Gary, she had found herself here, in this pocket of safety near the beach, where memories and gentle waves from the bay comforted her. Both had healed her heart and given her the strength to make a new life in Driftwood Bay. A life she was surprised to love as much as she did.

Now, it was time to turn the page and start a new chapter. One that would have the comfort of Mac at her side and where they would set out to make their dreams come true, together.

Saturday, Mac and his crew of friends arrived bright and early to load the furniture and boxes. Well before lunch, everything was moved.

Mel was off until the evening and had volunteered to help Lily so she wouldn't overuse her wrist or ankle. She and Mel stayed at Mac's house and once the downstairs furniture was moved, cleaned, and vacuumed, the men returned with Lily's furniture.

She stood back and admired the space, which seemed more like home to her with the additions of her things. She ran a hand over Gary's worn recliner. She liked having a reminder of him close by. Part of the reasoning behind the furniture shuffle was to make Kevin feel more at home with some familiar surroundings, but she also longed for the comfort of her things.

Everything looked fresh and welcoming and ready for Kevin and the woman she feared was about to replace her as the most important in her son's life. She tried to shake off the apprehension she felt at meeting Brooke. She wanted Kevin to be happy and while she understood that would come from making a life and family of his own, her heart hadn't yet come to grips with the idea.

After a quick trip outside with Mel to see Nibbles and Sweet Pea, who along with Marigold were settling in, intent on eating the clover and alfalfa in the pasture and making friends with Coco and Margo, along with Lucy and Ethel, Lily hugged Mel goodbye. "Thank you for all your help with everything today. We appreciate it."

"It was fun, and I'll call you if there are any problems at the cottages. I think Wendy has a handle on things now, though."

Lily laughed and said, "Yes, I think you're right. We'll talk to you soon and remember, next weekend is our family dinner, so be sure to request time off on Sunday. Tony, too."

"Already done," she said, hurrying to her car.

As soon as she drove away, Mac arrived with all three dogs. After a quick snack for lunch, they both changed clothes, made sure the dogs were set, and took off in Lily's car for the airport.

Over the more than two-hour drive, they chatted about Lily's plans to take the kids to Olympic National Park and anywhere else they wanted to venture. Mac still hadn't heard from Missy, which he took as a positive sign. With Cyndy talking to her, he confirmed she had received his email and hoped it meant she was thinking about everything he had said.

He was back to his old self, smiling and relaxed, while looking forward to spending time with Kevin and Brooke and to hosting the dinner at his house on Sunday. Cyndy was helping him, and they were putting together a huge spread with Mac in charge of the outdoor grill.

As usual, the traffic was horrendous as they approached the city. Lily had asked Mac about the best place to stop for dinner on the way home, and he made reservations at a popular place on Bainbridge Island, so they would be sure to get a table.

Lily hadn't been to Bainbridge Island since she was a kid, when her aunt and uncle took her. It was on the list of places to explore with Brooke and Kevin. Brooke had never been to the area, and Lily wanted to make sure she had a good time. Having dinner would give them a preview and let them decide if they wanted to come back to explore it.

They finally arrived at the airport just a few minutes before Kevin's flight was due. Mac parked, and they hurried to the baggage area to watch for Kevin.

With each group that entered the large area, Lily stretched her neck, hoping for a glimpse of her son. Her patience was waning when she spotted him and waved, hoping to catch his attention.

She kept her focus on him and imagined the spectacle she created as she made even larger arcs with her arm. He caught the movement and broke into a grin, increasing his pace, and closed the gap between them.

He dropped his carry-on bag to the floor and engulfed her in a hug. It was the best feeling ever. In that one moment, all was right in Lily's world, and her heart was whole. She never wanted to let him go.

After squeezing him tight, she released him and smiled. He extended his arm to the petite blonde next to him. "Mom, this is Brooke Durant."

Lily reached for her hand and was surprised when the young woman swooped forward and hugged her. "I'm so happy to meet you, Mrs. Reed."

"Lily, please. Call me Lily." Once released from Brooke, she stepped closer to Mac. "And, this is my fiancé Mac. Well, his real name is Jack MacMillan, but everybody calls him Mac."

Brooke treated him to the same type of hug and a smile. "Congratulations on your wedding and thank you for letting me come." Kevin reached forward and shook Mac's hand, and Mac pulled him in for a manly embrace, followed by a pat on the shoulder.

"It's wonderful to have you here, Kevin, and a pleasure to finally meet you, Brooke. You are just as lovely as we imagined."

Mac pointed to the luggage carousel. "Let's grab your bags and get on the road, shall we?"

Lily hung back with Brooke while Mac and Kevin claimed a spot along the conveyor path. "I bet you two are hungry and tired after such a long travel day."

Brooke smiled and nodded. "A little, and the time change makes it tricky, but Kevin has been so excited about this trip, I don't think he'll notice."

"We've got dinner reservations for a waterfront spot Mac knows, and it's on our way to Driftwood Bay."

Brooke's blue eyes reminded Lily of the darkest blue sea glass in her aunt's collection, dancing with excitement. "That sounds great. Kevin told me all about the gorgeous views of the water from everywhere. In Hanover, we're close to the Connecticut River, but our coastline is small and takes a couple of hours to get there."

"Hanover, that's where Dartmouth is, right?"

Brooke nodded. "That's right. It's a nice, small town. My dad is a Superior Court judge in Grafton County."

"So, he's probably part of the reason you're interested in law. What about your mom? Does she work outside the home?" Lily moved her head in the direction of Mac and Kevin, who were wheeling their bags toward the exit. "Looks like we can head out."

Brooke picked up her carry-on bag and nodded. "Yeah, Mom is a professor at Dartmouth. She and Dad are both looking to retire in the next few years. I'm the baby of the family and spent quite a bit of time at Dad's office or in his study at home. My older brother is a district attorney in Boston, and another one is a police detective in Maine. Kevin told me you and his dad were both police officers."

As they walked to the car, Lily nodded. "That's right. I never imagined retiring but have enjoyed running the bed and breakfast. It's a nice change of pace and change of scenery."

Mac and Kevin loaded all the bags into the back of Lily's SUV, and Kevin and Brooke slid into the backseat. Mac navigated the traffic and got them through the worst of it and to the ferry terminal where they would cross Elliot Bay to Bainbridge Island. His timing was spot-on, and they were just opening the ferry lanes when they arrived.

Both Kevin and Brooke were wide eyed as they boarded the ferry for the short crossing. It took just over thirty minutes to make the trip, and the views it offered were stunning. Kevin and Brooke were busy taking photos and had Lily take several of the two of them with Seattle as the backdrop.

Brooke insisted on taking some of Mac and Lily and of Lily

and Kevin and by the time they were done, it was time to disembark. The view of Seattle and the Olympic Mountains was awe inspiring, like a postcard. Mac drove them from the ferry landing to the marina district, where the Marina Grille was situated.

With Mac allowing for traffic and ferry delays, they were about thirty minutes early and took a walk along the waterfront. The early summer evening was perfect, with a subtle breeze and gorgeous bay views.

Lily eyed the condo properties tucked in along the shoreline and added a weekend escape as an idea of what she and Mac might want to do in the fall, once the summer tourist season was over. The island was bustling with visitors, and she imagined lodging was sold out for the season.

As they walked, Lily chatted. "This is a place that we could come back to one day if you two want to explore it further. I know the trip to Olympic National Park is at the top of the list, but we have several options for day trips."

Kevin nudged his shoulder against Brooke's. "What do you think?"

She laughed and said, "I'm up for anything. It's all new and exciting."

Lily reached for Mac's hand. "I'm at your disposal this week. We just have to be back at Mac's Sunday night for a celebratory dinner before the wedding on Wednesday."

They strolled back to the restaurant, and the hostess seated them on the outdoor deck, giving them a great view of the marina and beyond. The waitress handed them menus and took their drink order.

The restaurant was busy and filled with people dressed for a date night and families and couples in jeans and t-shirts. Lily studied the offerings and couldn't resist a juicy burger when she saw one delivered to a nearby table. They were famous for their clam chowder, and Mac encouraged them to start with a cup of it.

While they enjoyed their soup starter, Mac carried most of the conversation, pointing out landmarks and answering questions. One of the strengths Lily had honed over her career was her ability to size up people quickly. As she took in the conversation and watched, she realized her fears about Brooke could be put to rest.

She was a charming and sincere young woman and between the way her eyes rarely left her son and the sweet smile between them when their fingers touched, Lily could tell she was enamored with him. They were beyond cute together and as much as she longed for days gone by, she was pleased Kevin had found someone as lovely as the smiling young woman sitting across the table.

In talking with Kevin, along with the photos of their home and their mountain ski retreat, Lily surmised Brooke's family was wealthy. She and Gary weren't from money and hadn't amassed wealth. They were working-class law enforcement and while they had a comfortable life, they would never be in the same circles with judges and college professors.

Brooke wasn't arrogant or self-centered and showed genuine interest in what Mac was saying. Brooke had the gift of being able to make the person she was talking with the center of her attention and asked lots of questions. She was in a word —charming.

Kevin had a good head on his shoulders, and Lily wanted to believe he wouldn't have it turned by money or a lavish lifestyle but knowing she could never compete left her feeling vulnerable. Meeting Brooke helped ease some of her insecurities. Knowing they had a law enforcement connection with her family also helped.

Lily was jarred from her thoughts when she heard Mac ask, "What do you think about that, Lily?"

She focused on him. "Sorry, I was lost in a daydream and the gorgeous view."

He reached for her hand. "Brooke was saying her parents wanted to be sure to extend their congratulations and an invitation to visit the area. She says the fall colors are a great time to visit."

Lily nodded. "Oh, yes, that would be wonderful. I had some guests from Vermont last year, and they said the same thing. They told me about their little town with a famous Wishing Tree. It's called Linden Falls, I believe."

Brooke nodded. "Oh, yes. It's a real draw for tourists and everyone in the area. The tree sits in the middle of town, and people come from all over to tie wishes in the branches. It's been said to have a bit of magic and the ability to make wishes come true."

Lily met Mac's eyes. "I'd love to visit there and see the ladies. We should seriously plan a trip."

Brooke's eyes lit up. "My parents would love it. Maybe we could plan something when Kev and I would have time off during fall break. It's usually right around the first week of October, and we could join you. We have plenty of room for you to stay at the house. You could also come over Christmas and stay at our house in the mountains. You'd miss the fall leaves, though."

"Both options sound lovely. We'll have to make a plan. At the moment, we're just trying to stay organized and get through the wedding."

Mac nodded. "We'll keep it in mind. I'd like to cut back a bit, take more time off, and would love to make it happen."

They dug into their entrees, with Kevin and Brooke raving about the fish and chips and Mac singing praises about his prime rib melt. Lily's instincts had been right. Kevin was serious about Brooke and while the prospect of him getting married and creating a life far away from her loomed, he couldn't have found a nicer young woman than Brooke.

Not that she expected Kevin to make a huge announcement during this trip, but she sensed it wouldn't be long in coming. Instead of losing her son, she focused on the idea of gaining a daughter.

25

They got home as it was getting dark, and Mac helped Kevin and Brooke lug their bags inside. When Brooke got down on the floor with Kevin and let the three dogs maul her and lick her, Lily's already high opinion of her crept up a few notches.

Mac gave them a tour of the house, and he and Kevin carted their luggage downstairs. Kevin's eyes darted over the living area and rested on his dad's old recliner. He smiled at his mom and put an arm around her shoulder. "This is great. Your furniture looks perfect in here."

"We thought it would be a good fit. Mac transferred his old stuff back to the house for Wendy." Lily pointed to the hallway. "I've got the two guest bedrooms all set for you and fresh towels in the bathroom." Lily paused and added, "I put your slacks and shirt for the wedding in the closet, so be sure to try them on first thing. If we need any adjustments, we can get them done."

He smiled. "I'm sure they're fine, but I'll try them on just in case."

Brooke poked her head around the corner. "This is perfect."

Mac smiled and added, "We'll give you the grand tour outside tomorrow morning, but you can come and go as you please. There's a door over there. Just make sure you lock it." Mac pointed to the opposite side of the room.

Lily showed them the mini fridge and microwave. "We stuffed it full of drinks and snacks, but there is more food upstairs in the kitchen. Just help yourselves to whatever you want. If the dogs won't leave you alone, boot them up the stairs and shut the door."

Mac put his arm around Lily. "You kids are probably tired, so sleep as late as you like tomorrow. We'll have breakfast when you get up. We're just going to show you around the local area, so it will be an easy day of rest before you head out to the park with your mom on Monday."

"Sounds great. Thanks, Mac," said Kevin. "I think we'll get unpacked and get some rest." He checked his watch. "The time change is catching up with me."

Lily hugged Kevin. "Good night. I'm so happy you're here." She waved at Brooke, who was heading for the hallway that led to the bedrooms. "Sleep well, and we'll see you in the morning."

Mac wished them both a good night and checked the outer door to make sure it was secured. He and Lily herded the three dogs up the stairs and closed the door behind them.

Once the three furry friends were on the main level, they were hit with a serious case of the zoomies and ran all over the main floor of the house, chasing each other until they flopped down on the wooden floor.

Lily and Mac laughed at their antics. "Tomorrow, I'm not going to check to see if both bedrooms are used. I've decided I don't want to know. Sort of a see nothing, hear nothing, know nothing policy."

Mac chuckled as he filled the kettle. "Good plan. Almost sounds like the government." He paused and added, "Sometimes it's tough being a parent. It's beyond your control, and they're both smart young people."

She nodded and brewed two cups of tea and followed Mac outside to the deck. She noticed he had added twinkle lights to the railing of his deck and combined with the other pathway lights, it gave the space a wonderful glow.

"It's beautiful out here," she said, taking another sip from her mug. "Thanks for my twinkle lights."

"Are you doing okay?"

She nodded. "Brooke is a nice girl, but I think I was right that it's serious."

He bobbed his head. "Yeah, I would never question a mother's instinct. She does seem lovely, though. Very articulate and engaging."

"I agree," said Lily. "She's easy to like, and I can see why Kevin is so taken with her."

"I'm serious about planning a trip to visit. You've got Kev's school schedule, right? I can block out that week of their fall break. You've been talking about Vermont ever since the Winey Widows came to visit." He chuckled and added, "Like I said, I'm done waiting. We need to do all the things we want to do."

She smiled. "You're right. We need to do them before Mel grows up and flies the coop. She's so reliable and is always willing to watch the dogs."

"Good point." He pointed in the direction of the pasture. "You should have seen her with those goats. I think your prediction about pajamas may come true. She's like a mother hen with them."

"She's been out with her friend Tony a couple more times. She's bringing him to dinner on Sunday and to the wedding."

"Oh, do you think it's a serious thing?"

Lily shrugged. "I don't think so. It's her first boyfriend or friend who's a boy. She's so focused on her studies, I can't see much getting in the way of her plan to finish school and then move on to get a four-year degree. She's focused on becoming a school counselor."

"I can see that," he said, before finishing his last swallow of tea.

"Speaking of counseling makes me think of Missy. I don't want to hound you and ask if you've heard from her, so I'll leave it to you to tell me when you do."

He nodded. "You'll be the first to know. I'm glad she hasn't followed up with any nasty texts or messages. If she holds true to her pattern, she'll reach out to Cyndy first. After we have a blow-up, that's usually how it works."

She reached for his hand. "I'm always here and willing to listen. I just don't want to open an old wound."

"Honestly, for the first time in years, I feel at peace with the situation. I should have been braver years ago. I hope she comes around and reaches out, but now there's no question about where I stand."

She squeezed his hand before rising from her chair. "I'm going to call it a night. This has been a long week, and I think my adrenaline is wearing off, and I'm ready to crash."

"Get some rest, and I'll handle breakfast tomorrow. We can have a lazy day just puttering around here and showing the kids around."

She bent and kissed him. "I love you, Mac. Thanks for letting us invade your house and making Kevin and Brooke feel so welcome."

He pulled her closer, "It's our house, remember? I want Kevin to feel like this is his home. While I'm not trying to replace his dad, I do want him to know I'll always be there for him."

"I know," she whispered. "He knows, too."

~

The trip to Olympic National Park was awe inspiring, and Brooke, especially, took tons of photos, making them pose with trees and along the shores of Ruby Beach. In addition to two long days and a good part of the second evening spent there, Lily took them to Whidbey Island, where she and Brooke did lots of window shopping.

Brooke was fun to be with and down to earth, which eased Lily's fears about the disparity in her family's lifestyle and wealth. She asked Lily's advice in picking out some souvenirs to bring back to her family, and they had fun searching for just the right things. Kevin was a good sport and tagged along for most of it but escaped to watch the activity at the marina when they were on their last set of shops.

Brooke held up a beautiful sea glass necklace. The glass was the color of the dresses the ladies had chosen for the wedding, and it was wrapped in silver wire with an addition of a tiny silver starfish charm and a pearl. "Isn't this gorgeous? I think I'm going to get it to remind me of the cottages and your wedding."

Lily nodded. "It's lovely."

Brooke put it on the counter and continued to look for a few more things. Lily caught the cashier's eye, paid for it, and asked her to wrap it for her. Brooke returned with a couple more items, and Lily slid the bag filled with tissue and tied with a ribbon to her. "My gift to you. I'm delighted you came and happy to meet the young woman Kevin has spoken so highly of. You are even more lovely than I expected."

Brooke blushed and embraced Lily in a long hug. "Thank you, Lily. I feel the same way. I was nervous to meet you. Kevin loves you more than you can imagine and thinks so highly of you. I was worried you wouldn't like me."

When she let Lily go, Lily reached for her hand and whispered in her ear, "I'll let you in on a secret. I felt the exact same fear. I thought you might not like me."

They both laughed and after Brooke paid for her items, she looped her arm in Lily's, and they went to find Kevin. He was sitting on a bench not far from the store and broke into a huge grin when he saw them.

Brooke opened the box with the necklace and showed him. "Look what your mom bought me."

"Oh, that is so neat. It's perfect."

While she was putting it back in the bag and rearranging her purchases, Kevin put his arm around his mom's shoulder. "Thank you, Mom. That means the world to her. She really likes you."

Lily grinned and wrinkled her nose. "I really like her, too."

Much to Lily's delight, they opted to return to Bainbridge Island for a day of exploring and eating. She had enjoyed all their sightseeing together, but Bainbridge was her favorite. Having not seen much of it on their stop for dinner, it was relatively new, and they had fun checking the map and tour guides and picking out things to do and see.

They spent the lazy day strolling Main Street, ducking into bookstores, bakeries, and cafes, when they weren't walking along the waterfront to take in the gorgeous views. Lily's favorite though was the time they spent at the Bloedel Reserve.

Along with the eighteenth century French traditional residence, there were one hundred fifty acres of botanical gardens to explore. The grounds were meticulous and bursting with colorful flowers. It was relaxing and beautiful, and Lily couldn't wait to plan a return visit with Mac.

By the time Sunday arrived, Kevin and Brooke opted for a day of rest, and Lily was relieved. Although she had enjoyed spending so much time with them, she was exhausted from the non-stop touring.

Kevin and Brooke spent most of the day downstairs binging on movies, while Lily indulged in reading a book on the deck and sipping copious amounts of iced tea. Cyndy and Mac were busy in the kitchen and wouldn't allow her to lift a finger. They were intent on doing everything for the feast they were preparing.

The delicious aroma coming from the kitchen and the grill, once Mac started cooking, made Lily hungry. Before she could even consider getting up to get a snack, Mac delivered a bowl of chips and salsa to her, along with a sweet kiss and a refill of her tea.

"I could get used to this," she said, wiggling her brows.

He did an exaggerated bow. "I'm here to serve you, my lady."

She reached for his arm. "Don't overtire yourself today."

He shook his head. "Never. I love doing this, and Cyndy is doing the heavy lifting."

She tried to concentrate on reading, but the mouth-watering smell of marinated chicken and the steak and pepper kebabs kept distracting her. She gathered her book and went inside to change. Mac told everyone it was casual, but her shirt was rumpled from lounging around all day.

With a fresh shirt and a hint of lip gloss, she found Cyndy in the kitchen cutting up fruit. She offered to help but got waved off and took a seat at the counter to watch. Kevin and Brooke came up from downstairs, both sniffing as they came into the kitchen. "Something smells great," said Kevin.

Cyndy smiled and offered them a drink before shooing them out of the kitchen. Mac finally caved and allowed Kevin and Brooke to help set up the tables on the deck and carry out the plates and utensils.

Lily took the dogs for a walk while they readied things and by the time she returned, Jeff and Donna had arrived, as did Mel and Tony. Soon, Andy followed, and they were only waiting on Wendy.

Lily called her cell phone and after talking to Wendy, determined she had taken a wrong turn and was a few miles out of her way. She helped her get back on track and within ten minutes, she pulled into the driveway.

Lily relegated the dogs to the pasture and hurried to greet her sister and introduce her to Andy, Tony, and especially Brooke. Mac pointed at the metal trough filled with ice and invited everyone to help themselves to a drink.

Kevin remembered Andy, and Lily was touched by the way he took him under his wing and made sure he was part of the conversation. Brooke was a natural and charmed everyone as she asked them questions.

Wendy hadn't been to Mac's house, and Mel took her and Tony on a tour of the grounds while everyone else gathered on the deck and indulged in chips and salsa. Brooke volunteered to help Cyndy carry out all the side dishes she had been busy preparing. Before long, the makeshift buffet table set up along the house was overflowing with delicious salads, baked beans, crispy roasted potatoes, and a platter of thick, red tomatoes layered between creamy mozzarella, dotted with fresh basil from Mac's garden, and drizzled in balsamic.

Cyndy urged everyone to load up their plates and then proceed to the grill where Mac would add their choice of meat. The guests didn't need much arm twisting to dig into the mouth-watering spread.

Even Wendy couldn't resist loading her plate, and Mac assured her the chicken was organic before adding a piece to her plate. Simple vases held flowers snipped from Mac's garden, and candles glowed in mason jars spaced out along the middle of the huge table that matched the deck.

Once everyone was seated, Mac made sure everyone had something to drink and proposed a toast. "Thank you all for coming and sharing this special evening with us. As we embark on our new life together, Lily and I wanted to get our family together. Even though you're not all related by blood, we consider you all family and are so happy you're in our lives and will be a part of our wedding. Here's to hopes and dreams and most of all, love."

Everyone clinked their glasses, cans, or bottles together and cheered Mac. He took a swallow from his beer and sat. "A huge thanks to my sister Cyndy, who is an incredible cook. Let's dig into all this delicious food."

They ate and chatted and with each bite, Cyndy was the recipient of a new compliment. Everything she made was heavenly, but Lily was partial to the caprese salad and the roasted potatoes with hints of lemon.

The group sat around the table long after the meal had been eaten and the dishes cleared. Kevin and Brooke, along with Mel and Tony volunteered for clean-up duty, and made quick work of it, stowing the leftovers and leaving Mac's kitchen spotless.

After indulging in the chocolate raspberry cake Mac couldn't stop raving about, the guests filtered out and headed home. Mac and Lily hugged each one goodbye as they thanked them for coming.

Cyndy and Wendy were the last two to leave and as they were getting ready, Cyndy offered to lead the way, since she knew Wendy wasn't familiar with the route. Wendy smiled and thanked her and added, "Everything was scrumptious. You could make a fortune if you opened a café or restaurant."

Cyndy laughed. "Well, thank you. I love to cook, but I'm afraid if I had to do it for a living, it might no longer be so much fun. I'm so glad you enjoyed the meal."

Wendy hugged her sister and whispered, "Mac's a keeper. I see what you love about him." To Lily's surprise, she embraced Mac. "Thanks for a great evening. You've got a beautiful place."

Mac walked the ladies to their cars and saw them safely on their way. As soon as he retrieved the dogs and got back inside the house, he bid everyone good night, since he had an early morning at the clinic.

Brooke headed downstairs with a second piece of cake and left Kevin and Lily in the living room.

Kevin smiled as the door shut to the downstairs. "I don't know how she can still be hungry. I'm stuffed. That was the best meal I've had in a long time."

"Cyndy is the best, and Mac is no slouch."

"You definitely married up in that department." Kevin snickered.

She laughed. "I've had such a fun time with you. I was a bit worried when you said you were bringing Brooke. I thought she might cramp our style or might not like me, or I might not like her, but she's terrific."

His cheeks turned pink as he grinned. "She is. We have lots of fun, and she's a kind person. She's super smart and totally reliable. Her mom and dad are great, too."

Lily nodded. "Oh, yeah, speaking of that. I'm going to get plane tickets, and Mac and I are going to come out to visit, like you two suggested, that first week of October. I emailed the ladies who live in Vermont, and they're so excited. They already reserved a room for us at The Wishing Tree Inn, so we can come a couple of days before you get out of school and visit with them."

His eyes sparkled with excitement. "That's great, Mom. I want you to meet her family. Brooke is going to be so happy. I'll have her email you all the details about their place and how to get there from Vermont. That should be a nice drive for you during the peak of the fall colors."

She nodded. "That's what we thought. It sounds great and if she means what I think she means to you, I think I need to meet her family."

His cheeks reddened even more. "I agree." He jumped up

from his seat. "I'm going to tell Brooke right now. I can hardly wait." He kissed her on the cheek, grabbed a soda from the left-overs, and hurried downstairs.

Lily sighed. She had a feeling October would bring more than just fall colors.

26

Wednesday, an uncommon day for a wedding, dawned with a pristine blue sky. Mac was working until noon but would then be off for two whole weeks, so they could enjoy the rest of the week they had with Kevin and Brooke and then head to Friday Harbor for a vacation and honeymoon trip after dropping them at the airport Saturday morning.

Mac was long gone by the time Lily emerged from her shower and padded downstairs. He had assured her everything was in hand, and she didn't have to do anything today. He had arranged with Andy and Wade to handle the setup for the ceremony and the reception in the yard. He was meeting them as soon as he got off work to check on things. She was smiling at the pink box from the bakery her groom-to-be had left, when Kevin and Brooke came from downstairs.

Brooke pointed at the box. "Oh, how sweet. Mac drew hearts on the box."

Lily popped open the lid. "Help yourselves, and it looks like Mac has the coffee brewed, too."

Kevin poured two cups and hit the button on the kettle for

his mom's preferred tea. The three of them nibbled on cinnamon rolls and croissants while they took in the morning sky and the birds landing on the deck railing.

Brooke reached for her coffee and said, "This place is incredible. It's so quiet and peaceful, and the sunsets are magnificent."

Kevin nodded. "I wasn't sure you could beat the views at the cottages, but I like it out here. Much more secluded, and the dogs have a huge pasture."

Lily smiled and pointed out the window. "Don't forget the llamas and alpacas and now the goats. Mac used to have a horse. I think he'd have a whole zoo if he could."

Brooke smiled. "He's a kind person and has been so welcoming to us."

Lily nodded. "I'm lucky. After losing Kev's dad, I wasn't sure I'd survive, much less move all the way across the country, and at my age, get a second chance at love." A tear leaked from her eye. "It's overwhelming."

Kevin reached for his mom's hand. "You and Mac are great together, and I know Dad would be so glad to know you're happy and have such a great man in your life."

The tear turned into more, and Lily reached for a napkin to swipe at them. "I swore I wouldn't get all sappy today."

Brooke smiled at her. "Get it all out now before you get ready for the wedding, and ruin your mascara."

That made Lily laugh. "You're right about that. I don't want to be a blubbering mess."

Brooke was more than happy to accompany Lily to the salon where she was getting her hair and nails done for the ceremony. Cyndy and Mel, along with Wendy were joining her, all of them excited for a fun day of pampering before the big event.

They were the only party in the salon and amid the non-stop

chatter, the technicians treated them to pedicures and manicures before styling their hair and doing their makeup.

Cyndy had arranged delivery of charcuterie boards filled with delicious sweet and savory items and between treatments, the ladies snacked and sipped on champagne, with Mel being the designated driver for the group.

Lily laughed and enjoyed her time with the ladies, relaxing and admiring everyone's polish choices. Wendy chose an elegant updo style. Her freshly colored hair restored to the rich blond weave she always favored was styled in loose curls and then expertly arranged into a twisted low updo. The stylist added a beautiful rhinestone clip on one side to add the perfect touch of polish.

After watching Wendy, Brooke also elected to try an updo style and looked beautiful with her hair in a low roll with a few strands left loose. The stylist added in a few tiny sparkly combs in Brooke's honey-blond hair and together with the loose strands she was picture perfect.

Mel's transformation was the one Lily enjoyed most. Her thick, shiny hair looked fabulous in beach waves, and the stylist added a Celtic braid across the back of her head, along with small crystal combs tucked along the braid. The hint of bling added a bit of elegance to a beachy look. Mel's smile when she looked in the mirror made Lily's day. She never took much time with her hair or clothes but slowly had been developing more of an interest, and Mel couldn't quit using the handheld mirror to admire the back of her hair.

Despite letting her hair grow since coming to Driftwood Bay, Lily's hair wasn't long enough to do much with as far as an updo. Stacy, her normal stylist, added some highlights and curled her layers, giving her a more elegant look than usual.

Cyndy's dark hair was on the short side but not as layered as Lily's. After a bit of refresh to her color and some curling, she opted to have two longer pieces from the sides pulled to the back of her head and secured with a gorgeous Victorian crystal clip.

Late in the afternoon, when all the champagne had been drunk, and they were done admiring each other, the bridal party headed for the door, and Lily stopped at the reception counter to pay the bill. Stacy smiled at her and said, "Your sister insisted on covering it all. She wanted to surprise you."

Lily was speechless. She finally said, "Wow, I can't believe it."

Stacy kept smiling and said, "You look gorgeous, Lily. I'm so happy for you. Enjoy your special day."

Lily slid into the front passenger seat and turned and looked at the women in the backseat. Brooke was sandwiched between Cyndy and Wendy. They all looked beautiful. She didn't want to tear up again, but Wendy's gesture meant so much to her.

"Imagine my surprise when I went to pay the bill, and Stacy told me my lovely sister treated us today. Thank you for doing that, Wendy. That was a wonderful surprise, and I appreciate it so much."

Wendy grinned, and her eyes sparkled with enthusiasm. "Honestly, it wasn't much more than what I'm used to paying just for my treatments. I wanted to do something special. It's been a weird few months, but you've all been kind to me, and I wanted to treat you to something special today."

Each of the women showered her with praise and gratitude and as they did, Lily saw Wendy beam brighter. It eased Lily's mind to see Wendy happier and more settled.

When they arrived at the house, Andy's truck was in the driveway. Lily looked from the window overlooking the backyard. The tables and chairs were set up, the white cloths shifting in the gentle breeze. The beautiful sea glass color napkins matched the dresses Mel, Cyndy, and Wendy would be wearing and clear vases filled with sea glass and white hydrangeas and ranunculus looked perfect.

The catering staff was busy getting things ready and the

buffet tables set. Mac's band friends were situated in one corner, testing out their equipment. Her stomach fluttered.

With the chaos surrounding Missy, her impromptu trip to visit Friday Harbor, and Kevin's arrival, she hadn't had a minute to think about the actual wedding or be nervous. Now, it was only an hour away, and the butterflies in her stomach were spreading their jitters.

She shouldn't have drunk the champagne.

It was hard not to think of her first wedding.

Memories of her parents flooded her mind. She desperately wished they were here today.

And Gary. As she thought of him, she could swear she could smell him next to her. That hadn't happened for a long time.

She blinked her eyes a few times and breathed deeply.

Mel, Brooke, and Wendy went downstairs to get into their dresses and do any final touch-ups, leaving Cyndy and Lily to the master bedroom.

Cyndy's hand on her shoulder interrupted Lily's musings. "How about a nice hot cup of tea and then let's get you into that gorgeous dress."

Lily turned and gasped. She had been staring out the window longer than she thought. Cyndy smiled and twirled around in her dress. Lily had seen the gorgeous dress with the sheer jacket before, but with Cyndy's hair done and the sparkling flip-flops, she was stunning. "You look beautiful."

Cyndy smiled and took her arm. "Your turn."

Lily sat in the window seat and sipped at her tea. Like always, it made everything better.

Cyndy helped her into the beautiful dress she had chosen and with great patience, closed the long row of fabric-covered buttons that ran up the back of the lacy bodice. Lily's hand went to where the tiny pocket had been added inside the skirt of the dress. She felt for it and smiled. Inside, her something old, was her dad's wedding ring. She wanted him with her as she went down the aisle.

Lily looked in the mirror and smiled. The soft ivory dress was even more lovely than she remembered.

Cyndy reached into her tote bag. "And because you need something borrowed." She slipped a diamond tennis bracelet around Lily's wrist.

"Oh, that's gorgeous. Thank you for letting me use it." She held up her hand, and the sunlight caught the rows of diamonds.

Cyndy smiled and pointed at a small box on the dresser, wrapped with a white glittery ribbon. "Mac is taking care of the something new."

Lily's eyes widened as she took the box from her soon to be sister-in-law. She opened it and found a shimmering pair of diamond earrings. With trembling fingers, she managed to get them in her ears and held back tears. With the high neckline and beautiful embroidered lace bodice, Lily wasn't wearing a necklace, but the dangling stones were beyond gorgeous and absolute perfection.

With one more glance in the mirror, she followed Cyndy out the door. As they passed into the living room, she glanced out the window and saw Kevin waiting in the yard. Her heart fluttered at his profile. So much like his dad.

The photographer was waiting, as were the ladies. Mel and Wendy were gorgeous in their matching dresses and with Paula's help, Brooke had found the same color in a different design that was a more casual sundress type of style.

The three of them gasped. Wendy was the first to speak. "You look stunning, Lily. Absolutely perfect."

Jeanette, the photographer Mac had no problem using and arranged for her to handle the wedding, was all business and cut the gush-fest short. She hurried them along and posed them in groups and with the bride to capture several photos. She then called for Kevin and took lots of photos of him and his mom, him and Brooke, and the three of them together.

Jeanette was skilled at using humor and making them laugh and smile. She tipped her camera to Lily and showed her several of the shots. Cyndy was right; she was talented, and Lily saw several shots she could imagine in frames.

Cyndy was behind Jeannette and said, "It's time. We better get our seats and let this young man escort his mom."

The ladies, not wanting to risk making Lily cry or ruin her makeup, rushed to squeeze her hand and wish her luck before they disappeared out the door and down the back stairs.

Jeanette pointed outside. "I'll get in position. See you outside."

Kevin, looking handsome in his beige pants and sea-glass-colored shirt, handed his mom the gorgeous bouquet. The touch of a couple of blue forget-me-nots in the wrapped stems of white flowers supplied the something blue for the bride.

"You look beautiful, Mom," he said, taking her arm in his. "Ready?"

She nodded, determined not to cry, and set out for the trail that led to the beach. The only people in the yard were the catering staff, Jeanette, and Brooke, who was there to help keep Lily's dress from touching the ground. With her rhinestone flip-flops, the walk was easy, and Brooke did a great job of holding up the back of her dress.

The band was tucked in the corner, playing one of Mac's favorites, "A One-Man Band."

When they reached the actual beach, Lily's mouth gaped. There was a wooden, slatted pathway that led to the driftwood arch, dripping with the gorgeous white flowers she had imagined. Lanterns lined the edge of the pathway and were scattered next to the arch. The soft light from them combined with the pink and lavender sunset sky, and the water in the background took her breath away.

It was more beautiful than she imagined it could be.

The discreet speakers emitted the beautiful instrumental version of "A Thousand Years," Mac's pick for the processional.

Lily kept a tight grip on Kevin's arm and focused on the arch and Mac's smiling face. He looked so relaxed and happy in his beige linen pants and ivory shirt that matched Lily's dress, with a boutonniere that matched her bouquet. She risked a glance or two as they passed by the small gathering of friends, standing on the beach, waiting for her arrival.

As they got closer to the archway, Lily smiled. She and Mac had agreed they didn't want to have formal attendants, so she was shocked to see he had reneged. Sherlock, Fritz, and Bodie, all wearing blue bowties, sat next to him. All their tails making marks in the sand as they contained their excitement.

She and Kevin reached the end of the walkway, and her son kissed her cheek, while she blinked back tears. He took her bouquet and handed it to Wendy to hold. Mac held out his hand, and she slipped hers into it and stepped closer to the archway and the justice of the peace.

He was a friend of Jeff's and his dog, named Justice, was Mac's patient. The gray-haired man with twinkling eyes smiled at them as he welcomed everyone and began the short ceremony.

The water, shimmering with golden light, caught Lily's eye. It was hard to focus on what the judge was saying, but she knew her part was simple, and she let herself soak in the view she remembered from so long ago, the waves that had helped heal her heart, and the driftwood log where she had sat and talked to Gary each day.

This beautiful place where she had found hope, healing, and happiness.

She focused again on Mac and heard her cue. She said, "I do," and smiled at the man who she knew would make the rest of her life, the best of her life.

Minutes later, she was wrapped in a long embrace and given the sweetest kiss she remembered. Their friends cheered and clapped, and Mac slipped his arm around her.

The band played "Amazed" and the bride and groom, along with their three golden retrievers, led the way to the reception. Andy took the dogs, and the bride and groom stayed behind so Jeannette could capture photos of them together along the shoreline with the sunset background.

As she clicked the button on her camera over and over, she finally lowered it and approached them. With tears in her eyes, she reached out and took their hands. "This was absolutely beautiful, and I think Jill would be so pleased to see you this happy, Mac. She would have loved this. I only wish Missy could have been here."

Mac nodded, and Lily squeezed his arm in hers a bit tighter as she saw a tear slide down his cheek.

27

The band continued to play, and the upbeat tunes of "Stuck Like Glue" drifted in the air. Mac grabbed Lily for one more long kiss before they went up the trail. "I've had a few happy days in my life and some of the saddest I wouldn't wish on anyone. This one, this day right here, could be the best one yet. I love you, Lily."

"I wasn't sure this would happen or work, but I feel the same. I'm thrilled that we pulled this off and are married. I can't wait to start my life with you." She held his hands in hers. "I love you so very much and promise you I always will."

He dug into his pants pocket and pulled out his phone. "I have one more surprise for you. I didn't ask you about another addition to our family, but I know how much you're dreading giving up Bodie." He showed her a photo of a newborn golden puppy. "I put down a deposit on him, and he's yours if you want him. He'll be ready for his forever home in August."

She smiled and hugged him. "And I wouldn't have to train him and give him up?"

"No, sweetie. He'd be ours forever."

She touched her finger to her earrings. "I love these

gorgeous earrings, but I think that puppy is the best wedding present ever."

He wrapped her in a hug. "Let's get up there and eat so we can dig into that cake."

She laughed and gathered her dress, which he held for her as they made their way up to the yard. The lights along the deck and across the yard, combined with the firepit and the live music, made for a wonderful ambience. She noticed the dogs were on the deck, and Andy had put up the gate so they wouldn't bother anyone.

The band leader announced their entrance, and Mac guided her to the small dance floor Andy and Wade had installed. Lily wasn't a skilled dancer and tried to get out of it altogether, citing her ankle injury, but Mac insisted they have one short dance together.

She and Mac were both country music fans and when the notes for "Then" began to play, she smiled and kissed him. He took her in his arms, and they slowly swayed together as the lyrics that told their story were sung. After a round of applause when the song ended, the band invited others to join in for one more verse.

They walked hand in hand across the yard, amid congratulations and smiles.

The guests were filling plates or sitting and visiting. One of the caterers came by with a tray of champagne, and Lily waved her off. "No thanks, I've had enough of that." Mac opted for a beer, and she took a fizzy lemonade drink that tasted yummy.

Lily sought out Andy and Wade and hugged them both. "The arch and the walkway were perfect. Everything was. Thank you so much for doing all that work."

Wade shook Mac's hand. "It was our pleasure. It was a beautiful ceremony. You couldn't have asked for a better sky than tonight's."

Andy beamed as Lily complimented his workmanship and

then said he was going to sit with the dogs so they wouldn't be lonely. The band announced a quick break so they could eat and then promised an evening of music made for more dancing and listening.

The bride and groom milled around from table to table, thanking everyone for coming before they filled their own plates and took their seats at their table with Kevin and Brooke and Mel and Tony.

Cyndy sat with Jeff and Donna, along with Nora and Bree. Wendy had been sitting next to Cyndy but wasn't there. Lily scanned the yard looking for her sister. She finally saw her, sitting next to the keyboard player from the band.

She poked Mac with her elbow and tilted her head in that direction. He looked and then lowered his voice. "Ah, Mickey's a good guy. She's safe with him."

"It's nice to see her happier, but hopefully, she'll take it slow."

He squeezed her hand in his. "She's going to be okay, Lily. Who knows, maybe she'll end up liking it here more than she thought."

Cyndy appeared at Lily's shoulder. "It's time to cut the cake."

She and Mac made their way to the dessert table and admired the cake, that wasn't a huge traditional tiered cake, but a simple, rustic style. Mac was anxious to take their first bite and almost didn't wait for Jeanette to get into position for a photo.

Together, Lily and Mac sliced into the luscious cake and for the sake of tradition, fed each other a small piece. They were both very neat about it, taking care not to smear the whipped cream on the other.

The crowd laughed and cheered before helping themselves to the slices that the catering staff plated for them. Mac and Lily each took a huge piece and returned to their table to enjoy it.

The sweet berries, together with the rich cream and moist

vanilla cake were a hit. It tasted like Lily's childhood and the promise of summer.

The lights were on in the first cottage, as that was where Mac and Lily were spending their wedding night. Being the one night without guests, it would be the ideal spot to celebrate. Mel would take the dogs to Mac's and stay there, and Wendy would stay with Cyndy. They'd have the whole place to themselves.

The emotions and activity of the day was catching up with Lily. She looked forward to enjoying some alone time with Mac.

As she contemplated relaxing, the band announced a special mother-son dance, and Kevin invited her to the dance floor. The band played "I Hope You Dance," and she and Kevin made a slow trip around the wooden floor. A few of the guests joined them, including Andy, who grinned as he led his mom around the dance floor. Despite not being able to hear, he felt the beat and loved music.

Kevin returned his mom to her seat and grabbed Brooke for the next dance, a more modern rock one. Mac eyed the rest of Lily's cake, and she gave it to him. "Ah, true love," he said, smiling as he took it.

After another song, the band called for all the fathers and daughters to join in a dance. Lily reached for Mac's hand and at the same time, Cyndy came from behind them. She put her hands on her brother's shoulders and bent to whisper in his ear.

He snapped his head around and when Cyndy moved, Lily saw the young woman standing behind her. She couldn't believe it.

Missy.

After everything, she had come. Lily's stomach lurched, not sure if she should brace for a scene. She hoped with everything she had, Missy wouldn't embarrass her dad or cause him grief. She didn't want their perfect day ruined.

Missy smiled at him and put her hand on his shoulder. "How about that father-daughter dance?"

Lily had managed to contain her tears all evening, until now. As she watched Mac and Missy dance to "God Gave Me You," she couldn't keep them from flowing. She dabbed at her face, ruining the gorgeous sea glass-colored napkin but couldn't have been happier.

She knew how long Mac had dreamed of a day when he might reconnect with Missy. After giving up all hope after sending his email to her, she could only imagine his joy.

To see him smiling and the two of them together, filled her already overflowing heart with delight.

Kevin leaned over and said, "Is that who I think it is?"

Lily nodded, unable to find the words.

Cyndy slid into the chair next to Lily. "I've been talking to her and hoped she would come but wasn't sure. I didn't want to get Mac's hopes up. Her plane got delayed, so she was late."

Lily smiled. "You're the best sister in the world. Mac said you had magical abilities when it came to her, and now I'm convinced. I never expected she would come. I'm so happy for him."

"She's going to stay with me and has a flight back on Saturday morning. I knew you were taking Brooke and Kevin, so I thought it would work out if she had a flight near the same time. This first visit needs to be short and hopefully, sweet, and not encroach on your honeymoon."

Lily dabbed at her eyes. "It's perfect. Trust me, I'd gladly give up a few days of our honeymoon if it meant Mac could have a relationship with his daughter."

Cyndy reached for her and hugged her. "You're such a good person, Lily. Truly, the best. I think you were smart to confront Missy right off the bat. She has a bit of fear or maybe just respect for you, which is a good thing. The prenup showed her that you aren't after Mac's money, and that you love him. I think Missy understands that in her head, but her heart isn't sure.

She's got some old wounds related to the death of Jill, and it's going to take some time."

"I can understand that. I'm not sure your heart ever forgets or heals totally. It's taken me a long time to come to grips with the losses in my life. I like to think the heart just gets a little bigger and makes room for more people to love and more dreams to make."

The song ended, and Mac and Missy came up to the table. He reached for Lily's hand and said, "Lily, I'd like to introduce you to my beautiful daughter Missy."

Lily smiled and extended her other hand. "Wonderful to see you, and I'm thrilled you could come and spend some time here."

Missy nodded and glanced at her dad for a moment before saying, "I tried to get her earlier, but the plane..."

Lily shook her head. "Not to worry, the important thing is that you came and made your dad so very happy."

A tear trickled down Missy's cheek as she nodded. In a voice so quiet, Lily had to lean in to hear her, Missy said, "I hope you can forgive me for my email and the reviews."

Lily met her eyes and said, "It's forgotten. How about we start fresh from right now?"

Missy nodded and smiled at her.

Mac put an arm around each of them and leaned close to Lily, kissing her on the cheek. "Can you pinch me to make sure I'm not dreaming?"

She kissed him instead. He smiled and whispered, "This really is the best day of my life."

She leaned her head against his, listening to the music, taking in the gorgeous twinkle lights and the soft glow from the lanterns someone had moved up from the beach that now lined the walkways and dance floor. Her heart was full and her mind at ease. "I think this is only the beginning of what we dreamed."

EPILOGUE

Lily hopes you enjoyed the final installment of her story in the *Glass Beach Cottage Series*. If you're a new reader to Tammy's books, the characters in her *Glass Beach Cottage Series* visit the San Juan Islands and meet up with the characters from her *Hometown Harbor Series*. This is a bestselling series, and you won't want to miss reading the six books. Each tells the story of a different heroine and like this book, they all include dogs. If you've missed reading any of the Hometown Harbor Series, here are the links to the all the books.

Prequel: Hometown Harbor: The Beginning (free prequel novella eBook only)

Book 1: Finding Home
Book 2: Home Blooms
Book 3: A Promise of Home
Book 4: Pieces of Home
Book 5: Finally Home
Book 6: Forever Home

. . .

To read more about the Winey Widows, you'll want to check out a new series Tammy is part of called THE WISHING TREE SERIES. In WISH AGAIN and OVERDUE WISHES, you'll learn more about the Winey Widows in the quaint Vermont town of Linden Falls, where a fabled tree is thought to grant wishes and dreams.

If you haven't yet read the first two books in her *Glass Beach Cottage Series,* you can find them in digital and print here:

BEACH HAVEN
MOONLIGHT BEACH

ACKNOWLEDGMENTS

I always enjoy returning to Driftwood Bay and the characters in these stories. I especially like the dogs in these books and am in awe of the work organizations do that train dogs, like Bodie, to be hearing assistant dogs. If you're inclined, please look for an organization in your area and volunteer or donate to support their fine work.

I had lots of fun sending my characters in these books to visit those in my Hometown Harbor Series. If you've read them, you'll recognize them, but if you're new, it will give you a glimpse into the characters I've come to think of as friends in that series and I hope you'll try them.

My thanks to my editor, Susan, for finding my mistakes and helping me polish *Beach Dreams.* Like my other covers, I fell in love with this latest one. All the credit goes to Elizabeth Mackey for creating such an inviting and gorgeous cover. I'm fortunate to have such an incredible team helping me.

I so appreciate all the readers who have taken the time to tell their reader friends about my work and provide reviews of my books. These reviews are especially important in promoting future books, so if you enjoy my novels, please consider leaving a review. Follow this link to my author page and select a book to leave your review at www.amazon.com/author/tammylgrace. I also encourage you to follow me on Amazon and BookBub, where leaving a review is even easier and you'll be the first to know about new releases and deals.

Remember to visit my website at http://www.tammylgrace.com and join my mailing list for my exclusive group of readers. I've also got a fun Book Buddies Facebook Group. That's the best place to find me and get a chance to participate in my give-aways. Join my Facebook group at https://www.facebook.com/groups/AuthorTammyLGraceBookBuddies/

and keep in touch—I'd love to hear from you.

Wishing you a life filled with hope, happiness, and dreams,

Tammy

FROM THE AUTHOR

Thank you for reading BEACH DREAMS. Like my readers, I've fallen in love with the characters in this series and enjoyed writing this final installment of Lily's story.

If you enjoy women's fiction and haven't yet read my HOMETOWN HARBOR SERIES, I think you'll enjoy them. It's a six-book series, with each book focused on a different female heroine. They are set in the gorgeous San Juan Islands in the Pacific Northwest, and you'll recognize some of them from the trip Lily takes in MOONLIGHT BEACH and BEACH DREAMS. You can start the series with a free prequel that is in the form of excerpts from Sam's journal. She's the main character in the first book, FINDING HOME.

If you're a new reader and enjoy mysteries, I write a series that features a lovable private detective, Coop, and his faithful golden retriever, Gus. If you like whodunits that will keep you guessing until the end, you'll enjoy the COOPER HARRINGTON DETECTIVE NOVELS.

The two books I've written as Casey Wilson, A DOG'S HOPE and A DOG'S CHANCE have received enthusiastic support from my readers and if you're a dog-lover, are must-reads.

If you enjoy holiday stories, be sure and check out my CHRISTMAS IN SILVER FALLS SERIES and HOMETOWN CHRISTMAS SERIES. They are small-town Christmas stories of hope, friendship, and family. You won't want to miss any of the SOUL SISTERS AT CEDAR MOUNTAIN LODGE BOOKS. It's a connected Christmas series I wrote with four author friends. My contributions, CHRISTMAS WISHES, CHRISTMAS SURPRISES, and coming in 2022, CHRISTMAS SHELTER, are all heartwarming, small-town holiday stories that I'm sure you'll enjoy. The series kicks off with a free prequel novella, CHRISTMAS SISTERS, where you'll get a chance to meet the characters during their first Christmas together.

You won't want to miss THE WISHING TREE SERIES, set in Vermont, where some of the characters who visit the cottages, live. This series centers on a famed tree in the middle of the quaint town that is thought to grant wishes to those who tie them on her branches. Readers love this series and always comment how they are full of hope, which we all need more of right now.

I'd love to send you my exclusive interview with the canine companions in my Hometown Harbor Series as a thank-you for joining my exclusive group of readers. You can sign up www.tammylgrace.com by clicking this link: https://wp.me/P9umIy-e

ALSO BY TAMMY L. GRACE

COOPER HARRINGTON DETECTIVE NOVELS

Killer Music

Deadly Connection

Dead Wrong

Cold Killer

HOMETOWN HARBOR SERIES

Hometown Harbor: The Beginning (Prequel Novella)

Finding Home

Home Blooms

A Promise of Home

Pieces of Home

Finally Home

Forever Home

CHRISTMAS STORIES

A Season for Hope: Christmas in Silver Falls Book 1

The Magic of the Season: Christmas in Silver Falls Book 2

Christmas in Snow Valley: A Hometown Christmas Book 1

One Unforgettable Christmas: A Hometown Christmas Book 2

Christmas Wishes: Souls Sisters at Cedar Mountain Lodge

Christmas Surprises: Soul Sisters at Cedar Mountain Lodge

GLASS BEACH COTTAGE SERIES

Beach Haven

Moonlight Beach

Beach Dreams

WRITING AS CASEY WILSON

A Dog's Hope

A Dog's Chance

WISHING TREE SERIES

The Wishing Tree

Wish Again

Overdue Wishes

Remember to subscribe to Tammy's exclusive group of readers for your gift, only available to readers on her mailing list. **Sign up at www.tammylgrace.com. Follow this link to subscribe at https://wp.me/P9umIy-e** and you'll receive the exclusive interview she did with all the canine characters in her Hometown Harbor Series.

Follow Tammy on Facebook by liking her page. You may also follow Tammy on her pages on book retailers or at BookBub by clicking on the follow button.

ABOUT THE AUTHOR

Tammy L. Grace is the *USA Today* bestselling and award-winning author of the Cooper Harrington Detective Novels, the bestselling Hometown Harbor Series, and the Glass Beach Cottage Series, along with several sweet Christmas novellas. Tammy also writes under the pen name of Casey Wilson for Bookouture and Grand Central. You'll find Tammy online at www.tammylgrace.com where you can join her mailing list and be part of her exclusive group of readers. Connect with Tammy on Facebook at www.facebook.com/tammylgrace.books or Instagram at @authortammylgrace.

facebook.com/tammylgrace.books

twitter.com/TammyLGrace

instagram.com/authortammylgrace

bookbub.com/authors/tammy-l-grace

goodreads.com/tammylgrace

amazon.com/author/tammylgrace

Made in United States
Orlando, FL
02 October 2024

52241470R00161